S0-AGG-312

─────────────── ★ ───────────────

In half an hour, maybe less, it would be dark, dark enough for him to go to her house. Dark enough for him to open the back of the van and take out the burlap sack that lay on the vehicle's floor.

What a jolt that was going to give her when she came out to get the newspaper in the morning and found the sack, and looked inside. It would pay her back for those devious questions about if and when he was out of town, and what did he think was the reason that a man who murdered women cut off their tongues. That had been a bad therapy session, the worst of all, because he had seen her in the role of inquisitor. That was the means by which women castrated men, by asking question after question.

It would give her something to think about, all right.

─────────────── ───────────────

"...written with the certainty and restraint of a very seasoned hand."

—*The Milwaukee Journal*

Previously published Worldwide Mystery title by
C.J. KOEHLER

MIND GAMES

C.J. KOEHLER

PROFILE

W☉RLDWIDE.

TORONTO • NEW YORK • LONDON
AMSTERDAM • PARIS • SYDNEY • HAMBURG
STOCKHOLM • ATHENS • TOKYO • MILAN
MADRID • WARSAW • BUDAPEST • AUCKLAND

If you purchased this book without a cover you should be aware that this book is stolen property. It was reported as "unsold and destroyed" to the publisher, and neither the author nor the publisher has received any payment for this "stripped book."

To Ruthann

PROFILE

A Worldwide Mystery/April 2000

First published by Carroll & Graf Publishers, Inc.

ISBN 0-373-26345-7

Copyright © 1994 by C.J. Koehler.
All rights reserved. No part of this book may be reproduced or transmitted in any form or by any means, electronic or mechanical, including photocopying, recording or by any information storage and retrieval system, without permission in writing from the publisher. For information, contact: Carroll & Graf Publishers, Inc. 19 West 21st Street, Suite 601, New York, NY 10010-6805 U.S.A.

All characters in this book are fictitious, and any resemblance to actual persons, living or dead, is purely coincidental.

® and TM are trademarks of Harlequin Enterprises Limited. Trademarks indicated with ® are registered in the United States Patent and Trademark Office, the Canadian Trade Marks Office and in other countries.

Printed in U.S.A.

PROFILE

PROFILE

ONE

THIS THERAPY SESSION, like the ones which had preceded it, was not going well.

The patient, a twenty-five-year old white male named Philip Schroeder, must have sensed her hesitation, her uneasiness, because he grew more hostile and manipulative with each ticktock of Wylie Frymark's antique grandfather clock.

Dr. Lisa Robbins shifted her attention to the clock for a moment, as if by concentrating on it she might be able to tap its owner's wisdom, or at least his cerebral detachment. But neither the clock nor any of the other masculine furnishings with which Mr. Frymark's therapy room was adorned communicated with her. She was on her own. She could hear him chiding her: trust your instincts. Sadly, her instincts functioned with no more precision than the grandfather clock.

"Why do I resent Develice?" Schroeder said. It was a habit of his to repeat her questions aloud before he answered them, not to gain time to form a lie as most of her patients did, but rather to mock her and to ridicule her profession. "I don't think that I resent her. She isn't worth the effort."

World-weary cynicism: another trench in his defense network. "But you said she tried to put you down by criticizing your work," she reminded him.

His prominent Adam's apple bobbed as he swallowed. While she watched it, the terminology from her medical school anatomy class came back to her: epiglottis, esophagus, trachea, larynx. Adam's apple wasn't medical. She forced herself to stop looking at his scrawny neck, and shifted her attention instead to the notebook which lay on her lap. The open page contained almost no notes. Lisa became aware again that he was staring

at her legs. She fought down the urge to recross them, which
he would have counted as a victory.

"What she complained about was trivial, silly," he said.
"What difference did it make which column I put the per-
centages in? It was clear from the heading what the formula
was. You see, it didn't matter whether it was in the third or
fourth column. She knew that. She only made a point of it to
prove she was the department head. It didn't mean anything."

"Does Develice do that sort of thing often?"

"Does she do it often?" He fell silent, letting the old clock
reclaim auditory supremacy. His hooded eyes watched her from
what seemed a great distance, from his tiny island of blue
leather chair, across the sea of gray carpet; he had the ability
to distance himself, to dissociate himself from her to such an
extent psychologically that he distorted the actual physical separation. She didn't control the situation, he did. "She does it
only when I won't submit to her. She can't deal with any kind
of challenge to her authority. A typical woman. You all act the
same way."

This was the most overt revelation of his hatred of women
to date, and she noted it eagerly on her pad. Wylie had recorded
numerous instances of the same attitude in his progress notes,
but Schroeder had been careful during her earlier sessions not
to talk about women in a derogatory way. She hoped this
breach meant he was becoming less guarded with her, although
she doubted it. The remark did confirm once more his underlying compulsive syndrome. She reviewed in her mind some
of the other evidence: his record for breaking and entering; a
fetish about women's undergarments; the bizarre episode of
defecating on a woman's bed during one of the teenage break-
ins; a preoccupation with the morality of sexual conduct; feel-
ings of isolation. And, most telling of all, the love-hate relationship he had with his mother.

"Can you give me an example of another woman who acted
like that?" Lisa asked.

"Can I give you another example of a woman who acted

like that?'' He paused for a moment, then said, ''My mother, of course. Dr. Frymark liked it when I talked about my mother. All you shrinks do.''

''Relationships with parents are important. They're our whole universe when we're small children.''

''My mother is a bitch. She drove my father out of the house when I was little and he never came back. All I ever saw of him was the alimony check once a month. She'd leave it on the hall table so I would see it. She did that on purpose. I don't know why. Do you know why she did that?''

Lisa shook her head.

''My mother knows how to use power,'' Schroeder said. ''She was much more adept at it than my father. I finally figured out why. Men don't administer power as well as women because of egotism. Women aren't burdened by ego baggage, so they use power in a pragmatic way. England's power leaders were women: Elizabeth I, Victoria, Thatcher.'' He watched her intently with his slate-gray eyes, waiting to see if she was impressed by his sagacity.

To avoid his eyes, she glanced at Wylie's clock and was dismayed to see that their session wasn't over. For some reason the clock claimed her full attention again. Odd about time, she thought. We took it for granted now, but whoever first discovered you could measure its passage had performed an impressive feat of abstract thinking.

Quite unexpectedly, Schroeder announced that he had to leave. Relieved, Lisa didn't object. She confirmed the time and date for his next appointment, which he carefully entered in the small appointment book he carried with him. She doubted that it contained any other appointments.

After he departed she returned to her office and sat down at her desk with his file. She reviewed again the test results, looking for some clue that might unlock his personality. When he had taken the ten-card Rorschach test, he had only made eighteen responses, a lower number than patients usually entered. Most of what he ''saw'' in the ink blots were prehistoric animals, a subject which fascinated him. In the draw-a-person exercise he drew only heads—never whole bodies.

She picked up a folder which contained his TAT, the Thematic Apperception Test. In this examination the subject was shown twenty pictures and told to make up a story about each. One of the photos depicted a woman in bed while a man was standing in front of the window with an arm shading his eyes. The usual response was that the man had gotten out of the bed in the morning, opened the blinds and found the sun shining in his face. Schroeder had embroidered the situation by concluding that the man had tried to have sex with the woman, and had been rejected. In Wylie's notes it quoted Schroeder as saying the woman was trying to emasculate the man. "He's looking out the window, but he's really thinking about killing her," Schroeder claimed.

Philip Schroeder was a very disturbed young man. And possibly a dangerous one.

WHEN LISA LOCKED the back door of the clinic and turned toward the parking lot, a wind gust whipped the hem of her overcoat and sent swirls of fresh snow caroming off the brick building. Her three-year-old Volvo crouched in forlorn solitude beside a snow bank scalloped by the wind.

For a few moments, as she listened apprehensively to the sluggish sound of her starter motor, she feared the vehicle was going to betray her. Somehow she had to find time to buy a new battery, she reminded herself, as the engine finally turned over.

She wanted to go home directly, but St. Luke's was on the way and she hadn't visited Wylie in several days. She decided to stop for a few minutes. He was in intensive care on the fifth floor, where in all probability he was going to die. The stroke had left him in a coma for, how long now? At least two weeks, she decided. There had been so much confusion, so many of his patients to see, that time had become distorted. She fixed her concentration on Jack; for some reason she was able to sort out what day it was by remembering his schedule. He'd be back from New York on Friday, the day after tomorrow.

As she left the elevator, she happened to glance at the smoking room and saw Wylie's wife Terri sitting alone in a corner sifting through magazines on a coffee table. Lisa walked into the room, which was otherwise unoccupied, and peeled off her overcoat. Terri looked up then and smiled in a shy, tentative manner. Her eyes were dull with worry.

Lisa tossed her coat on a chair and sat next to the older woman. "How is he tonight?" she asked.

"Unconscious," Terri answered, "but he's had a bad day. The respirator again..." She was a small, neat woman with short gray hair and a rosy complexion despite her age, the kind of seventy-year-old woman about whom people said, "She must have been a knockout when she was thirty, because she's still beautiful." Wylie loved her very much. "You look tired," Terri said, studying Lisa's face as if it revealed in fine detail the day's tribulations at the clinic. "I suppose it's all those extra patients of Wylie's that you have to look after. Such a shame."

"No, it isn't—it isn't so bad. We're all managing to cope with the patient load, but we miss Wylie's spirit. He's the heart of the place."

Terri squeezed her hand gratefully, then unexpectedly let out a gasp. Lisa glanced up, following Terri's gaze, and was astonished to see Philip Schroeder standing in the doorway to the little room. He wore a navy-blue peacoat and held a stocking cap, which he twisted in a menacing fashion in his long, effeminate hands. "Hello, Mrs. Frymark. Hi, Doc." Having offered his greeting in the studied manner of someone who was reciting a password, he came forward and stood directly in front of Terri.

Lisa sensed her friend recoil from the young man even though she didn't move physically. Ever the clinician, Lisa made a mental note that Schroeder was one of those unfortunate people who had no sense of when he was invading another person's space. Because she was seated, she found herself staring at the young man's hands, which continued to wring the stocking cap in a slow, methodical way. There was something obscene in the tic, something that made her think of wringing a cat's neck. Immediately, she realized why she had thought about killing a cat; psychopaths often resorted to torturing and killing animals, especially cats.

Terri and Schroeder exchanged ritualistic comments about Wylie's illness. After a pause, Schroeder concluded that since Wylie was still in a coma, there wasn't much sense in going to his room.

"No, I'm afraid not," Terri said. "He wouldn't recognize you."

"He wouldn't even know I was there, would he?" His intonation made it sound as if he knew a conspiracy was afoot to keep him from communicating with his former therapist.

Schroeder stood in front of them for a few more awkward moments, then abruptly bid them good night and departed. Terri watched him disappear from view into the elevator before she exhaled and said in a tight, childish voice. "I'm glad he's gone. Why does he keep coming here?"

Lisa nodded and clasped her friend's hand in her own. As soon as she withdrew it, Terri reached for a pack of cigarettes on the corner coffee table and lit one. She inhaled deeply and sent a puff of blue smoke toward the ceiling. She smoked three packs a day, according to Wylie, and had quit trying to control the addiction. It was strangely out of character, this dependence on tobacco, because in every other aspect of her life, willpower ruled. Her smoking had worried Wylie enormously, both because he loved her to the point of obsession and because of his unstated male terror that she would die before he did. Men wanted a woman at their bedside when they died.

"That boy is now one of your patients, isn't he?" Terri asked rhetorically. "You should turn him over to someone else. Wylie wouldn't want you to treat him."

"Oh, why do you say that?"

"Wylie didn't talk about his patients—he was very concerned about confidentiality—but this young man troubled him. He didn't tell me his name, but this must be the one."

"What did he say about him?" Lisa asked.

"He said society can't deal with people like him."

Exactly the kind of personality Larry Kimble had been asking about in that awkward phone conversation they had two or three weeks ago, Lisa thought, the kind of man who might have been responsible for the murder of Nancy Sorgel.

PHILIP SCHROEDER DECIDED for no specific reason to stop off at the West Ridge Mall on the way back to his apartment. The stores would be open for another couple of hours. There would be no people about; not as many as on a normal Wednesday night because of the storm, but enough. He liked it better when fewer people were shopping; it was easier to watch them.

He found a bench in the central concourse which had been designed to resemble a city park. It had trees, pebble walkways, and a small bandstand—and all inside the buildings!

A middle-aged couple, laden with several large cartons, emerged from an electronics store off to his left and hurried toward the exit. They were having an argument, something about money. A covey of teenage girls emerged from the Penney's store on the opposite side of the park and came toward him. He looked down at his shoes and pulled the collar of his jacket up around his face; he was afraid they would notice him and start to talk about him. Stupid little bitches, he thought, noisy and stupid. One of the girls, a slight, pale creature with bangs that curled well down on her forehead, smiled at him as she passed. He scowled at her with disapproval, knowing that his effort would be wasted; she would go on smiling at men until one of them smiled back, then she would castrate the poor blighter. He liked the phrase "poor blighter." It was so English.

After a while he began to feel the urge to make a phone call, but he tried to put it out of his mind because the impulse inevitably made him think about the phone in his own apartment, which even now was blinking its insistence that he call his mother. That was the real reason he didn't want to go to the apartment; it was still connected to his mother by the umbilical phone cord and the accursed red eye that was always blinking when he returned. He tried without success to extinguish the red eye in his mind, and with it his mother's unrelenting love. He would have to go back there and call her.

But first he went to the bank of phones near the exit doors to the parking lot and dialed a number from memory.

A woman's voice answered almost at once. Not Hers. Another woman, the one who always answered. The mother.

"Robbins residence," the mother-voice said.

Philip Schroeder didn't say anything. He waited until he heard the sound of the disconnect signal, that steady, monotonous hum of someone who didn't want to talk to him. In his mind's eye the red light remained lit, no longer blinking. Steady, like the disconnect sound.

TRAFFIC ON THE FREEWAY had been so badly snarled into a glutinous mass by the storm that Lisa was more than an hour later than usual getting home. As she came in sight of the sprawling ranch house, she caught a glimpse of cheerful lights in the kitchen and felt her day-long tension begin to dissipate. She fumbled along the sun visor for the garage-door opener, pumped the button, and marveled once again that the heavy door began to rise. Having no real confidence in mechanical gadgetry, she was always amazed that the garage door responded to such a minute amount of force on her part. She turned gingerly into the driveway, which sloped gently downward, and schussed into the garage. She pushed the tiny button again, and watched in the rearview mirror as the door descended. Another victory.

As she kicked off her boots in the foyer, she caught a glimpse of her six-year-old son Kevin hunched over a plate at the kitchen table. He was wearing his yellow Mickey Mouse sweatshirt, the last of his booty from a trip to Disney World the previous July. He didn't notice her.

The aroma of some Italian delicacy drifted into the foyer, reminding Lisa that she hadn't eaten since breakfast. Although she was famished, she forced herself to take her briefcase to the den, the one area of the house which was off limits to everyone but her husband Jack and herself. The case contained the medical records of Philip Schroeder.

When she got to the kitchen, Rose left the table to put something on the stove for her. Usually Rose and Kevin waited for her until six-thirty, then, following a long-standing policy, her mother-in-law fed the boy. Even so, Rose never ate until Lisa sat down at the table. Whenever Lisa chided her for waiting, she answered that it made her sad to see a woman eat alone.

Kevin wiped some sauce off his lips with a napkin and raised his dark head to accept his mother's kiss on the cheek. He put a thin arm gently around her neck and embraced her for a moment. Again, she felt a momentary regret that his embrace was dutiful where once it had been enthusiastic.

"That looks good," she said, glancing down at his plate.

"'Talian stuff," he explained, looking at his grandmother expectantly.

"Costolette di Maiale ai due Vini," Rose said, laying on a mock Italian accent for the boy's benefit.

Kevin giggled and waved his fork gleefully. "Por' chops," he translated.

Rose put two salads on the table and seated herself opposite Lisa. "We had a busy day," Rose said. "After school I took Mickey Mouse out to the dentist to have his tail trimmed. His tail didn't have any cavities. He's got your teeth, not Jack's. *His* mouth is solid silver."

Kevin giggled again, picturing his father's solid silver teeth.

Lisa smiled to show she understood, but she was aghast that she had forgotten Kevin's dental checkup. She had been forgetting domestic concerns with depressing regularity lately. Ever since Wylie got sick, she thought. What she would have done without Rose she had no idea. Her mother-in-law did their shopping, came to their home each weekday to be there when Kevin arrived, took him out every Thursday after school for his piano lesson, and managed a multitude of other chores which Lisa probably was not aware of. And despite her pervasive presence in Kevin's life, she scrupulously avoided supplanting Lisa in the boy's emotional life.

Lisa's gratitude was boundless and had caused Jack to remark on more than one occasion that "You married me for my mother."

There was more truth in that than she liked to admit.

After Kevin had finished eating and departed to watch television, the two women talked about their harrowing driving experiences on the icy streets and made plans for a shopping expedition on Saturday; Kevin wanted to stay at a friend's house, so they would have the afternoon free.

Later, as they were clearing the table and loading the dishwasher, Rose remarked casually that she had received another ominous phone call just before Lisa arrived.

Lisa immediately felt the same frustration and anger that always followed such news. She suspected Rose didn't always tell her when she had a call because of how upset it made her, but even allowing for these considerate lapses, the calls seemed to be coming more frequently. "Like the others?"

"Yes, he—if it's a he—just breathes. He never says anything."

"You don't try to talk to him, do you?" Lisa asked.

"Not when I don't get a response to 'hello.'"

"I'll call the phone company."

"I did," Rose told her. "They suggested that we have an unlisted number, but I explained how impossible that was because you're a doctor. There's not a lot they can do, I'm afraid."

"No, I suppose not." Lisa had discussed the problem herself with a supervisor at the phone company, who reassured her by saying that such calls were rather common, but that they usually stopped as long as the called party didn't show any alarm. He had quoted her statistics which proved that while such calls were annoying, even frightening, they were not often the prelude to real physical harm. Like all statistics, the telephone man's gave Lisa little comfort, just as knowing that the odds were heavily against being struck by lightning didn't make electrical storms less frightening.

Even though Rose's apartment was no more than ten minutes away, Lisa prevailed on her to spend the night rather than risk driving on the icy streets. While her concern about the weather was genuine, she also wanted another adult in the house tonight; if Wylie were inside her head he would have commented in the affectionate, indulgent manner he had often adopted with her that her child was taking over. That was true. Something about Philip Schroeder made her ache for security. She thought of Jack and wished that he would come home tomorrow, instead of the day after. She wanted to feel his arms around her, to lay her head against his chest and hear the strong heartbeat.

Kevin inveigled his grandmother into playing a new game she had brought him, one in which each player attempted to advance tokens by outguessing his opponent about intended movement strategy. The boy, as competitive as his father, was devilishly clever about disguising his tactics and had proven to be almost unbeatable when he played with the women of the household. He liked the game enormously.

After a while Lisa went to the den, opened her briefcase, and took out the files she had brought home from the office. Histories of several of Wylie's patients were in the briefcase, but the only one she reviewed was Philip Schroeder's. Attached to the file jacket was a note in Cathy Jakes's flowing, Spenserian handwriting giving her the phone number of Dr. Larry Kimble at the state university. Lisa stared at it for a long time, trying to fix Kimble's features in her mind. She had only met him once, following a presentation he made at a luncheon of the state psychiatric association. He had discussed autism, as she recalled, a subject on which he had written frequently in several national medical journals. Kimble also prepared personality profiles of homicide suspects for law-enforcement agencies. It was in his capacity as a police consultant that he had phoned her. Despite her protests, he had insisted on giving her a profile of Nancy Sorgel's killer. Incredibly, he had asked if the profile fit any of her patients.

After working up her courage for several minutes, she dialed Kimble's number. She was relieved not only to find him at home but receptive to the idea of a luncheon appointment the next day. He suggested they get together at twelve-thirty in the faculty dining room at Baldwin Hall.

She had rehearsed an explanation, but he didn't ask for one.

BALDWIN HALL, WHICH HOUSED, in ironic juxtaposition, the psychology department, ROTC, and faculty dining room, stood atop a small hill near the center of the original campus. It was a daunting, fussy Victorian structure that had taken on an aspect not only of age but of eccentricity, so much did it contrast with the horizontal, aggressively modern, tan brick buildings which sprawled in all directions from the base of the hill.

Dr. Larry Kimble mirrored the architectural anomaly. He had sixty-year-old skin, lined and furrowed on his face, loose and flaccid on his neck, yet his clothing, which consisted of a striped cotton shirt and a pair of Jordache jeans with cargo pockets below his hips, proclaimed a youthful, contemporary look.

Lisa was still young enough to feel embarrassed in the presence of anyone so driven to deny his real age. She had noticed the tendency before in college professors, and attributed it to the pressure of having to associate constantly with genuine youth.

Kimble greeted Lisa with exaggerated warmth and gaiety, as if they were old friends. His effusive welcome put her on guard; people who displayed more friendliness than social convention dictated made her uncomfortable.

At his suggestion, they descended immediately by elevator

to the lower level and went to the faculty cafeteria. Lisa, going first through the serving line, took a tuna-salad sandwich and a cup of coffee. She was amused by the care Kimble took in choosing, after prolonged deliberation, a chef's salad and a glass of skimmed milk. He allowed her to pay for both orders.

After they had located a table and seated themselves, he asked, "What is it about your patient that brings you to me?"

She hadn't mentioned that she wanted to talk about a patient, so she was caught off guard by the question. Still, why else would she be here? She fought down the impulse to be coy and said simply, "He's been apprehended breaking and entering. He has a lot of hostility toward women. During one of his break-in episodes he defecated on the victim's bed."

"Fetishes?"

"Yes, women's undergarments."

For the moment that satisfied Kimble. He attacked his salad without the benefit of any dressing. Youth was thin.

Lisa picked up one half of the sandwich and took a bite.

At length he asked about some of the standard tests, grunting occasionally while she summarized what they revealed. "Did he ever talk about murder?" he asked. "I mean, did he ever specifically say he might kill someone?"

"Not to me. My colleague—this individual is really his patient—made several references to serial killers in his notes, though. The patient was fascinated by them."

"And your colleague is—"

She told him.

"Ah, how is Wylie? I understand he had a heart attack."

"No, a stroke," Lisa said. "You knew—know—him, I gather?"

"We were interns together. A good man, Wylie. How is he doing?"

"He's dying." She hoped her bluntness would convey somehow just how painful it was for her to talk about him.

He looked shocked for a moment, then went back to eating

his salad. He ate in quick bursts as if the intake of food repelled him and he had to finish before revulsion overcame him.

Between these bursts of feeding, he said, "I called you, among other therapists, because the police are stymied on the Sorgel killing. You probably think that's unprofessional, but the investigating team asked me to make the effort. The police hope you know of someone who fits the profile I gave you. Based on what I've heard so far, your man fits my profile like a glove. So tell me more about him."

When he realized that she wouldn't respond, he began a soliloquy which sounded like the beginning of a lecture. "He's a psychopath probably, from what little you've told me, but is he dangerous? That's what *you* really want to know, isn't it?" He didn't wait for an answer. "Dangerous? Who knows? Probably he isn't. Even with all the emotionally disturbed walking the streets, very few turn into Boston Stranglers and Charles Mansons.

"In the extremely slim possibility that your man is one of them, there's no way to tell it in advance. You can say with some certainty that the sticks of dynamite are in place, but you won't be able to predict what the fuse is, or what will set it off. Maybe nothing will. Maybe he'll die with his potential for mass murder unfulfilled.

"Which brings us to you. Even if you were pretty certain he was going to kill someone, you'd be reluctant to give his name to the police. If he says he's going to kill some specific person, you have a moral and ethical responsibility to warn that person. Usually that situation never develops. If he kills someone, it will probably be a stranger, or a group of strangers, each of whom is in his mind the woman he really hates." Kimble stopped long enough to put some more salad into his mouth. He ate it quickly. "But you know all that," he said. "So what do you intend to do?"

"You're a consultant to the police. I'm sure you have information on cases like the Sorgel killing."

"Yes, that's true. I review major cases and provide psychological profiles of killers. Some of the local police think that can be helpful in solving homicides.''

''What do *you* think?'' Lisa asked.

''Perhaps they are, perhaps not. It depends on how the cop leading the investigation uses the profile.''

Both of them concentrated on eating their lunches for a while. At length Lisa said, ''I read everything about the Sorgel homicide, including your profile of the killer.''

Fastidiously, he wiped his mouth with a paper napkin. ''It didn't help much unfortunately, which is why I wound up calling my colleagues.''

''Do the police have any real leads?''

Kimble shook his head. ''They don't have a clue. I wouldn't have made those calls if they weren't desperate.'' He studied Lisa thoughtfully, assessing the consequences of what he had said. Psychologists knew about consequences. ''County cop named Koepp is heading the investigation.''

She asked him to spell the name, then wrote it down in a notebook. Kimble, watching her, was amused. ''What do you plan to do, turn your patient over to Sergeant Koepp?'' His tone was condescending.

Lisa answered evenly that she hoped to examine the investigation file. Admitting her intent aloud forced her to confront the absurdity of what she was doing. Kimble studied a crime and created a psychological profile of the unknown killer; she had a psychological profile and was trying to find a crime to fit it. She had it backward.

''He won't let you see his file,'' Kimble told her.

''No, I suppose he wouldn't—''

The psychologist grinned. ''I have a fairly complete report on the murder, however, which I could share with a colleague, particularly one as attractive as you.''

She fought down the tart rejoinder his chauvinistic remark called for because she didn't want to ruin her chances of getting her hands on the investigation file. Sensing her eagerness was probably what had emboldened Kimble to make the remark.

But if he was foolish enough to talk like that, he was foolish enough to be useful.

"I would be most appreciative," she replied. She squeezed out a small smile and let it melt provocatively.

On their way back to the elevator Kimble said casually, "One other thing you might find interesting."

"Yes?"

"Sergeant Koepp thinks the Sorgel case is one of several murders with the same M.O."

"But you only talked about one case."

Kimble punched the up elevator button. "Koepp only has the Sorgel murder in his jurisdiction," Kimble told her, "but he's turned up at least two other homicides that are similar, one in Indiana, and one in Chicago, I think it was."

"What links them together—at least in Koepp's mind?"

The arriving elevator car was empty, so they continued their conversation on the way to the fourth floor. "Each victim was mutilated in the same way," he told her. "But the murders occurred so far apart your man may be off the hook."

"You mean because my patient isn't a transient, because he lives here?"

"Exactly," Kimble said. "You have to stay in one spot to undergo therapy."

"The other two homicides only matter if we accept Koepp's theory," Lisa said. "You know him. Can I rely on his being right about a connection between all three murders?"

"He's usually right," Kimble said. "Very thorough. When he makes an arrest, the D.A.'s office almost always gets a conviction." He looked oddly at her for a moment before asking, "Why are you so determined to get into this?"

"Because of some things Wylie wrote in his notes," she answered. "Our patient is obsessed with serial killings."

When they arrived back at Kimble's office, he had to search through a file cabinet for several minutes before he could produce the brown manila envelope which contained the background on the Sorgel murder. He handed the envelope to Lisa without looking at its contents.

"Do you know when the Indiana and Chicago murders occurred?" Lisa asked.

Kimble smiled. "No, but I have the feeling I'm going to call Koepp to find out." He looked very pleased with himself.

"It would be helpful," she assured him. She fixed her eyes on his when she smiled, suggesting an incentive.

TWO

JOANNE WHALEN INSPECTED herself in the full-length mirror in her bathroom with dispassionate objectivity. She pretended to examine the image in the mirror as he would see her. Hair falling loose over her bare shoulders. A generous amount of pink lipstick to disguise the smallness of her mouth. A touch of eyebrow accent and only the barest suggestion of shadow on her lids. She was satisfied with the result. She could never be as beautiful as some women, certainly not as lovely as his wife, but she knew he wouldn't be displeased. She opened the white peignoir and surveyed her lithe, white body. By dedicated dieting and a rigorous training program she had managed to keep her forty-year-old figure within its twenty-year-old dimensions, and that's what mattered most to a man four years younger than herself.

"Form follows function," she said to the mirror. Then she giggled.

She went to the wet bar and mixed some martinis in a metal shaker. She measured the gin and vermouth as meticulously as she had applied the eye shadow and lipstick. Five to one. If she did everything to please him, and did it perfectly, he would have to fall in love with her. Love her as she loved him, to the exclusion of everyone else.

When Jack called from the airport, he had said he had to pick up his luggage and catch a bus to the parking lot. Considering that he would be embroiled in rush-hour traffic, she had estimated he would be there in forty-five minutes, an hour at most.

She poured herself a drink, dropped a cocktail onion in it, and arranged herself on the couch. She wouldn't have to answer the door; he had keys for the downstairs hall and for her apartment.

His phone call had settled her nerves; before then she had agonized that this day they had planned so carefully might be destroyed by a missed airline connection or a last-minute "must attend" meeting at his company's New York headquarters. Now he was on the way to her. Just anticipating the evening ahead and the quiet intimacy of the morning gave her a languid, sensual feeling. She let her imagination develop the scene in her bedroom, the peach-colored sheets askew, his hard, naked body pressing down on hers, and later the faint aroma of fresh coffee brewing, the spear of morning sunlight beneath the lowered shade.

She would be good then, a woman to make him forget all other women. Pleasing men was what she did best, because she understood that all men were egotistical and that what they required more than beauty or sex or understanding was to be admired. He would succumb to that irresistible attraction, just as other men had, and then he would be hers.

With quickening excitement she heard the key being inserted in her door. She watched the handle turn and felt the shudder of desire.

To LISA'S SURPRISE, Larry Kimble called her the evening of the day on which they had lunched together at the university. He gave her the dates of the homicides in Chicago and Elkhart, Indiana, the first having occurred about three years earlier, the second fourteen months previously. Lisa jotted down the dates, then made a quick calculation. Nancy Sorgel had died eight months ago; the Elkhart homicide happened six months before that, the Chicago killing almost two years before the one in Indiana. All the cases were still open, according to what Sergeant Koepp had told Kimble.

Lisa remembered his saying the cases had the same M.O., but she hadn't had the presence of mind to ask for details. The similarities might be evident from the files he had given her, but she asked for his assessment.

"Same murder weapon—thin-bladed knife," Kimble said. "Multiple wounds in the chest and abdomen. All the women were living alone, all were in their thirties or early forties. No evidence of rape. No evidence of forcible entry into their apartments. All of them were killed at home, by the way. It's all in the files I gave you."

"I haven't had a chance to look at them yet," Lisa told him defensively. "That's odd about no evidence of forcible entry. It means that three women let him in. They must have known him."

Kimble laughed. "Don't try to play detective, Doctor," he told her. "You're interested in psychological profiles, remember?"

For a change she arrived home before six, so she was able to eat dinner with Rose and Kevin. Although her son greeted her warmly when she entered the house, she noticed almost at once that he was uncharacteristically glum. She looked at Rose, seated opposite her in the dining nook, questioningly, but the older woman shook her head slightly, warding off further discussion. During dinner Rose made a determined effort to reawaken the boy's interest in the snow sculptures they had seen in a city park after school. A local artists' association sponsored the event each February to raise funds for the Children's Hospital. Because Jack was on the hospital board, Rose loyally served on the volunteer committee which publicized the snow sculpture competition. As a treat for Kevin she took him each year to the official judging by a group of local celebrities. "I liked the Statue of Liberty," Rose said. "It was just like the one in New York, wasn't it, Kevin?"

"I guess so," he answered, with more politeness than conviction.

"Kevin liked the horse and sleigh the best, though," Rose said. She smiled then, and nodded toward her grandson's plate, calling Lisa's attention to the fact that the boy was fashioning his own tiny sculpture with a pile of mashed potatoes. Whatever it was he had in mind to build, his efforts were frustrated by the vegetable's lack of body. He didn't comment on the horse and sleigh.

Instead he said, "We tried to call Daddy, but he wasn't at the hotel anymore." It was clear from his manner that he felt betrayed and expected reassurance from his mother.

"Well, they must have been confused," Lisa said. "Of course he's there. We'll try in a little while and I bet we can talk to him." She looked at Rose expectantly. "He's at the Sheraton. That's where you called, isn't it?"

"Yes, like always," she said. "I tried later. He checked out." Rose's normally animated face was drained of expression; it reminded Lisa of the faces in a wax museum.

With more hope than she felt, Lisa suggested that he might have finished his meeting early and had decided to come home that day. But Kevin shook his head.

"He would have called, Mama. And I turned on the message 'corder. We didn't have any messages except from the stupid ol' clinic." He watched his mother abstractedly. Kevin was beginning to learn that grownups couldn't always be counted on after all.

Lisa fell silent for the moment, giving up hope of changing the boy's mood immediately. She silently cursed the adolescent male's compatibility with gadgets such as telephone recorders. Men often were intimidated by electronic wizardry; small boys never were.

Kevin was right. Jack would have called if he were coming home today. She didn't know where her husband was at the moment. What was worse, Rose knew it, which made it difficult to pretend she wasn't annoyed and resentful.

It wasn't the first time either.

A HIGH PRESSURE SYSTEM FROZE the brittle refuse left by the storm and bathed the city and its sprawling suburbs in glistening light Friday morning. Sunlight bounced off the crystalline landscape with such ferocity that Lisa actually experienced some discomfiture whenever she looked directly out of her office windows. Her young patient, however, seemed oblivious to the light as she stood, her back to Lisa, in front of the south window and gazed fixedly at some object in the distance. As she waited for her patient to regain control of her emotions, Lisa thought of Van Gogh working feverishly in the merciless sun of Provence. The beginning of his madness. Oh, not madness. An ear infection, they said now.

Her name was Pauline Boushard and she had recently been divorced. Lisa thought of her as young even though she was thirty-eight because the woman was pathetically immature in her dealings with the important people in her life. She was one of the unlucky people who are genuinely surprised to find that their marriage had disintegrated. After several weeks of therapy, Pauline was making the transition from bewilderment to anger, but as yet she had not gained any insights into how her clinging passivity had contributed to the divorce.

"It's true, isn't it?" Pauline said in a voice thick with phlegm. "Some men can't help themselves. They just aren't capable of monogamy. Robert is incredibly good-looking. I always knew that. I could see other women throwing themselves at him—in fact we used to joke about it after we'd come home from one of those dreadful parties his firm put on at Christmas. He would make fun of the women who did that. He actually felt sorry for them!"

"What did you say when he said that he felt sorry for them?" Lisa asked.

"I would kid him, but also flatter him, by telling him that he was so attractive they couldn't help themselves. I'd say maybe he should take pity on them—make love to a different secretary each year. A special Christmas bonus, I'd call it." She began to sob again, then rushed back to the couch so she could grab another Kleenex from the box that Lisa always kept on a nearby end table.

Lisa smiled reflexively, remembering Wylie's puckish claim

that the clinic bought more Kleenex than any other medicinal aid. "Sometimes," she told her snuffling patient, "we insist on giving something in a relationship which the other person doesn't want. Then we get a different result than we expected."

"What do you mean?"

"You said that you flattered Robert when you both talked about the overtures he got from other women. What did you intend for Robert to do when you acted that way?"

"I didn't intend for him to go to bed with them," Pauline said indignantly. "I wanted him to be faithful to me like I was faithful to him. We took vows—"

"Did you think what you said might have encouraged him to be unfaithful? You implied the women couldn't help themselves because he was so attractive. Maybe he used that argument on himself when he met a woman he found physically attractive."

"Are you saying his infidelity was my fault?"

"No, I'm simply trying to offer an example to show that communication is not what we say or intend but what the listener understands us to say and intend. Sometimes these can be very different. Sometimes they're opposites."

"I don't know why we're talking about Robert. That's over, the divorce decree is final. What's the point?"

"The point is that we learn from a failed relationship," Lisa said gently. "You're young, you have a full life ahead of you. You're going to meet other people, perhaps fall in love with someone. You can prepare for that by using the experience you had with Robert to, ah, make your expectations conform more closely with reality." Lisa realized immediately that she had gone too far. She had started to lecture the subject. As Wylie would have said: "The patient's insights are gold, the therapist's are dross."

Pauline underscored the failure by reverting back to anger. "I should have known what the bastard was up to. I used to know where he was all the time. The unexpected meetings, the times when he had to stay late at the office, the unexpected trips out of town. You can tell when a man is playing around if you want to.''

She might have been describing Jack, Lisa thought uneasily.

As soon as the session ended, Dr. Tom Luchow came into Lisa's office. She knew after one glance at his face, which was normally animated and aglow with puppy-dog friendliness, that he brought bad news. Even before he opened his mouth, she knew what he had come to tell her.

''It's about Wylie,'' Lisa said. ''He's dead, isn't he?''

Tom nodded, but his eyes never left hers; it was as if he expected to find something there to reassure himself. After a few seconds he departed, as silently as he had entered, and as bereft of reassurance.

Lisa felt calm, almost relieved, now that it was over. Her mind functioned with remarkable lucidity. She called Cathy Jakes on the intercom and instructed her to cancel her appointments for the balance of the day. Then she went to St. Luke's Hospital.

She found Terri in the business office on the first floor where she was signing a release form so that Wylie's body could be transferred to a local funeral home. When she saw Lisa she rose to her feet, keeping a hand on the back of her chair to steady herself, and embraced her. They held each other for a long time, saying nothing, and Lisa felt the tiny spasms of Terri's sobs.

For the rest of the day Lisa stayed at her friend's side, waiting in Wylie's book-laden den while Terri called relatives, driving her to the funeral home, accompanying her to a small boutique downtown to help her select a black dress for the memorial service. It had taken Lisa the better part of an hour to convince Terri that shopping for a new dress was not an inappropriate activity for a woman on the day her husband died. She won the argument when she finally had the good sense to ask, ''Would Wylie object if he were here? Would he feel dishonored?''

Terri, remembering, had agreed that Wylie not only would

not have objected, but would have insisted on it; he had been a great believer in activity as a means of relieving stress.

Late in the afternoon, driving home on the freeway, Terri talked about how Wylie had died. "When I got there he was conscious, just lying there calmly waiting for me. As soon as I came into the room he smiled without opening his eyes and held up his hand for me to take it. He was completely lucid and spoke as clearly as I have ever heard him. We talked about the trip we made to Switzerland and Austria on our thirty-fifth anniversary, then about the kids, then about you."

"Me?"

"Oh, yes. I think sometimes he thought of you more like a daughter than he did of his own Joyce. I told him that you were looking after some of his patients, which I thought might make him feel, well, like there was continuity, something to go back to. It's strange how we try to find ways to reassure those we love that they aren't dying even when they know they are. We must do that for ourselves, I suppose. Anyway, he became agitated when I told him that and made me promise to tell you not to treat the 'mama's boy.' He couldn't remember the name. My mind went blank and I couldn't help him, either, but I knew who he meant."

"He meant Philip Schroeder," Lisa said.

"Yes, I'm sure that's the one," Terri said. She held the box which contained her new dress tightly in her lap and gazed out the car window with a drawn, defeated expression. "He was afraid for you, Lisa." After a long time she added, "He died in my arms. He never opened his eyes the whole time, but I knew he could see me just the same. I know that sounds crazy—"

"No, it's not. He could see you. Wylie always saw more than other people. He saw with his heart."

Several times during the day, as they drove from one place to another, Lisa had noticed the same blue minivan in her rearview mirror.

But she did not then attach any significance to the vehicle. Or its driver.

THE CAT'S PAW WAS an undergraduate hangout across the street from the "old gym," the one where intramural basketball games were played, so the tavern smelled not only of tap beer but of sweat, wintergreen oil, and talcum powder. Detective Sergeant Ray Koepp saw his partner wriggle her nose with distaste as soon as they were inside and inundated with the athletic aroma. He didn't mind. He was glad it smelled like a man's place.

Margaret, surveying the crowded bar and the booths along the wall opposite them, said at length, "I don't think he's here."

"How would you know?" Koepp asked her. "You don't know what he looks like."

'Yes, I do. I met him once in the lieutenant's office, three, maybe four years ago." She glanced at Koepp, saw that he was still skeptical, and added, "Early sixties, red hair that goes in all directions, wire-rim glasses, built like Ichabod Crane, imperial nose—"

"Okay," Koepp said, chastened. "I was a fool to doubt."

"That's all right," she answered sweetly. "But he's not— oh, oh—check the guy coming out of the boy's room. Larry Kimble or I'm Mother Theresa."

"Impressive," Koepp said. "Would you like to be my partner, Detective?"

"Yes," she responded. Deadly serious. She was always doing things like that, being grave when he expected her to make a joke, laughing unexpectedly in the middle of tense situations. "What's he doing with those coeds?" She was referring to two college girls who were seated across from Kimble when he settled into one of the booths.

"He's trying to get laid. They're trying to get an A in psych." Koepp managed to catch Kimble's eye, and waved. The professor said something to the girls, who turned and looked up at Koepp with expressions of mild reproof. They climbed out of the booth.

"They could be his granddaughters!"

"He knows that," Koepp said. "But he claims he has no choice. He told me that women in their thirties and forties think he's too old for them. Girls of twenty think he's a challenge."

Professor Kimble stood up to shake hands with Koepp, then with Margaret. Before anyone could perform introductions, he addressed her by her first name. This feat of memory momentarily unsettled Margaret's composure; she wasn't used to people whose memory for details and names was as accurate as hers. Koepp, whose recall was unexceptional, allowed himself a moment of malicious satisfaction. Kimble held Margaret's slender hand in his own for a long time, challenging her to withdraw it. But she remained passive, compelling him at length to let go first; it wasn't easy to intimidate Detective Loftus.

They sat down, Kimble on one side, the two detectives on the other. "I suppose you're here because I asked you about the Sorgel case?"

"You didn't ask me about Sorgel," Koepp said. "You asked me about the cases in Chicago and Elkhart."

"Ah, yes, so I did."

"Don't be cute with me, Larry," Koepp said. "What have you got to tell me?"

"A colleague asked me about unsolved murders. I mentioned Sorgel. I also discussed your theory that her homicide might be linked to the others."

"That's police business, Doctor. You had no right to—"

"This person is a physician. There's no possibility that your investigation will be compromised."

"That's for me to judge."

Kimble was not offended by Koepp's tone. He laughed softly. "You must be desperate indeed to come over here on a day like this."

"We were in the neighborhood. Besides, it was quitting time

and we're on our way home. Why is your colleague interested? He's a therapist?''

"Yes, as a matter of fact. A patient exhibiting some disturbing symptoms. A psychopath.''

Koepp pulled his notebook from a pocket of his sport jacket and opened it. As he felt around the inside of the pocket for a ballpoint pen, he asked, "Who is your friend?''

"I'm sorry, I can't tell you that. I would be violating a confidence.''

"Sometimes that's necessary," Koepp said. His partner had found a pen, which she handed to him. When he saw that Kimble wasn't going to respond, he considered making threatening noises about obstructing justice. Almost at once he discarded that tactic. Kimble was too intelligent to be intimidated. He shifted to a new topic. "You have my notes, a photostat of the ME's autopsy, copies of the files from Chicago and Elkhart—you didn't share that with your colleague, I trust?''

Kimble paused for a moment before he answered. "No.''

He's lying, Koepp thought. He glanced at Margaret to see what her reaction was. But her face revealed nothing. Koepp felt the beginning of anger, his inevitable reaction whenever upright citizens refused to cooperate in an investigation. He had more patience with criminals than with unsupportive civilians.

Kimble seemed to sense his growing irritation and attempted to mollify him. "Believe me, if anything comes of it, you'll know right away. I'll insist on it. But you must realize that therapists often come across people who have the potential for criminal actions. It's worrisome, but we can't turn every unbalanced person in to the police.''

"Your friend is obviously going to see if the patient has an alibi. Will you tell me what he determines?''

"Perhaps. I can't promise. You'll have to trust me.''

"And your friend," Koepp said.

Later, when he and Margaret were walking back to her car, he asked her if she thought Kimble lied about not showing the investigation records to his "colleague." Margaret was usually skeptical if a witness was too glib. This time she surprised him.

"I don't know," she admitted. "If he was lying, he's good at it. Maybe psychologists have to lie to patients—tell small lies to arrive at the greater truth. They might get to be very adept at that sort of thing."

Maybe, Koepp thought. He felt almost certain that Kimble had shown the file on the Sorgel case to the unknown psychiatrist. On previous cases Koepp had come to respect the psychologist's professional acumen but not his judgment. Kimble tended to look on criminal activity as a fascinating aberration of the human mind, not as something that was a threat to society. Koepp wished now that he had followed accepted police procedure and held back one essential fact from the information he gave Kimble. He had agonized over his decision at the time, but in the end had included the medical examiner's reports about the mutilations because they had such pronounced psychological implications.

He was sure now that he had made a mistake. He had trusted Kimble.

THREE

PHILIP SCHROEDER LEARNED that his therapist, Dr. Wylie Frymark, had died about ten o'clock Friday morning. He had called the clinic to talk to Lisa Robbins and was informed by the receptionist that she had canceled her appointments for the day. Philip could tell from the girl's voice that something bad had happened because she sounded as if she had been crying. Only something dramatic would have caused Lisa to cancel her appointments. He began to feel excited.

"Is she sick?" he asked.

"I'm sorry, I'll take a message—"

"I'm a patient," Philip said harshly. "Tell me how to reach her. I demand to know where she is."

He could sense the girl's hesitation, and knew she would tell him what he wanted to know. He remembered that her name was Cathy Jakes. She was an airhead.

"It's Dr. Frymark, the man who started the clinic," Cathy told him. "He died this morning, and Dr. Robbins—"

Philip didn't wait for any further explanation. He told his supervisor that he was not feeling well and was going home. But he didn't go to his apartment. Instead, he drove to St. Luke's Hospital and idled slowly past the entry gate for the physicians' parking lot. As he had suspected, the Volvo was parked there, looking out of place flanked by a Camaro and a Porsche.

He found a parking space from where he could see the exit driveway clearly. He had to leave the motor running so he could keep his van warm, but he didn't think she would be there very long; hospitals didn't like having dead bodies around. Now, with time to fill, he considered what might happen to him because of his leaving work. The bitch who claimed

to be his boss didn't believe he was sick. He could tell by the
expression on her face. By now she had discussed the matter
with the MIS department head, Mr. Bates, and demanded that
he be discharged. Bates, if he ran true to form, would promise
to take the matter under consideration. That meant he would
do nothing. This time Develice would go higher, talk to the
vice president of finance as she had threatened to do, because
Develice was the polar opposite of Bates. He never did anything; she always did something. Eventually, even though she
was a woman, they would have to fire Bates and put her in
charge of the systems people. Philip didn't want to be there
when that cataclysm occurred. He wanted to be fired so he
could spend more time watching Her. He couldn't just quit
because of his mother, but if he got canned she would blame
the company, not him.

Of course, it wasn't just following Her that occupied him
now. The New Messianic Church had begun to open its doors
in the afternoons so members could study in the library or
watch tapes of the television shows, or, on Tuesdays and
Thursdays, participate in a biblical discussion group. A plan
had been forming in his mind for weeks now, and it had become so compelling and engrossing that he knew he was re-
ceiving Divine Inspiration. God had spoken to him in his
dreams, as He had to Joseph, told him to go into his own Egypt,
become a deacon of the New Messianic Church. To do that he
couldn't just wait for a bolt of lightning to come down from
Mt. Ararat. He had to help, prove his worth to the elders of
the church, show by his zeal that he had the Calling. He had
come to the attention of the church leaders because of his assistance in setting up a new computerized accounting system
for them, but in the process he had seen other ways in which
he could use his computer skills for their benefit. However, his
plans depended on being available during the day. This was
his chance to finally do what he wanted, to get his mother out
of his life for good. He had to make time.

Lisa left the parking lot within half an hour of Philip's arrival. Dr. Frymark's widow, driving her own car, preceded her. Philip followed them, keeping several car lengths between himself and the Volvo. When they stopped at a home in Collinswood—he assumed it was Frymark's—Philip pulled his van over about half a block from the driveway and parked so he could survey the front of the house in his rearview mirror. He waited until, at last, they came out and drove to a funeral home. He spent the rest of the afternoon following them by car to a mall, then by foot as they shopped in several women's clothing stores.

When he realized they were looking for a dress for Frymark's wife, he was shocked. He couldn't believe anyone was so callous that she would go shopping the day her husband died. Almost at once he decided that the Frymark woman was doing it because she was under Her influence. Maybe She was celebrating because She would control the whole clinic or something. Why not? It had happened before. She had driven his father out, made it impossible for him to live with them. The weak little man got nothing, while she and her vulture lawyers took the house and all the money, so much money that she hadn't worked a day since and had more money today than when she divorced him. Now she was taking over the clinic, getting control of that, too, so that he'd have no place left on earth.

No place anywhere on earth.

He realized then that he was mixing the two of them together, his doctor's wife and his mother. They were so much alike.

For a few minutes he lost sight of them inside one of the shops, so he edged up to the store window, pretending to look at an outfit on one of the mannequins. His attention was arrested momentarily by the elegant black sheath dress on the unrealistically slender plastic woman. Lisa turned toward him as she held up a dress for Mrs. Frymark to examine. At that instant, before he could back out of sight, he thought she might have recognized him.

JACK WAS HOME when she arrived, standing at the sink in the kitchen and talking in an animated manner with Kevin and Rose. As soon as she entered the house, he came to her and wrapped her in his arms.

"I'm sorry about Wylie, darling," he whispered in her ear after he had kissed her. He continued to embrace her so firmly that she began to feel uncomfortable; she couldn't rid herself of a sense of embarrassment whenever he was too intimate, too sexual, in front of their son. It was healthful for Kevin to see that they were affectionate, but she couldn't help how she felt.

Jack thought her attitude prudish and sometimes held her too long just to tease her.

Sensing her tension now, he released her and stepped back.

"How did you know?" Lisa mumbled.

"I told him," Rose said. "Cathy Jakes called while I was doing the housecleaning. She gave me some other messages for you. They're on your desk in the den."

During Rose's dinner of spaghetti and meatballs they talked about Wylie and Terri, then about Jack's trip to New York. Kevin listened with his usual solemnly intense expression to the adults' conversation for a while without comment, then, to Lisa's dismay, he told his father about their unsuccessful attempt to reach him by phone the night before. Jack answered his son's question with grave detachment, as if he were speaking to another adult. "I intended to tell you that I wouldn't be at the Sheraton last night, but things just happened so fast. Our eastern regional manager asked me to call on Dearman Associates in Connecticut. So we went up there last night. That way I could meet them this morning and still get back to Kennedy in time to catch my flight." He chuckled grimly. "It was a wasted trip, though. We're still going to lose the account."

"What was the problem?" Rose asked. It was a curious question, because she normally showed little interest in Jack's business. Lisa assumed she was trying to help her son shift the conversation away from the change in hotels.

"They have a new hot-shot controller," Jack said. "He

thinks we're managing their pension money too conserva-
tively." Jack made it sound very plausible.

Kevin didn't understand the explanation, but he appeared to
be satisfied with it, for which Lisa was grateful; she never
wanted her son to lose faith in his father. She knew from first-
hand experience how desolating that could be.

Later, after Rose had gone back to her apartment, Lisa
helped Kevin start his homework, then joined Jack in the family room. Her husband folded up the evening newspaper and
patted his lap invitingly. Even in these strained circumstances
she couldn't stop being a psychiatrist; was the invitation to
physical contact a means of assuaging guilt or just an attempt
to allay her suspicions? She smiled but sat on the hassock in
front of his chair.

"I have to tell you about something else that happened,"
she said. "But I want you to promise not to overreact."

His eyes warmed with amusement as he reached out and took
her hand. "You totaled your car."

"Nothing that simple, I'm afraid," she said. Now that she
was committed, she couldn't wait to get it out. "One of my
patients is following me."

Although Jack didn't say anything at first, she could tell by
the expression on his dark, angular face that he was shocked,
which did nothing to bolster Lisa's confidence. She had anticipated bland reassurance. Instead, he asked uneasily, "Who is
he?"

Apparently it never entered his mind that the patient might
be a woman. Did women ever follow other women? She
thought about the question briefly and decided that it would be
awkward and possibly dangerous for a woman to shadow anyone; errant behavior was always more difficult for females.
"He was a patient of Wylie's actually. I've only had a few
sessions with him."

"It's not coincidence?"

"At first, when I saw him in front of a clothing store at the
mall, that's what I thought. He jumped back when he saw me

looking at him, but I told myself he was just embarrassed at meeting me outside the clinic. Patients are like that—they don't expect to run into you in other circumstances.''

He nodded. He knew the truth of what she said because he had witnessed several clumsy attempts by her patients to avoid her at cocktail parties. ''So why worry?''

''He followed me home tonight. I recognized his van.''

''You mean he's outside on the street right now?'' He started to get up, but Lisa grabbed his hand.

''No, he drove past the house and kept going. I turned off the garage light and checked the street. He's gone.''

Jack's face tightened into an expressionless mask. ''I'll check again in a little while. What's his name?''

That was the second time he had asked that question, although he should have known that she wouldn't tell him.

''Is he dangerous?'' Jack asked rather tentatively.

''No more than any other patient,'' she answered. She hoped she sounded more confident than she felt.

''Maybe it's an infatuation. You've experienced that before. Every therapist has.''

Kevin came into the family room, announced that he was ready to read, and looked expectantly at both parents. He excelled in reading and didn't need adult help, but he wanted to show off. Jack signaled he would supervise tonight's lesson by standing up and walking toward the couch. Kevin, elated that he would command his father's full attention, raced ahead of him and bounced onto the couch.

Lisa took Jack's chair and listened for a while to the misadventures of a robot named Bob. Seeing that the pair was absorbed, she went to her study to look at Larry Kimble's file in her attaché case. Although she recalled leaving it on top of her desk, the case now stood on the floor next to a wastepaper basket. She was momentarily confused until she remembered that Rose cleaned the room on Fridays. She sat at the desk and laid the case on its side so she could read the combination-lock numbers. The five digits displayed on the face of the lock

were the same ones required to open it. That was odd. She
habitually rotated the numbers until a line of five zeros showed.
She paused, trying to remember when it was exactly that she
had closed the case. Had she been interrupted while she was
locking it? No, there had been no phone call or other intrusion
that might have caused her to forget to return the numbers to
zero. She stared at the case, trying to find a logical explanation.
She sometimes brought home medical records in the case, so
she always kept it locked. She wouldn't have forgotten something like that. As Jack said, she was compulsive.

Rose?

That possibility seemed almost as unlikely. Her mother-in-
law neither pried into her professional life nor violated their
privacy.

The only other person in the house had been Kevin, and
while he might have been curious enough to try to open the
case, he didn't know the combination. Nor did Rose, for that
matter, as far as she knew, but the combination was in the back
of her address book. Just the five numbers, with no explanation
of what the digits represented.

She looked inside. Kimble's file was on top of her other
papers, where she remembered leaving it. She opened the
brown manila folder and carefully reviewed its documents.
Nothing was missing.

Holding the file had the effect of bringing Philip Schroeder's
nimbus into her study: she could hear his sarcastic voice, feel
his penetrating, obtrusive stare so vividly that a tiny convulsive
reaction, much like a shiver, went through her body.

She was glad Jack was home. She hoped that he would take
her in his arms when they were in bed, hold her close and tell
her that she had nothing to fear from Schroeder.

For the first time, she felt the stirring of a very unprofessional anger toward her difficult patient. He had reminded her
that she was a member of the vulnerable sex.

THE MOURNERS AT Dr. Wylie Frymark's brief, nonreligious funeral ceremony overflowed the available seating in what the

tall, avuncular funeral director called the visitation parlor and spilled over into the hallway. Most of the clinic staff were on hand, as well as several of Wylie's sisters and their husbands. The others, doctors and therapists for the most part, were known to Lisa, with one or two exceptions. One stranger was a tall man in his late thirties with sandy hair, a slightly hooked nose, and a thin, sensitive face. She noticed him because he looked out of place. Not out of place in the role of a mourner, but out of place in the late twentieth century. She imagined him as an eighteenth-century French bureaucrat, then as a character in a Chekhov play, a Russian landowner with greatly diminished resources. Neither role fit him. He was one of those people who shed personal identity.

Philip Schroeder had also arrived to offer his respects to the deceased counselor. He looked strikingly different in a neat, dark-blue suit and conservative, striped tie. Dressed as he was, some might even judge him as rather good-looking. He avoided eye contact with Lisa whenever she glanced in his direction, but she felt the pressure of his stare on the back of her head once she turned away.

Wylie's sister Peg self-consciously gave a short eulogy, which consisted of a recitation of Wylie's professional accomplishments, his medical philosophy, and a few unrevealing and insipid anecdotes from their youth in a small town in Indiana. She made a good choice as a spokesman for the Frymark family: as a dean of women at a small private college she had gained enough experience at public speaking to be conversational and self-effacing; she was the only other atheist in the family, so she was less apt to make some tasteless remark about the Deity; and she was the only one of Wylie's four sisters with whom he did not get on, making it less likely that she would be overcome in mid-eulogy by a crying spasm.

Lisa, who was on the edge of tears, was grateful for Peg's detachment. She thought the other mourners might be also because they seemed uneasy throughout the brief service. She had noticed this phenomenon before at cremations and had always attributed it to the abruptness of disposal of the loved one's mortal remains. A cemetery burial had the virtue of unwinding the tension of the onlookers in a logical, predictable progression. Cremation, on the other hand, not only occurred with unpredictable suddenness, but visited physical destruction on the loved one's body as well. In terms of human psychology, cremation was flawed.

The dreadful moment arrived. Peg finished speaking, bowed slightly as if she had finished her recitation in a forensics contest, then turned to watch a purple drape enclose Wylie's casket. Lisa imagined that hidden from view a pair of workmen were even now trundling the casket to an oven in the bowels of the funeral home. Inevitably the staff would refer to the crematoria furnace as Dante's Inferno. The thought moved her; Wylie would be amused. Quite unexpectedly, she began to cry.

She had arranged earlier to ride to the office with Tom Luchow so that Rose could go home in her own car directly, without having to take Lisa to the clinic. Tom stood a few feet away, reluctant to intrude on her grief. Finally, he said he would bring his car to the front of the building and departed. She shook hands again with Wylie's brothers-in-law, hugged his sister Eileen for a moment, then embraced Terri.

"I'll call you in a day or two," Lisa said softly. Terri, her eyes fulgent with tears, nodded jerkily.

Among the professional people who attended, she had noticed Larry Kimble from the university. He was standing near the exit door, obviously waiting for her. Lisa dabbed at her eyes with a hanky, then walked toward him. She was surprised to see him there because Wylie had never mentioned him.

After he mumbled something about condolences, he stood in awkward silence for a moment. Neither of them could think of anything to say, perhaps because they felt as though they should talk about the deceased, yet they had no shared Wylie experiences.

Lisa became aware that another person had joined them, the

tall, sandy-haired man she had noticed in the audience earlier. He stood expectantly near her right elbow.

Kimble looked at the stranger blankly, and Lisa thought, a little rudely, for a few seconds, then cleared his throat and said, "Dr. Robbins, this is Sergeant Koepp."

She made a quarter turn to her right and put out her hand, which Koepp took with exaggerated gentleness. He smiled sympathetically while his eyes hurried around her face, cataloging details. His expression suggested that he was on the verge of apologizing for something. Her only impression was that he appeared to be too esthetic for a policeman. Her earlier assessment that he was not a twentieth-century product was reinforced.

With as much dignity as she could summon, she turned an accusatory stare at Larry Kimble and felt genuine satisfaction when he seemed to blanch. "Is the price still thirty pieces of silver?" she asked.

Although he opened his mouth to answer, Sergeant Koepp spoke up first. "Meeting you was entirely my idea," the detective said. "We both have a problem. It seemed sensible that we meet to see if we can help each other. I promised Dr. Kimble that if you weren't in a position to help, I wouldn't press the issue."

"This is an inappropriate time, don't you think? Why didn't you just make an appointment to come by the clinic?"

"Would you have seen me?" Koepp asked.

"No," Lisa said. "But it would have saved all three of us some embarrassment."

"I'm sorry," Koepp said, "I didn't mean to embarrass you."

His concern was so genuine and unfeigned that Lisa was momentarily taken aback; from a policeman she expected either no apology, or a practiced, professional one. She wondered if he was that considerate of crime suspects.

"It's all right," she muttered. "We can use the lounge near the entrance."

"Fine," he said, holding out a hand to signify that she should lead.

They went into the hallway and walked to a room near the front of the mortuary which was reserved for grieving smokers. Several stuffed chairs and two couches were arranged in a conversational grouping. The walls of the room were adorned with three Barbizon school landscapes—Corots perhaps—chosen no doubt to match the carpet's earth tones. Koepp actually looked briefly at each of the prints. The air smelled of cigarette smoke and the faint, astringent scent of some kind of industrial carpet cleaner.

When Larry asked if he could stay, Koepp shrugged and looked at Lisa. She nodded. The men arranged themselves so that the three of them formed a triangle, signaling, perhaps unintentionally, that they were not going to gang up on her.

Oppressive silence ruled for several seconds, until Larry, feeling the obligation of a host, said pointedly to Sergeant Koepp, "You said you were interested in Dr. Robbins's profile of a serial killer, not in any particular patient—"

It was an absurdly transparent attempt to excuse his own treachery in arranging for Koepp to meet her, and to Koepp's credit he didn't play along with it. "If I gave that impression, Larry, I didn't mean to," Koepp said. "I am very interested in the qualities of abnormalities in one of Dr. Robbins's patients that prompted her to inquire about the Sorgel murder."

"Any murder," Larry said. "I was the one who mentioned the Sorgel case." He was still trying, for Lisa's benefit, to show that the detective's inquiry would be generic, not specific.

"Right," Koepp agreed. He was smiling faintly. "What pattern do you recognize as suggestive of sociopathic behavior, the kind of behavior which might lead to serial killing?"

"A history of mistreatment of women or fantasies about assaulting women," Lisa said. "Violence against animals. A fetish, like destroying women's clothes." She paused, unsure of what he wanted, but he only nodded encouragingly. "Potential serial killers might have some kind of religious obsession—

think God is speaking to them, for example. Often such people have sexual identity problems and reality is blurred—''

"Blurred?"

"They aren't sure where reality ends and their fantasies begin," she said. "I don't see how this can be very helpful. You could find out what I just told you by reading a textbook on the subject. I'm sure Larry could recommend a number of titles for you." This last remark was condescending and Lisa knew it, but she just couldn't help herself; Koepp had a quality of disingenuousness that challenged her and antagonized her at the same time.

"A textbook wouldn't tell me which of these traits you thought were predictive," Koepp replied patiently. "I'm interested in your subjective evaluation of the behaviors which your profession says are important."

"Not so. You want me to finger a specific patient. You've got an unsolved murder on your hands that's beginning to get moldy and you think I can give you a suspect."

"Precisely."

From the corner of her eye Lisa saw Larry Kimble shift uncomfortably in his chair. Sergeant Koepp, however, studied her with a bemused expression, as if he were watching the antics of a precocious preschooler. But he wasn't offensive about it, she had to give him that. His candor disarmed her; she had expected him to dissemble about his real intentions.

"It would be unethical for me to betray the trust of a patient that way," she told him. "Psychiatry depends totally on the patient trusting the doctor. If I compromise that, it could do irreparable harm to the person I'm treating. Surely you must understand that?"

"I can appreciate that risk, but there is risk also for an innocent person if you conceal the fact that a patient has homicide in mind."

"There is no evidence of that in any of my patients."

"If you were as confident as you sound, Doctor, you wouldn't have made inquiries about unsolved murder cases

through Dr. Kimble," Koepp said. "Still, you're the best judge
of the condition of your patients. I understand that you won't
reveal the identity of a specific patient, but I would still like
to have you review the Sorgel case and give me any impressions you might form about the kind of person we're looking
for."

Lisa had little interest in doing what he asked, but she happened to look out the front window, then at a passing automobile carrying mourners back to the routines of the living.
Somewhere in the parking lot Philip Schroeder might still be
waiting in his dark van. Even if he were not, she knew that he
would follow her home tonight, or be waiting for her in the
morning. That thought put a little lump of dread in her stomach.

The dread spoke for her. "I'll review what you have and
give you my impressions. But no suspect names."

"Deal," Koepp said. He looked surprised.

BEING IN THE SAME ROOM with Philip Schroeder, Lisa discovered three days later, was less intimidating for her than she had
expected. She speculated that she might feel more secure because they were in her patient conference room at the clinic
where she maintained territorial supremacy. Or was it simply
that other people, professional allies, were close at hand?

Because he had spoken of God several times, she encouraged
him to express his religious views and his affiliation with a
fundamentalist church he recently had discovered.

"Do I think God speaks to us individually?" he said, repeating her question. He grinned at her. "You want to know
if I think like that guy in Chicago, John Wayne Gacy, the guy
who killed all those kids and put them in his basement. He said
that God told him to do it."

Lisa was startled by the connection he had made with the
infamous Gacy. She kept silent, encouraging him to continue.

"He used God as an excuse. God didn't talk to him. He
couldn't because He doesn't exist."

"If you believe that," Lisa asked, "why are you going to a church?"

"Oh, I believe in God. You're the one who doesn't."

"What I think doesn't—"

"Doesn't matter? Yes it does. You don't believe in God. You study Freud and pretty soon you think like he did, that the only reason to believe in God is to keep from being neurotic."

She tried to regain the initiative. "You said that you are going to a church, yet you said God doesn't exist. I don't understand that. Do you believe in God or not?"

"Do I believe in God or not?" He rose suddenly and began to walk aimlessly around the room, stopping to examine things which could not have interested him, such as the top of a bookcase, the cord which controlled the venetian blinds. He traced his finger along whatever surface he was contemplating. "God exists because I believe He does. God does not exist because you do not believe He exists."

"That's contradictory. Either God exists in reality or He doesn't. Our perceptions of His existence don't agree. All that proves is that one of us is wrong."

"But that's my point—perception *is* reality. I exist because God wills it. God exists because I will it."

"Philip, if God does not exist because I don't believe He exists, then He can't will that I exist. Therefore I do not exist. That's absurd."

He slammed his fist down on the arm of the sofa and cried triumphantly. "That's right. That's right. You don't exist."

FOUR

ON WEDNESDAY EVENINGS after the watch was relieved, the proprietor of O'Malley's kept the corner booth available for the watch commander, Lieutenant George Tarrish, and his party. It wasn't because the lieutenant was such a loyal customer that this accommodation was made but rather because Vito Gianelli, the ethnically inappropriate owner, didn't want to lose the other policemen who were habitués of his bar. Cops were the backbone of his business, and he feared that a word from Tarrish could discourage them from coming in after work.

The lieutenant only appeared on Wednesdays because that was the day his wife played bridge with her girlfriends. It was his night "out."

On this particular Wednesday, the lieutenant had two guests, Sergeant Ray Koepp and Detective Margaret Loftus. This was somewhat unusual because neither Koepp nor his partner spent much time in O'Malley's; certainly not on Wednesdays because it was an unwritten rule that if somebody in the squad room had a personal problem that couldn't be worked out in Tarrish's office, he could bring it up on Wednesday at O'Malley's. Everyone else was supposed to stay away. Koepp and Loftus, as everyone knew, didn't have personal problems; they were both single.

The corner booth served approximately the same function as confessionals in Catholic churches, Koepp thought idly as he watched the smoke curl up from Tarrish's cigarette. The lieutenant had given up smoking several years earlier except for Wednesday nights at O'Malley's, so he savored his first smoke in a week. It was not considered prudent to bring up requests for a boon until the nicotine was well into his system.

"Ahhh, that's good," Tarrish said. "I start thinking about it on Sunday night."

"About what, Lieutenant?" Margaret asked.

"About the cigarettes, the damned cigarettes," he said, inhaling heavily again. "Forgive me, Margaret, but I'd rather have a smoke than a woman."

She smiled indulgently at him the way she did when one of the other male officers made a pass at her; her expression conveyed both amusement and pity, as if she recognized some strain of crassness inherent in all men but had learned to overlook it. Her eyes moved restlessly behind her long, dark lashes. Finally, she said in the disarmingly direct way which she had perfected, "Take me off the school tour, Lieutenant. I served my time."

"Sorry, Maggie, but I can't do that. The sheriff's department has to think about community relations—"

"You can if you make enough noise," she told him impatiently. "Substitute somebody else, Kline or Alfanti, or somebody you're mad at."

"Then what would be my argument? I'd be replacing one detective from my squad with another one. There wouldn't be a net gain."

Koepp intervened. "Sure there would be. You'd be sending a gumshoe to do a PR job so you could get an artist back solving homicides," he said.

"Oh, ho, so Maggie's an artist now. Well, well—" He grinned at her.

Margaret stared back at him in stony silence. She hated it whenever anyone called her "Maggie." None of the other cops, not even Koepp, dared use that nickname except Tarrish. Which was why he did it; he was trying to irritate them, not her.

"You know what I mean," Koepp said. "Margaret solves major cases—homicide cases."

"She's also very good in the drug ed program," Tarrish said, sounding more authoritarian. "The chief says he gets all kinds of compliments from teachers, parents, the school principals. Maggie keeps talking to the kids, maybe you won't have so many homicides you can't solve, Koepp.''

"Wouldn't it be better community relations to solve an open murder case?" Koepp asked.

This conversation wasn't going any better than it had the last time, Koepp thought dismally. Drugs were the bane of every cop's existence, but were particularly offensive to Tarrish. He'd been a city cop for years, then had transferred to county to get away from drug-related crime. But coke had followed him to the suburbs. Unlike some cops, Tarrish believed there was value in having a young, "with it" cop like Margaret talking to kids about addiction.

But they had planned their attack in advance, anticipating his negative response. Margaret was sure that Tarrish could be persuaded to take her off the drug ed detail if he thought progress could be made on the Nancy Sorgel homicide. Koepp began to steer the conversation in that direction. "We're stymied on some cases because we need some fresh thinking, some creativity," Koepp said.

"We need an *artist*, is that what you mean?" Tarrish asked. He exhaled a miasma of thin, white smoke. "Which cases?"

"The Sorgel case for one," Koepp said. "It's getting moldy." As soon as he said it, he remembered that the term "moldy" was the one Lisa Robbins had used. He noticed with satisfaction that the lieutenant's cheeks puffed in and out as he clamped his jaws together, a sure sign of inner conflict. Sorgel, a thirty-eight-year-old nurse at the VA hospital, had died of multiple stab wounds at her condo several months before. Despite intense efforts by county detectives, no suspects had been identified. This was unusual because the conviction rate for homicides was higher than for any other crime, and Tarrish's team had been notably successful in apprehending murderers; since he had become a watch commander in the sheriff's office, only four or five homicides had gone unsolved on his shift. The Sorgel case rankled him.

"Have you got any new leads to follow up?" Tarrish asked.
"Not exactly a lead—"

Margaret became impatient with the leisurely pace at which
Koepp was proceeding. "You've got a serial killer, Lieutenant,
somebody who's almost certain to kill again. It's going to be
a big stink when he does."

Koepp was both amused and awed by the way his former
partner went for the jugular. Telling Tarrish "you've got"
made it sound as if he had the sole responsibility for finding
Sorgel's killer, while her suggestion of a media circus played
on his innate dislike and fear of the press.

Tarrish finished his cigarette with a sigh and tamped out the
butt in a dented metal ashtray. He stared at it for a moment
with a baleful expression, as if it had somehow betrayed him.
But Koepp knew he was reviewing the Sorgel case in his mind.
Tarrish didn't contradict Margaret's declaration that it was the
work of a serial killer. The victim's tongue had been slashed
after she was dead, a fact which had been brought to the attention of the FBI's National Center for the Analysis of Violent
Crime. A unit at the center collected reports on major unsolved
crimes, filed them in a computer data base, and could compare
M.O.'s on new cases with existing case profiles. Koepp had
filled out a form on the Sorgel murder and sent it to the FBI.
A few days later he received summaries on two cases, one in
Chicago, one in Indiana, with nearly identical characteristics;
multiple stab wounds in the chest and abdomen, no evidence
of sexual assault, no evidence of theft. In both instances the
victim's tongue had been mutilated. A serial killer, unmistakably.

For that reason Tarrish had pushed the chief of detectives
for additional manpower and had investigated the case vigor-
ously for several weeks. But the lieutenant was too experienced
to "drill in a dry hole," as he put it, for long, especially when
the object of a manhunt was a serial killer. Serial killings were
notoriously difficult to solve because, from an investigative
standpoint, they were motiveless crimes. That was not strictly

true, because no one killed without a reason, but it was only after the killer was apprehended that it was possible to learn why he had committed the crimes. Detection was further complicated by the fact that the victims were usually either complete strangers or acquaintances of short duration.

At last Tarrish asked Koepp, "What did you mean by 'not exactly a lead'?"

"A local shrink in that clinic on Fairfield Avenue contacted Larry Kimble and made an appointment to talk to him. The psychiatrist was one of those he called for us."

"Did he have a suspect for the Sorgel homicide?"

"Maybe. Kimble loaned *her* the Sorgel file," Koepp said.

"That stupid son of a bitch," Tarrish growled. "'Scuse me, Margaret." Tarrish's sense of gallantry permitted him to swear in front of female officers as long as he apologized. "A woman shrink?"

"Most definitely," Koepp said. He was aware that Margaret had shifted her attention to him, although her face had remained impassive throughout this exchange.

"You talk to her?" Tarrish asked.

"Yes, but she won't tell me the patient's name. Doctor-patient confidentiality."

"What's this got to do with Margaret?"

"For starters, I'd like her to talk to the psychiatrist. Maybe she can get the patient's name. We could put him under surveillance."

"Not a chance. It's too flimsy and we don't have the manpower. I'm surprised at you, Ray. I mean, we're talking a real long shot here."

"We don't have anything else."

"What if she won't reveal his name?"

"We can still find out who it is," Margaret said. "There are other ways."

"Sure, check the license tags of everybody who goes in and out of the clinic. See if one of the patients has any priors.

That's surveillance. That takes people. You're not listening any better than Koepp.''

''That's a good idea about checking the license plates with DMV, George,'' Margaret told him brightly. She looked wholly sincere to Koepp, who could never be sure when she was patronizing someone.

Tarrish studied her suspiciously, but seemed unable to make up his mind, too.

''Maggie stays on the drug ed detail for now,'' Tarrish said at length. ''But she's off the drugstore holdups. Vinnie and DeMoss should be able to make an arrest in a day or two. That'll give her some time to annoy this doctor, what's her name?''

''Dr. Robbins,'' Koepp said helpfully.

''Yeah, but keep me posted. I don't want to waste a lot of time on this theory. The other tongue-slashings occurred in pretty widely spaced locations, so the chances are this guy is moving around. By now he's probably out of our jurisdiction.''

Margaret shifted uneasily in her chair when their supervisor mentioned jurisdiction. She had been a detective for seven or eight years, but she still retained the rookie's fervor about apprehending criminals; a case was over when a criminal went to prison. Tarrish, who had been a cop for thirty years, had more modest goals. If he couldn't get a conviction, he counted it a victory if the criminal moved to a different neighborhood.

Koepp was sure Tarrish was going to be disappointed. The tongue slasher was still around. He could feel it in his guts.

As soon as Lisa pulled out of the traffic into the visitors' parking lot behind the Safety Building, she regretted her promise to review Sergeant Koepp's serial killing. She wasn't worried about the grisly details and photographs that she might have to look at—medical school anatomy class had prepared her for anything—but she hated pretense. She wasn't there to help the police find a killer; she wanted to get enough details so she could try to trap Philip Schroeder into some kind of admission that would prove he was at the murder scene. Or, lacking that, she could safely conclude that he was innocent. The only justification she could find for her actions was the fact that Koepp was acting falsely as well. He wasn't interested in her psychological insights, only in finding out which of her patients she suspected.

She was directed by a uniformed officer on the second floor to wait in a conference room nearby. "I'll get Detective Loftus for you," the young woman said.

"No, I'm here to see Sergeant Koepp."

The policewoman nodded knowingly. "Sergeant Koepp has had a schedule conflict. He said Detective Loftus could talk to you. He'll get there as soon as he can."

Lisa considered just leaving, thought better of it, and found the meeting room without difficulty. It was empty when she arrived. She sat down near the middle of a long table surfaced with a linoleum type material printed to look like wood. The wall which she faced had a bad crack in the plaster in the shape of the state of Florida. She could hear water running in the pipes inside the walls.

A tall, striking woman with short dark hair and wearing a tweedy knit pantsuit came into the room, carrying several thick file folders. She set the files next to Lisa and said with genuine warmth, "Margaret Loftus."

Lisa identified herself. She was slightly taken aback when the detective decided to sit in the chair next to her; she had assumed they would be seated across the table from each other. She liked to keep a little physical distance between herself and other people.

"Perhaps we should start by my giving you a quick summary of the Sorgel homicide," the detective began, "and also the other two cases that we believe were done by the same man."

"The ones in Chicago and Indiana?"

"That's correct, Doctor. I forgot you saw Dr. Kimble's record." Was there a suggestion of disapproval in the last statement?

"Call me Lisa, please."

"Fine. I'm Margaret."

"You seem certain that the murders were done by a man," Lisa said. "Is that just an assumption, rather than a fact? There was no evidence of rape, for example—"

"Oh, we're looking for a man, all right. In each case there is evidence that the victim was facing her assailant and made some effort to ward him off. Each of them was overpowered. And Sorgel was a quite large and, from what other people at the hospital say, very strong woman. Perhaps you knew her?" Margaret suggested.

"I may have met her. I didn't *know* her. I don't see many patients at Veterans Hospital." Too late she realized that this sounded elitist, as if she only ministered to the carriage trade. The detective appeared not to notice.

While Margaret went to fetch coffee for both of them, Lisa began to read through the medical examiners' summaries, detectives' reports, inventories of the contents of the victims' homes, and myriad other official and unofficial documents, faxes, and news stories. She was impressed with how much paperwork had accumulated from each homicide. Her first search for a common theme, a thread that might tie the homicides together, proved fruitless, so she went reluctantly to the psychological profiles provided by the FBI and by Larry Kimble. She had promised herself that she wouldn't read their profiles until she had formulated her own, but she now decided she needed some stimulus. Maybe their ideas would spark some of her own.

Margaret returned with the coffee, excused herself and promised to check in from time to time.

The speculations of the psychologists seemed even more arid than the other reports. Both profiles discussed some of the same characteristics as those she had given to Koepp at the funeral home: sexual identity problems, fetish, cruelty to animals, a history of abuse of women. She started to concentrate on the victims rather than on the details of the murder scenes. All three women were about the same age, all of them white Caucasians, all of them without spouses. Jane Holloway was divorced, Sorgel had never married, and Zeto's husband worked in construction and was away from home for much of the year. Their singleness accounted for their vulnerability, but revealed nothing about why they attracted a psychopath's notice. That was one of the theories that Lisa had planned to explore, the contention by some students of psychopathic behavior that certain personality types were natural, even inevitable, victims; you could define the killer by his victims, rather than by his modus operandi. One characteristic emerged that had not been remarked on by either Kimble or the FBI: all the women had been caregivers: Sorgel was a nurse, Holloway a social worker, and Zeto an independent insurance agent. The latter occupation perhaps was stretching the "caregiver" classification a trifle, but Lisa decided to pursue the concept. She began to make notes on the lined yellow tablet which Margaret had left behind: *Caregivers represent means by which women dominate and emasculate men? Bad experience with caregiver? Mother was a nurse or social worker or equivalent occupation?*

When Margaret returned, she had Sergeant Koepp with her. Both of them sat this time on chairs on the opposite side of the table from hers. This put them somewhat in an oppositional stance, but she preferred it to having them next to her. Koepp smiled sympathetically. "I appreciate your coming down. This isn't very pleasant, I know—"

"That's all right," she assured him. "Anyway, I learned quite a lot about the Sorgel case, which was my primary reason for coming here."

"What do you plan to do with that information, Lisa?" Margaret wanted to know.

"Work it into my therapy sessions with the patient who might be a suspect. Theoretically a suspect."

"With respect to your professional qualifications, Lisa, there are safer ways to evaluate a suspect," Margaret said. "We could discreetly look into his whereabouts on the days of the murders. Probably we'd find he had an alibi. Then you could quit worrying, and we could start looking somewhere else."

This was Lisa's moment of truth. While she still felt doctor-patient confidentiality superseded other considerations, she told herself that Philip Schroeder had put that relationship in jeopardy by the bizarre act of following her. And making the phone calls. That had to be him! Had he not violated the trust so much already that she was fully justified in giving his name to the police? And what of her safety and that of her family—and other innocent people for that matter?

The two policemen waited in silence for her answer. Lisa listened to the rings of telephones in the adjoining offices, the dull drone of people talking, the gurgle of water inside the cracked walls. It struck her as remarkable that they seemed so different from each other, yet were partners. Koepp's light, nondescript eyes moved languidly inside their narrow sockets, which heightened the medieval aspect of his long, homely face. In repose, his features suggested amused perplexity. He almost never blinked. The woman's face was exquisitely proportioned from softly modeled planes of near perfect skin. She had a wide, sensuous mouth, a long, graceful neck, and blazing dark eyes. Lisa couldn't be sure of the color, but they appeared to be black. They moved back and forth quickly. Restless eyes, Rose would have called them. In most circumstances she would have concluded that they were nice people, people who could be trusted. But here they exuded a faintly ominous quality, the menace of enforcers.

They were cops. They had a uniquely different agenda from herself and everyone else. They could not be trusted.

She sensed they knew what her answer would be before she opened her mouth because they stiffened almost imperceptively in their chairs. "It violates a trust if I were to identify the patient I'm concerned about. You'll have to wait until I'm convinced this person is really dangerous."

"We understand," Margaret said with a trace of weariness in her voice, "but we believe you're making a mistake."

"Have you any insights to offer us, now that you've seen the psychological profiles?" Koepp asked.

She mentioned the fact that each of the victims was a caregiver and suggested that they keep that in mind when questioning suspects. It didn't sound very useful, but both detectives listened respectfully to what she had to say. When she had finished, Koepp leaned forward and handed her one of his business cards. She wondered if that's what they called them; was putting people in jail a "business"? "Let me know when you're ready to talk about your patient."

Lisa was already beginning to regret her decision. If she told them about Philip, she could also tell them that he was following her. They could have warned him off, let him know that he would be the prime suspect if anything happened to Lisa or her family.

She walked back to her car, hollowed out with depression. As she unlocked the door of the automobile, she noticed a slip of paper stuck under her windshield wiper. At first she was incredulous that a policeman could give her a ticket while she was parked in the Safety Building lot. But it wasn't a notice of a violation. It was a note from him. It said: *You shouldn't have told them about me.*

FIVE

SHORTLY AFTER LISA ROBBINS left the sheriff's department, Detective Margaret Loftus drove to the clinic on Fairfield Avenue, parked across the street from the patients' driveway, and began to note the license numbers of departing cars. After two hours she called Ray Koepp on her car radio and gave him the numbers she had collected so far. Koepp called them into a clerk at motor vehicle registrations and requested identification and home address of each car's owner. Just before the shift change, Koepp received a second call from Margaret with another list of license numbers.

After reading off the patients' license numbers, she told Koepp that one more number should be checked. "This isn't a patient," she said. "But it's the license for a dark-blue Ford van parked down the block from me. There's a man in it who seems to be waiting for something. But it's not a company vehicle, like a service truck, because it has no markings. He's been here for about twenty minutes, so it could be he's just waiting for his wife to get off work. But I think we should find out who he is."

Koepp gave the number to DMV, along with the others which Margaret had given him. He got the same clerk as on the previous call, but this time her cordiality was strained by the fact that it was quitting time. "I'll do them first thing in the morning," she told him. "This is a bunch, so I'll fax them over to you."

"Great, Wendy, but could you punch up just one right now?" Koepp asked. When she started to protest, he broke in and pleaded that it was urgent.

"Everything is urgent in the sheriff's department," the girl said. "C'mon, give me the damned number."

Koepp stayed on the line. He could hear her punching savagely at her computer keyboard, punctuated from time to time by muttered complaints. In a few seconds, she said crisply, "Eighty-nine Ford van, registered to Mrs. Sarah Schroeder, 15134 Lancaster Place, Hillside."

"Got it," Koepp said, scribbling furiously. Margaret had identified the driver as a male. Spouse? Handyman? Son?

Wendy, an experienced bureaucrat, sensed from his hesitation that her answer had not fully satisfied him. But she ended the dialogue before he could frame his follow-up question: "Gotta pick up my kids at the day-care center. Call me in the morning if you need anything else." She hung up.

For a moment Koepp twisted the cord of his phone in his hands in frustration. He banged the phone back into its cradle. The Sorgel killing had been on his mind for weeks, which was bad enough, and there hadn't been a worthwhile line of investigation to pursue, which was worse. Now some clerk had brought to a halt the one flimsy lead he had. He wanted to do something, even if it had little chance of success. Then he remembered Jim Ruguso. He headed downstairs to the records room.

Ruguso was a kindred spirit, a young graduate student who worked full-time in records on the second shift. Like Koepp, he was capable of fanatical persistence when he was given a challenging problem. The difference between them was that Koepp found his answers in interminable bouts of interviewing witnesses and suspects while Ruguso sought truth within the county's computer data banks. He was sitting in front of his PC when Koepp arrived, and waved a hand mechanically, as if it, too, was activated by the computer's hard drive. But he didn't look up. He punched a function key and watched with distaste while the screen went blank. Koepp, who hated computers, sympathized with him. In a few moments a complex display of figures in columns emerged. Ruguso moved the cursor about, changing digits. The screen went blank again while the computer digested the new numbers. Then Ruguso spun his chair slightly and looked at Koepp. "Haven't seen you around, Sergeant," he said. "Heard you retired."

"I'm only thirty-seven."

"I'm going to retire by the time I'm thirty-seven," Ruguso said in a matter-of-fact tone.

Koepp had no doubt that the young man was serious. "Here's my problem." He handed the note he had made about Mrs. Schroeder to Ruguso. "I got her name from DMV after we called in the tag number on her van. Except the driver of the van is a young male Caucasian."

"Fascinating, Sergeant. Where you headed with this?"

"I want to know who was driving Mrs. Schroeder's van."

For a few seconds Ruguso pondered this conundrum in silence, then he ran a long, bony hand through his long, ill-kempt hair, a sure sign that he was about to leap into action, and muttered to himself, "Anybody named Schroeder who lives at that address who has a record." He punched up a menu screen. "Get yourself a cup of coffee and come back in about ten minutes."

Koepp walked down the corridor to the small room where the vending machines were kept and put a quarter in the coffee dispenser. The place was empty, which added to its mean, desolate aspect. On a table next to the coffee machine was an open bakery box, half filled with crullers and Long Johns. He took out one of the crullers and examined it for ants. Satisfied, he bit off the end. It was dried out but edible. While he waited for his coffee to cool, he ate the pastry in tiny, measured bites. That was how he did everything, he thought with detachment, in tiny, measured bites. Unlike Margaret, who painted life with broad strokes.

Ruguso sat on the stool as before, staring at the monitor. He didn't look up as Koepp approached, but nodded his head slightly at the screen in front of him. "You're hitting from the three point line tonight," he said.

Koepp read over his shoulder. A twenty-five-year-old male named Philip Schroeder lived at the Lancaster Street address.

He showed two prior arrests for breaking and entering, one when he was seventeen, another at the age of twenty. In the first case, charges were dropped because of insufficient evidence. Schroeder was convicted of the second B and E but given a suspended sentence. Koepp found it particularly interesting that after both arrests he was required to undergo psychiatric evaluations. The findings of the psychologists were not included in the record on the computer screen, so Koepp wrote down the case numbers for both incidents. Using the numbers, he could get the investigating officer's case files in the morning. He thanked Ruguso and asked for a printout of Schroeder's arrest record. The young man tapped the "Print Screen" key lightly.

Koepp went back to the communications center on the second floor and asked one of the dispatchers to get Margaret Loftus for him. "I'll be at my desk. Patch her through when you get her." The radio operator nodded.

His phone was ringing when he arrived back at his desk in the squad room. As soon as his partner identified herself, he asked where she was. "Going west on Montgomery," Margaret responded.

"How come? You gotta boyfriend out there?"

"I'm following the van."

"What for?"

"Because he's following Dr. Robbins."

IT WAS ONE of those ominous company parties, the kind that senior executives of Muldoon-Craddock Investments like Jack had to attend. This one was at the home of Wilson VanDam, the newly appointed president of the division. Like VanDam, his luxurious duplex condo was new and untried. It was on the thirtieth floor of the Rampart, a tiny lakeshore development that offered spectacular views of the lake and central city. It was said that the VanDams had engaged an architect more than two months before Paul Cotney, the former president, had been dispatched; the office philosophers considered it obscene that

VanDam had known about Cotney's fate so long before he did. Although VanDam had arrived alone, the expectation was that he would recruit his own "team." Jack was certain to be judged a Cotney man and was therefore at some risk personally. He hoped his record would save him from the "restructuring" axe; he had increased the number of his accounts by thirty percent in the past three years despite the obstacle of mandated increases in management fees.

She watched her husband across the huge living room as he sat on a granite ledge and carried on an animated conversation with a young man from the bond department. Lisa couldn't remember his name; after they were with the firm for a while, their individual identities melded into the M-C stereotype. Lisa assumed that the younger man was trying to bond with Jack— or was it "networking"?—as a means of advancing his career in the firm, unaware perhaps that Jack might soon be a corporate outcast, a member of the older, discredited regime. Any firm that was in trouble, that had lost its entrepreneurial spirit, required the services of a repairman like VanDam, and what was there to fix except the disgraced prince's court?

Jack's hands, one of which held a Manhattan (a brandy Manhattan of all things because Jack had come from Wisconsin), moved with serpentine grace as he spoke to his acolyte. They were long and elegant, the kind of hands one expected to see in artists' self-portraits. They were firm and gentle hands when he made love, and she felt a stirring of desire now as she experienced their remembered caress. Was there someone else in the room, one of the affectedly severe young blonde associates who also remembered his touch? Or one of the wives? So many married women slept with other men these days, she had learned in the intimacy of therapy. She had been shocked by several of them, not because they had chosen to take a lover, but because they took so many, and did so with such casualness. Was it one of them? Talmadge's wife, the buxom one with the southern accent? Or Linda Abrams, the exotic-looking attorney with the Wellesley pedigree? It surprised Lisa to realize that she was identifying the wives as one might describe cats or horses; for her at least the wives were not real, either.

She had been listening to one of Elliot Dowden's golf stories with insufficient interest to be certain when she was supposed to laugh, so she drifted away from the group in the center of the room and stood near a window. She looked down at the city lights. In a few moments she caught sight of a reflected print dress in the glass and felt Jill Koenen's presence at her elbow. Jill was about fifteen years older than Lisa, but she was also the closest of all the M-C wives. Despite their age differences, they found that they had a great deal in common. Jill was a treasure, a woman with whom she actually enjoyed shopping. They had gone to the ballet on several occasions, and lunched together on the rare occasions when Lisa came into the city alone. Jill's husband Paul was fifteen years her senior and close enough to a lucrative retirement that office politics held no terrors for him. Jill reflected her husband's serenity. But her innate vitality forced her to seek other outlets now that she no longer had to be an adjunct to her husband's career. One of these was overseeing some aspects of Lisa's marriage, career, and child-rearing responsibilities. After commenting on the view from VanDam's windows, she inquired about Kevin.

"He's fine," Lisa said. "He likes school, which surprises me. I thought boys hated school."

"Mine certainly did," Jill said. "Richard kept leaving class in the first grade. He'd just walk out the door during recess and try to come home. The police were always bringing him home, then I'd have to haul him back to his school. His teacher thought he was weird." She chuckled softly. "I guess he was." Richard was a pre-med student at Georgetown University now, where, presumably, he attended class regularly.

"What do you think of the new president?" Lisa asked, keeping her voice low.

"VanDam? A cold fish. When you talk to him he stares at you for a few seconds to establish eye contact, then looks past your shoulder at whatever's behind you. It's as though he's planning the next move. Paul doesn't like him.''

"I thought Paul liked everyone," Lisa said. She saw her friend's smile reflected in the window.

"What does Jack think of him?"

"He hasn't said. We don't talk much about our jobs. I don't think he's all that happy at the firm anymore. He says it's gotten too political. I know a doctor isn't suppose to diagnose a family member, but I think he's under more stress than usual.''

"Your husband's problem is that he's an honorable man in a dishonorable world," Jill said, sighing. "That's why the politics get to him. Unfortunately, all businesses are political. Life is political. And speaking of politics—''

Warned, Lisa turned toward the center of the room. She saw that Grace Talmadge was headed toward her. Grace was in her forties but always tried to dress ten years younger than she was; tonight that attempt was defined by a mint crepe chemise with a sprig of Venice lace at one shoulder. Folds of material draped across her ample chest. She embraced Jill first, then Lisa in a practiced, affected manner which illustrated what Jill had once said about her: "She's one of those women who can do emotional things like hugging and kissing in public without any real emotion. Grace strives for artificiality.''

The conversation, with Grace at the helm, veered onto the Children's Hospital Charity Ball, which was taking place in six weeks. Grace was a co-chairman again for the annual event and desperate for a committee chairman. She studied Jill pointedly.

"Sorry, Grace," Jill said, "but Paul and I will be watching a Maui sunset about then.''

"But now is when we need the help." She slurred her words badly.

"Sorry.''

Grace turned her attention to Lisa and seemed about to try to recruit her. She must have remembered that Lisa was a phy-

sician and would not possibly have enough time to help. Perhaps like some women who spent a lot of time doing volunteer
work she resented Lisa's career, because her manicured cordiality evaporated. "It's unfortunate that the medical community can't spare any time for things like the Children's Hospital
since I believe it is a medical facility," Grace said.

"We're lucky to have people like you to take up the slack,"
Lisa said, trying to sound genuinely appreciative. And failing.

Jill attempted to suppress a grin by pursing her lips. The
result made Lisa think of Kevin trying to get bubble gum off
his teeth. She felt like giggling herself.

Even while inebriated, Grace Talmadge was no fool; she
knew when she was being patronized. Her round, smooth
cheeks colored. Her voice began to rise in pitch and volume.
"Oh, yes, I'm sure you doctors are very appreciative. I'm sure
you have staff meetings at your clinic where you all sit around
and congratulate each other that you have dumb housewives
raising money so you can have hospitals to send your patients
to."

"Lighten up, Grace," Jill said quietly.

Several of the other guests had turned their attention in
Grace's direction, Lisa noticed with growing alarm. One of
them was Jack.

"Your efforts are appreciated, Grace," Lisa said. "Believe
me, they are."

"I doubt that, but I really do understand your reluctance to
get involved in any community activities. If you're away too
much at night, your husband might have a lot of time on his
hands." Her voice had taken on a hard edge, rising in pitch
and volume.

"Perhaps you can explain that to me," Lisa said. The last
thing she wanted was an explanation. She wished she could
call the words back.

"I shouldn't have to explain it to a psychiatrist. You certainly must know all about straying husbands."

"Grace, for God's sake—" Jill muttered.

To Lisa's dismay, Grace's eyes filled with tears. She turned suddenly and hurried out of the room in the direction of the foyer, the location of the nearest bathroom. Jill and Lisa watched her departure in mortified silence.

Jack suggested immediately afterward that they leave. It was the only course of action available to prevent further embarrassment, but Jack's face was dark with resentment as he helped Lisa into her coat in the foyer. VanDam stood near the door, making the good host's valiant effort to convince them to stay longer. Jack mumbled something about having to get the babysitter home early, which was a total fabrication; his mother was staying with Kevin and planned to spend the night.

Because they knew the hazards of driving an automobile when one was in an emotional state, they waited until they got home to start their fight. It began in the kitchen as soon as they entered the house and spread to the other rooms as arguments are inclined to do. She supposed that was because one or the other of them was walking out of the room in a vain effort to bring his or her temper under control. The first subject was her inability to get on with his business associates' wives, which was followed by her sarcastic denunciation of Muldoon-Craddock "power parties." To inflict real punishment she repeated Grace's innuendo in the broadest southern drawl she could affect. When he had made fun of the infidelity insinuation, Lisa only became more angry, and demanded to know why he had left the hotel in New York a day early.

He explained it again. By then she wasn't listening. It had been weeks since had made love and she had hoped that tonight, after the party, he would want her as much as she wanted him. In the early days, the best sex they ever had was after they got home from a party. It was that disappointment more than anything else that made her not listen, made her scream at him, "I don't believe you. There's another woman. Who is she?" She knew what words to say; her patients had taught her well.

Later, after she had gone to bed, she berated herself for los-

ing control. It was pathetic that someone who spent her days
guiding people to better marital relationships could do nothing
about her own.

With a sense of shame and dread she realized that Rose must
have heard them.

KOEPP AND MARGARET had been sitting in the glass cubicle
that Lieutenant Tarrish called his office for almost fifteen
minutes before the watch commander arrived. Koepp had been
eating a chocolate-covered doughnut before Tarrish entered the
room. He licked the chocolate residue off his fingers quickly
so he could hand Philip Schroeder's rap sheet to Tarrish. Margaret, who couldn't look at pastry without gaining weight, began to chew on the nail of her little finger.

Tarrish, wearing a new suit, accepted her invasion of his
office amiably. He was a morning person. Margaret, who made
a study of all her superiors, had told Koepp once that Tarrish
didn't get cranky until noon during winter, but that ten in the
morning defined the limits of his good humor in the summer-
time.

"Why is that?" Koepp had asked.

Margaret had explained that the glass box he called an office
isolated him from the air-conditioning. She was nothing if not
analytical.

"I thought we had this conversation last Wednesday," Tarrish said. He tossed the print-out on his desk, took off his
overcoat, and hung it on a clothes tree.

"This is a different conversation," Koepp said. "This is the
conversation in which you become aware that your astuteness
in putting Margaret back on the street has paid immediate div-
idends."

"Ah shucks," Margaret said.

Tarrish donned his reading glasses and glanced at the rap
sheet. He studied it reverentially, as if he were looking at the
original text of the Magna Carta, then peered at Koepp over
the top of the eyeglass rims. He could see Koepp better this

way and it gave him a professional air; years of command had convinced him of the value of such affectations. "I give up," he said, enjoying himself.

"Philip Schroeder, the subject of that rap sheet, is a patient of the psychiatrist I was telling you about, Dr. Lisa Robbins," Koepp explained.

"She's the one who responded to Larry Kimble when he called around town to get nominations for psychopath of the month?" Tarrish apparently still thought it was a goofy idea.

Koepp nodded. "I assumed she must have good reason to suspect one of her patients."

Tarrish shifted his thick body in his chair, which creaked in response. "Assume is a little strong, Sergeant. Fantasize would be more accurate, I think."

"All right, fantasize," Koepp said. "At any rate, Margaret staked out the clinic last night, noticed that this guy was waiting around and asked for an ID on his vehicle. Then she followed him."

With theatrical gravity the lieutenant turned his attention to Koepp's partner. "And where did he go?"

"He followed Dr. Robbins to her home," Margaret said.

"How do you know he's her patient?" Tarrish asked.

"I called the clinic and said I was with an insurance company—checking on his current address—"

For a few moments he sat watching Margaret over the top of his glasses, saying nothing, showing no expression. Tarrish wasn't mentally quick, but he was methodically sequential in his thought processes. Finally, he picked up the rap sheet and read it again, more carefully. When he got to the second paragraph of the B and E conviction, he looked up at Koepp and said with astonishment, "He shit in her bed?"

Koepp waited for him to apologize to Margaret for his vulgarity before he said, "That's rather bizarre, isn't it? I wonder if Dr. Robbins knows about it."

"Probably," Tarrish grunted. "A good shrink always knows how your potty training went down."

Margaret laughed, which seemed to please Tarrish. He looked at her approvingly. "Okay, it's bizarre, but all it proves is that he's probably spending his money wisely on therapy." It was an encouraging sign that Tarrish had switched to his devil's advocate mode.

"It's probably his mother's money," Margaret said. "He can't seem to hold a job and Dr. Robbins is expensive."

"He lives with Mom?" Tarrish asked, studying the sheet.

"Not at the moment," Margaret said. "Two months ago he took an apartment just off Ridge Avenue. We got his current address from his driver's license."

"You've been a busy little girl," Tarrish said.

"I'm working on my detective's merit badge."

Tarrish turned his attention back to Koepp. "So we have a lady shrink who is inquiring about open murder cases because she has a very funny patient. The funny patient has a record for breaking and entering—and curious elimination habits. The funny patient follows the doctor home at night. All of which may be cause for concern. What's it got to do with the Sorgel case?"

Koepp admitted that he hadn't been able to make any connection. "But we don't have any other leads," Koepp said.

"What do you want?"

"Surveillance on Philip Schroeder."

"So you can create a lead? Sorry, Ray, but the good citizens of this county don't give us enough money to be that extravagant."

Koepp hadn't expected to get a surveillance team. His request had been a negotiating ploy. Because Tarrish had turned him down on one request, the lieutenant might bend the rules another day to give him something else.

"You better let the doctor know the kid's following her," Tarrish said. "Tell what's his name—Schroeder?—tell him we found out he's following her before he does something to her."

Koepp nodded. Tarrish's orders made sense, but they ran counter to what Koepp would have preferred, at least in one particular. He agreed that Dr. Robbins should be told that Schroeder was following her. Perhaps she knew already. Warning Schroeder to stay away from the doctor, however, might cause him to run for cover, or worse, shift to another victim. He would also be on his guard once he became aware that the police were watching him.

Koepp was convinced that sooner or later young Mr. Schroeder was going to come to the attention of the police again. It wasn't just because he had no sustaining relationships with family or friends, but rather because he had no personality. Throughout his life people would dislike him; crime would be the means of paying them back. He might not have something as drastic as murder in mind, but he certainly meant to break into Dr. Robbins's home. And crap in her bed maybe.

A clerk had delivered the fax from DMV with the vehicle registrations for all the cars Margaret had spotted leaving the psychiatric clinic. Koepp picked it off his desk, glanced at it, and tossed it onto Margaret's desk.

"What's this?" she asked.

"The owners of the vehicles you called in to me last night," Koepp answered. "I guess we don't need to follow up on them. Schroeder has to be the guy Robbins is concerned about."

Margaret put the fax into a file folder in her desk drawer. "When are you going to talk to him?" she asked.

"Let's do it right away. Give him a call. If you get him, tell him we'll be there in half an hour, maybe forty minutes. I'll call Dr. Robbins." They both began looking up their assigned phone numbers.

It was Dr. Robbins's day off, Koepp learned, when he called her clinic. He tried her home phone, which was answered by an older woman who was decidedly cautious about letting him talk to the doctor. At length she seemed satisfied that he was who he said he was and brought the psychiatrist to the phone.

Koepp explained as matter-of-factly as he could that Philip Schroeder had followed her home the previous evening. She listened to his information in silence. Finally, she said, "Yes,

I know. I've been noticing his van behind me on occasion lately.''

''Why do you think he's following you?''

''He's not really following me. I mean—he doesn't do it all the time—''

''Any idea *why* he's doing it?''

''None whatever, Sergeant Koepp.''

''Doesn't it frighten you?'' Koepp asked. ''Why didn't you report it?''

''No, it doesn't frighten me especially, so I had no reason to tell the police about it,'' she answered. ''It's my job to deal with disturbed people, people who do things you and I wouldn't do. Philip Schroeder hasn't threatened me or done anything that would cause me to suspect that he's dangerous.''

She's lying, Koepp thought. *She's scared as hell.* By some process that he couldn't analyze, he could often tell when a witness was afraid. ''Forgive me, Doctor, but this is the patient who caused you to start asking questions about unsolved murders,'' Koepp said. ''That makes him dangerous in my book.'' Koepp wasn't certain Schroeder was the reason she went to see Larry Kimble, but he risked nothing by pretending that was the case.

Her silence for several seconds confirmed his suspicion. Then she said lamely, ''You should leave psychoanalysis to psychiatrists, Sergeant.''

Koepp felt more confident now. ''We're going to talk to Schroeder and find out why he's following you,'' he told her. ''We'll also be asking him where he was the night of the Sorgel murder.''

''What gives you the right to interrogate him about that? You don't have any reason to suspect him.''

''He's got a conviction for breaking and entering. And he was pretty kinky while he was robbing the victim. Maybe he broke into Sorgel's place, she surprised him, he killed her. That's enough cause to question him.'' Koepp found it interesting that while she objected to them interrogating Schroeder about a homicide, she hadn't objected to their talking to him about following her. That confirmed what he had decided earlier. She was afraid.

"He's not a serial killer, Sergeant."

"Maybe you should leave detection to detectives," he told her gently.

After a moment of silence Koepp heard a short, nervous laugh. Then she said, "Touché!" and hung up.

SIX

WHEN THE POLICEWOMAN had called him, he almost panicked. It was something about listening to a stranger, an unknown voice, that unnerved him. But now that she was here, along with another cop, he wasn't afraid at all. They weren't anything special. The girl was pretty, but other than that they could have been anybody you meet on the street or at the mall.

He also felt more confident because he had outsmarted them. Shortly after the woman called him, he tried to call Lisa at her home, but the line was busy. That meant the cops were talking to her about him. She must have complained that he had been following her.

Almost as if she had been reading his mind, the girl cop asked him, "Why did you follow Dr. Robbins home last night?"

"Why did I follow her home?" He was sitting in the straight-backed chair facing the two cops, both of whom were seated on his sofa, the old, sagging sofa he was ashamed of. He studied the face of the man, wondering if he approved of what his woman partner was trying to do. "I was in the neighborhood and wanted to see that she got home safely. That old car she drives isn't very reliable and she keeps saying she has to get a new battery. In this weather she's bound to get stranded. I don't want anything bad to happen to her."

"That's very considerate of you, I'm sure," the woman detective said. "but what about all the other times?"

"The other times?"

"We know you've followed her before."

This time it was the sergeant who spoke, Sergeant somebody or other. The woman's name was Loftus. He knew because he had written it down. "No, I didn't. Last night was the only time. Even if I had, is that against the law?"

He thought if he asked questions, he could put them on the defensive. "Do you remember reading about a murder of a woman named Nancy Sorgel in the city about eight months ago?" the woman asked. "Last June it was, the sixth to be precise."

"Do I remember reading about Nancy Sorgel? No, I don't think so. I don't read the papers very much. Or watch television news. It's boring."

"The victim, Nancy Sorgel, was a nurse. She was killed in her apartment by an intruder. There was a lot of publicity. You must have seen something about it."

Now she was trying to pressure him, just like women always did. A pushy broad, trying to get him into a corner, trying to humiliate him, just like his mother. Women had to do that to men to justify their own existence, but it was profane for her to be doing that in his place. She had no right to be here, the bitch. He had to get rid of her. He'd never had a woman come to his apartment until she came. Don't answer any more questions, he counseled himself. Then she'd have to leave.

"You must have seen something about it," the woman cop insisted.

"No, nothing."

"Were you here then, living here, I mean?"

"No, I was staying with my mother. I was between jobs, so I needed a pad for a while."

"You're between jobs now, but you're living here. Does your mother pay your rent?"

"None of your business, you bitch." He waited to see if the other cop would object, come to her defense. But he didn't do anything. Schroeder told them to get out.

"Where were you on June sixth?" she asked.

"Get out!" This time he shouted at her. He had promised himself when she called that he wouldn't shout at them, but they went too far. He had a right.

It worked! They both stood up and walked to the door. The man looked as if he might have one more question and paused. Then he apparently thought better of it. They left.

He watched the street through the front window of his living room until the two policemen appeared directly below him. They dodged traffic to cross the thoroughfare and climbed into an unmarked police car. It was parked next to a curb painted yellow, which denoted a "no parking" zone. That was one advantage of being a policeman: it was easy to find a parking place.

He watched the car drive away. When he was sure they had gone, he went to the telephone and called Lisa Robbins again. This time she answered the phone. His intention had been to simply listen until she hung up, but he found that he wanted very much to talk to her. So he identified himself.

"Hello, Philip," she said. Did she seem relieved to hear him identify himself, or was that just his imagination? He couldn't be sure without seeing her face.

"Could we make an appointment?" he asked.

"You know this is my day off, Philip. I can't see you until your regular appointment. Is something wrong?"

"The police were here," he said in a tone of accusation.

"Oh—"

"You knew they were going to."

"Yes, I did—"

"I knew it," he cried bitterly. "You told them about me."

She waited for a moment for him to get control of himself, then she said, "No, I didn't. They saw you outside the clinic yesterday. You followed me home. They followed you."

"Why were they waiting outside the clinic?"

He had hoped desperately that she would have an explanation for him that made sense, something he could believe. But she hesitated, searching for a lie, which confirmed that she had been involved in bringing the cops there. Philip hung up before she could think of a plausible false answer.

LISA WAS DETERMINED not to let the unpleasant phone conversation with Philip Schroeder ruin her day off. She had too much to do to lose time brooding over his strange behavior. She had an early appointment to have her hair done, then she went to the supermarket to do her weekly shopping. She still did the cooking three or four nights a week, and always on Wednesday nights. Jack was out of town again, but she still planned on baked salmon for dinner; it was one of her rules to keep cooking when he wasn't around. If she didn't, she knew they would soon become fully dependent on Rose for that chore also.

By noon she was driving back into her driveway. To her surprise she found Rose sitting in her car in the drive with the motor running. Lisa parked next to her. Both women got out of their cars simultaneously. "Why are you waiting out here?" Lisa asked. She had been expecting her mother-in-law because Rose wanted to have her Buick serviced; Lisa had agreed to bring her home after she had delivered the automobile to the garage.

"I lost my keys," Rose said. She smiled. "Again." That was not unusual. Rose had a penchant for misplacing things, which seemed like an anomaly in someone as well organized in other respects as she was. She opened the back of Lisa's car and took out two bags of groceries. Left with only one bag to carry, her daughter-in-law was able to manage the front door. They went directly to the kitchen without taking off their overcoats.

"Thank goodness I have car keys scattered around the place," Rose said, "and another house key in the garage. I can't imagine what I did with them."

"Check your purses, then check them again. That's where all lost items are." The women set the bags on the kitchen table, took off their coats, and tossed them over the backs of two chairs.

"I've checked purses—every purse in the house. I think I must have dropped them in the snow when I took the trash out last night. They're definitely not in the house or garage. I'd better get some new ones made for your place."

"Sure, if you really can't find them." Lisa began to put some of the canned goods away while Rose started searching through the bags for frozen food packages, which she deposited carefully in the freezer.

"There's a locksmith down the block from the Buick garage," Rose said. "If I can borrow Jack's keys, I'll get some new ones made."

"Sure, if he left his here. Sometimes he takes them when he goes out of town, sometimes he doesn't. I'll check. If they're not here you can use mine." Lisa went to the bedroom to look for Jack's key ring. The keys were on top of his dresser. She took them back to the kitchen and dropped them into Rose's purse. "They're in your purse." Both women laughed.

After lunch, Rose departed for the garage alone. She had suggested that Lisa wait for an hour before coming to the garage because she planned to get the new keys made before she dropped off the car. Lisa spent the time opening mail, throwing away circulars, and paying bills. She was still writing checks by the end of the hour. As always, she was astonished by the number of financial transactions that occurred each month in a household of just three people. Fortunately, with Jack gone again, she would probably need something like bill paying to keep her mind occupied that evening. She laid the unopened envelopes on her desk in the den and went to the hall for her coat.

As soon as she opened the garage door, she caught sight of the dark van parked several houses down the street. She wished she didn't have to go out. It would have given her a good deal of satisfaction to back out to the street, then return to the garage and not go out for the rest of the day. Perhaps if he were frustrated that way he might lose interest. Then again, he might not; disturbed people sometimes exhibited extraordinary patience.

The van followed her down Mandrake to Collins Avenue,

staying half a block away. Fifteen minutes later, she pulled into the service lot behind the car dealership, where she quickly surveyed the locations of other driveways. Rose had been watching from the service shop waiting room and came out immediately. She pulled the collar of her cloth coat tightly around her neck, and stepped gingerly across a patch of ice. A violent north wind tugged at her brown hair, dragging a few strands across her face.

Rose, enveloped in frigid air, plopped into the seat next to Lisa. "It's awful out there," she said, stroking back the unruly hair.

Lisa circled behind a cluster of parked cars and went around behind the building, hoping to find a driveway onto the side street. Rose glanced at her in surprise, but said nothing. Fortunately there was a driveway. Lisa drove into the residential street and turned left, opposite the direction which Rose anticipated she would take. She pushed down on the accelerator hard, which caused Rose to vocalize her curiosity. "I've no idea where we're going, but you're certainly in a hurry to get there."

"Someone is following me. Keep your eyes open for a blue van." Lisa recited Philip's license plate for Rose, unaware until now that she had memorized it. Rose glanced out the rear window, but there were no other vehicles moving on the street behind them. Lisa made two more left-turns before she emerged onto a thoroughfare. When she came to an intersection and a stop sign, she paused for a moment to consider which way to go. As she was deciding, the blue van appeared on her left and made a sudden stop at the curb. A compact car, which had been trailing the van, swerved to avoid ramming it in the rear. Lisa noticed that the face of the driver in the small car was ashen. The van remained at the curb, waiting for Lisa to commit herself. She turned left again so that she was headed in the opposite direction in relation to it. In her rearview mirror she watched with dismay as the van easily completed a U-turn and fell into position behind her.

Rose had been observing all this with intense concentration. As she relaxed in her seat, she said, "Care to tell me what this is all about? It reminds me of 'Starsky and Hutch.'"

Lisa explained who the driver of the van was.

"How long has he been following you?"

"He was waiting for me outside the house."

"Of course. Now that you mention it, I saw it! He's done it before, hasn't he?"

"Yes, for the last week or so. Not all the time." Lisa considered trying to lose him in traffic, but realized how futile that would be. If he lost her, he'd just go home and wait for her. *You're behaving hysterically,* she told herself. *Pull yourself together.* Once she became calm she suggested to Rose that they stop at one of the malls and try to get some trousers for Kevin.

Rose agreed readily, although her mind was still on the van. Now and then she glanced out the rear window. Lisa made another left onto Collins and pulled into a shopping mall. Rose pointed at a large department store. "They're usually good for children's clothes. Why don't we start there?"

An hour and a half later they slid gratefully into a booth at the Copper Kettle, where they ordered coffee. On the bench seats next to them they piled their packages, which consisted not only of corduroy slacks for Kevin, but dress shirts for Jack, a pair of earrings for Rose, and jeans for Lisa. They both laughed when they saw how much space their casual purchases took up.

"Did you call the police about your shadow?" Rose asked at length. Her effort to sound casual wasn't effective.

"No, they found out on their own."

"They did! How? Does he have a record for doing this kind of thing?"

"Not that I know of. I'm not sure how they got onto him," Lisa lied. She felt she had compromised her patient enough with Sergeant Koepp, and didn't want to add to her guilt by explaining about Philip to Rose.

"He's a patient," Rose concluded confidently. She was inclined to making frequent and usually accurate intuitive judgements like that.

"Yes."

"Is he just a nuisance or is he dangerous?"

"In the right circumstances most people are dangerous," Lisa said. She regretted the remark immediately. It sounded condescending, the sort of thing a psychiatrist would say.

The coffee arrived, along with a check, which Rose pounced on. "What are you going to do about him?"

"Wait him out, I guess. I can't have him arrested. He hasn't committed a crime."

"Can't you get a court order or something? That isn't normal behavior."

"The police said they were going to talk to him this morning. Either they didn't, or it didn't do any good. I'm going to recommend that he see another doctor. We can't continue therapy with this going on." Until now, Lisa had been determined not to let Philip Schroeder's bizarre behavior jeopardize their patient-doctor relationship. Talking about him with Rose had changed her mind. Rose, always sensible, often had that effect on her.

"How can I help?" Rose asked. It wasn't a gesture; her mother-in-law was one of those rare people who went beyond the polite gesture.

"Let me know whenever you see him hanging around. And call the police if he ever comes onto our property."

"You needn't worry about Kevin. I'll see that nothing ever happens to him."

Lisa reached out impulsively to clasp Rose's hand, which was curled around the handle of her coffee cup. She squeezed it gently. "I don't know how I'd manage without you."

Rose flushed and stared fixedly at the coffee. She was as genuinely warm as anyone Lisa had ever known, but she had difficulty accepting compliments gracefully. Women of her generation had never learned to value their contributions.

"It's good you're going to stop treating him," Rose said.

"It's always best to take action when a serious problem develops. Little problems go away if they're ignored; big ones just get bigger. You have to take action."

KOEPP FOLLOWED KIMBLE down two steps into a family room dominated by a huge stone fireplace in the wall opposite them. The room was comfortable but in some disarray, with magazines, stacks of paper, and books scattered on modern furniture and around the floor. In that respect the place was oddly similar to Philip Schroeder's messy living room. Kimble pointed toward a chair near the blazing fire and headed toward a wet bar in the corner of the room.

"Scotch, right?" he asked. When Koepp hesitated, Kimble reminded him that he was off duty.

"No, I'm not, I'm meeting with the official department consulting psychologist. But the Scotch sounds pretty good." While he waited, Koepp glanced idly at the shelves of books next to his chair. He noticed a large number of titles having to do with forensic medicine, and several dealing with forensic hypnosis. He remembered then that Kimble had hypnotized witnesses in several county cases to help them recall details about criminal events.

Koepp had never used the psychologist in that capacity, but, unlike some of the other detectives, he had no bias against the technique. Kimble found a nearly full bottle of Scotch with some difficulty and filled a glass. He fixed a martini for himself.

As he handed a glass to Koepp, he nodded toward the folder which Koepp had laid on the hassock in front of him. Koepp picked it up again and handed it to the psychologist. Kimble sat down, put on a pair of reading glasses, and began examining the file's contents. After about ten minutes he put the folder back on the hassock and looked thoughtfully at Koepp for a few moments. "Is this guy Lisa's patient?"

Koepp nodded.

"I didn't think she'd tell you which patient she suspected," Kimble said.

"She didn't. In fact, she denied that he's the one. She's lying. But it's him."

"I think you're right," Kimble said. "This guy has classic symptoms. No wonder she's worried."

"Schroeder has been following her around."

For a moment Kimble was stunned. "Christ," he said with genuine concern. "Can't you do something?"

"He knows we know about it. Maybe that will scare him off." Koepp leaned forward. "That's our problem. You've seen those evaluations. What do you think?"

Kimble wrinkled his face with displeasure. "These things are always pretty sketchy, shallow. Court-appointed psychologists get a lot of these kinds of cases, but they don't have much time with the patient. It's not their fault. The system's overloaded, and it isn't sympathetic to people with emotional problems."

"But you agree he's disturbed?"

"Of course," the psychologist said. "Any reasonably bright layman could read these summaries and figure that out. Is he capable of killing people? Who knows?"

"That's not very precise."

"Goddamn it, Koepp, this is not a precise business. He does have some very disturbing attitudes about women. His mother looms large in all this, and she's probably the cause of his misogyny. He doesn't have any normal sex life, no real friends. The classic loner." Almost as if he had just thought of it, he added, "A lot of serial killers are loners, but not all of them. John Gacy was very gregarious, had a lot of friends. He's the guy in Chicago—"

"I know," Koepp said. "All I'm going to get is a qualified maybe, right?"

Kimble smiled wanly. "One of my graduate students put it rather well—if pretentiously—in a dissertation: 'Scientifically, the human mind is farther from us than Orion or the Pleiades.'''

As Koepp sat watching the fire, questions tumbled around in his brain, but he didn't need to ask them because he knew they would generate ambiguous responses from the police consultant. Despite his frustration, he didn't hold Kimble accountable. In his own life, back in the days when he was a priest, he had practiced the same ambivalence in theological matters, which were not after all far removed from psychological concerns. God was also more remote than the Pleiades.

"Does Schroeder have the potential for seriously harming or killing another human being?" he asked. He felt some satisfaction that he had asked the question the way Assistant District Attorney Tom Styles would have.

"Yes," Larry Kimble said firmly. Then he ruined everything. "So do you."

HE DIDN'T HANG AROUND the shopping mall for very long after he saw the two women go inside the big department store. Women could spend an eternity fingering merchandise and carrying dresses to the changing rooms. He remembered all the times when he was little that he had to wait while his mother tried on clothes. She rarely bought anything, as he remembered those trips, but she spent hours going from one shop to another. The clerks, all of whom were fat and chewed gum, looked at him as if he was some kind of bug. He was a boy in women's territory, and they always resented an intrusion by any males, even little boys. Women were turf protectors. Men weren't like that at all, which was probably why his father had left the house and never come back. He hadn't belonged there. Their house was his mother's turf.

He drove out toward the church now, but changed his mind when he was halfway there. Instead, he stopped at another mall and went to a movie. It was called *Pretty Woman* and was about a man who took a prostitute to a fancy party and then fell in love with her. It was an incredibly stupid movie, but he stayed through to the end. He almost never watched a movie on television until it ended, but he never walked out of a movie no matter how bad it was. He hated to lose the money. Thinking about money caused him to remember how badly he needed some. He hadn't been working now for almost two weeks and he hadn't been to his mother's house in a long time. Those were two of the ways he got money. The third was to break into an apartment somewhere, but he was afraid of doing that. For one thing, he had trouble picking a lot of the locks. For another, if he got caught again, the judge had told him he'd be sent to prison. More and more it looked as if he might have to go back to living at home. With her. Some choice, he thought, feeling very sorry for himself: prison or his mother. He started to laugh out loud. If those were his only choices, he'd take prison. In prison there were only men. Maybe he'd run into his father there.

He began to drive down some of the side streets, looking at the houses, trying to find one that was hidden from view from the street. A house might be easier than an apartment because he could smash a window and reach in to unlock it. It would be dark soon, which would give him more cover. On the other hand, the occupants of these empty houses would be coming home before long.

For some reason, trying a break-in right now just didn't feel right. You had to know inside you were going to be successful, or you could never keep your nerve up long enough to find where they had hidden the money. That's why he had been caught that time, because he panicked when he thought the person who lived in the apartment was coming home, and he ran right into the super on his way out. And that stupid old man, the bald guy with the limp and a foreign accent, had picked him out of a lineup with no trouble at all. He had been sure the old geezer couldn't see his hand in front of his face. That would never have happened if he had felt right when he went into the place. His biorhythms were screwed up.

Instead, he drove back to Lisa Robbins's house and parked

on the opposite side of the street about two hundred feet from their driveway. It had started to snow again, but two boys were shoveling their sidewalks anyway. He thought that was stupid; the snow was just going to cover up the walk again. He watched them, even though they were stupid. He made a pact with himself, that he would stay there until they finished shoveling and went away. There was no point in staying because it was obvious that she wouldn't go out again tonight.

Then he got a surprise. A sliver of light appeared at the bottom of the Robbinses' garage door and expanded into a yellow rectangle. For a moment, as he watched the garage door rise, he imagined that a giant yellow eye was raising an eyelid. He giggled aloud; metaphoric concepts always struck him as wildly absurd.

He put his truck in drive gear and started up the grade past the Robbinses' house. Where in the hell was the stupid bitch going on a night like this? he wondered. And where was her old man? He had noticed that the garage's left-hand stall was empty when she backed out.

Sleet had begun to mix with the snow, making the streets even more treacherous. Philip could keep the taillights of the car in sight now, but it would be difficult in traffic. He decided that Lisa Robbins couldn't distinguish his headlights from those of any other vehicle, so he reduced the distance between them. She turned at Collins just as she had earlier in the day, only this time she swung off after four blocks onto the East-West Freeway. The freeway access ramp was so slippery that the car threatened to stall. If it did, he would be trapped behind it with no way to pass her or back up. But she made it to the top and slid into the sparse traffic. Philip began to feel more obscure; there wasn't enough traffic to cause him to lose her.

He could focus his mind less on driving. Why was she out on such a night? Perhaps with her husband out of town she was meeting a lover. That hadn't occurred to him before because she seemed so cool and cerebral, but the idea titillated him, giving the evening a new dimension of pleasurable anticipation. Maybe he could find out who the man was, then use the information to get money from her. That would solve all his problems. Instead of going to her for advice, he could make a weekly visit to the clinic and get a check. His breathing became raspy just thinking about how she would look as she pleaded with him. He could dominate her for a change.

The two vehicles stayed on the freeway for a long time, running at only thirty-five miles per hour, moving as though they were connected.

Before long, Philip's excitement began to dissipate, to be replaced by the nagging fear that he could have a bad mishap under these conditions. With his luck, if he did have an accident, it wouldn't be a quick, fatal one. He was far more likely to be injured badly, which was a prospect that filled him with dread because he couldn't bear physical pain. He wished she'd turn off, but she kept resolutely to the freeway's center lane. The darkness, the swirling snow, and the desolation of the roadway combined to create a surrealistic atmosphere so that Philip's imagination began to perceive a roadway through a terrifying void. The faint lights of the city below were images only, lingering specters of human habitation that momentarily would be blotted out, leaving an infernal highway to infinity. Soon the lights of the oncoming cars would disappear, isolating only Robbins's car and his own. Then, in a single sweep of his ice-crusted windshield wipers, her vehicle would be gone, too, leaving him alone, propelled by inexorable, unseen forces to nowhere. In a panic, he tried to read the green direction signs to learn how far the next exit was. They were a confused jumble. He maneuvered the van gingerly into the right-hand lane and slowed to twenty miles per hour. He determined to take the next exit no matter what.

Miraculously, as if taking its cue from him, the other car pulled into the right lane as well. Its turn signal began to blink. Almost at once the car ahead skidded badly, recovered and began to descend in a shallow arc to the right. Philip no longer worried about getting too close and being discovered; the driver

ahead was too preoccupied by the weather. Moments later they
found themselves back in the reality of the airport boulevard,
headed north toward Shepherd Hills. They were near the west-
ern edge of the county, about fifteen miles from the central city
and the lake.

Lisa Robbins drove hesitatingly, as if she were unfamiliar
with the area. She acted, in fact, as if she were unfamiliar with
her own car. Clearly, she was looking at street signs as she
passed each intersection. After driving north for seven blocks
she turned right, then right again into a large complex of apartment buildings. Philip was confronted with a dilemma: should
he follow her inside the complex and risk exposure, or park on
the street, go in on foot and hope that he could figure out which
apartment she was visiting? He decided on the former course.
The entry road wound past the snow-shrouded, two-story brick
buildings in serpentine fashion. Side roads branched off left
and right. The Volvo headed into the third one on their left and
came to a stop in front of the corner building. Philip parked
on the main access road because he could see the apartment
from where he was and, in case he decided to leave in a hurry,
wouldn't be trapped in a dead-end cul-de-sac. He kept the engine running.

Then her car began to move again. She plowed up a driveway and disappeared behind the building.

His mind raced frantically through a list of possible actions.
Should he go inside and try to determine where she was
headed? If so, how could he unlock the outside door to the
building? There must be a parking lot in the back. Maybe he
could wait for one of the occupants to arrive, then enter when
that person did, pretending that he belonged there but had simply forgotten his keys. He had done that before; most people
were foolishly trusting if you acted boldly. Then he remembered his key collection and reached into his glove compartment to pull out a cigar box. Its contents jangled reassuringly.
Sometimes the door locks on apartment buildings got so worn
that almost any similar key would work.

Even as he pondered his next move, she solved his problem by turning the lights on in the apartment on the second floor, which was closest to him. It had been completely dark before that. Her lover hadn't arrived yet, so she was just making herself at home to wait for him. He sat still in the van, his hands gripping the steering wheel, while he felt the excitement spreading through his body. Despite that momentary terror on the freeway, this was going to be one of those times when everything went his way. He could feel it.

A big man in a leather car coat appeared from behind the building and trudged toward a similar structure about seventy yards to the north. He pulled up his collar to protect his head from the wind, then he stopped at a car and opened the trunk.

In Philip's racing mind the whole scenario began to take shape. One way or the other he would have to get into the building so he could learn the name of the occupant of the corner apartment. Once he had that information he could find out everything else he needed to know by following the occupant for a few days. While he was in the building, he might try to pick a lock to one of the other apartments and lift some cash. It would put the fear of God in her to know that he had broken into one of the apartments in the same building as her lover. That would be a delicious prospect—seeing her reaction at their therapy session, knowing she could do nothing about it because he had a way to blackmail her. Perhaps he would force her to play patient while he acted as her analyst!

Buoyed with new confidence, he selected several keys which he could try on the outside door.

He was right to have waited. By following his instincts he had avoided a mistake this afternoon; now he was going to be paid back for his patience. He put his pick, flashlight, and gloves in the pockets of his coat.

SEVEN

JOANNE WHALEN'S STATUS as a senior partner in the auditing firm where she worked provided one perk which she valued above all the bonuses, the firm's contribution to her pension plan, the four weeks of vacation, and the stock options: she could manage her own time. True, she spent more hours on her business career than she ever had, but the flexibility the new job gave her was ample compensation.

At times like now, when Jack's schedule enabled him to come to her unexpectedly, she could leave work early and make whatever arrangements for his comfort she felt were necessary. Nobody at the firm cared. After all, the other partners slipped out to spend time on their yachts or at the golf course under the guise of servicing their accounts. Rank had its privileges.

Jack was due back around seven from a short trip to Des Moines. As in the past, he had informed his family that he would return the day after he actually intended to come back. That meant that they could spend the entire night together instead of just a few hours after work. These times were precious to her, and she was determined to make tonight special for him as well. His birthday was Sunday, so she had arranged for a cake with the number "37" in blue frosting on top.

She found a can of condensed chicken broth at last and added it to the other ingredients she needed for Cantonese Pork. She double-checked the items on her list against the produce in the cart: peanut oil, celery, a green pepper, a can of pineapple chunks, cornstarch, pork, and rice. Everything else she needed was in the pantry in her kitchen. She picked up the cake, wrote out a check for the groceries, and followed the bag girl out to the parking lot. At first she had trouble identifying her car because all the vehicles, humped with new fallen snow, looked alike. While Joanne tried to remember exactly where she had left her automobile, the girl hunched over the shopping cart to fend off the wind. The light tan jacket she was wearing seemed woefully inadequate for the weather. She reminded Joanne of herself at the age of sixteen—scrawny, unsure of herself, wearing her sister's hand-me-downs, trying to get through the Michigan winter with a thin jacket and two sweaters. The girl's similarities made her feel guilty.

The car was crouched behind a red pickup truck with one of those cab things over the back.

They piled the groceries in the trunk of her little car, then Joanne gave the girl a ten-dollar tip. For a moment the girl looked at the bill, uncomprehending and slightly apprehensive. Joanne knew what she was thinking. If somebody gives you something you don't expect, you better find out what else you had to do to earn it.

To put the girl's mind at ease, she blurted, "Thanks a lot." She got quickly into her car to signify that they were going to part without further obligations on either side.

On her way back to the condo she kept thinking about the girl and her reaction to the ten dollars. Despite her hangdog appearance, she clearly was no fool, at least where money was concerned. And if she wasn't a fool about money, she probably wasn't a fool in other ways, either. She was the right age to be Joanne's daughter, if Joanne had gotten married like the rest of her classmates at the University of Michigan. She felt a stir of melancholy again, only this time it was caused by regret, not guilt. She would have liked having a child, but she had never been willing to pay the price. Unlike Lisa Robbins, she would not have had a devoted mother-in-law to take care of a kid. That meant she would have to scrimp at some menial job or get married to somebody with a good job, a job that would provide what a child of hers was entitled to. But marriage was bondage for a woman, no matter how luxurious the circumstances.

Once a woman married she became a man's possession, even if she was successful in her own career. In Joanne's mind, becoming a possession was the worst fate that could befall any woman. She was the possessor, not the possessed. Even on those occasions when she went to bed with a man to further her career, she had kept control of the situation. She never allowed herself to be vulnerable, no matter what the outcome of the lovemaking.

It had paid off handsomely. No better evidence of that existed than the fact that she could afford finally to take a lover for the pleasure and enjoyment of it. She had even allowed herself the luxury of falling in love with him.

Marriage, of course, was unthinkable.

She parked in her assigned garage across the parking lot from her condo, opened the trunk and took out only one bag of groceries. She also fished her house keys out of her purse. With one bag she would be able to unlock the door. Then she'd push the two-by-four against the jamb so that the door wouldn't shut automatically behind her. This would facilitate bringing the second bag from the car. When she arrived at the back door, she found that the block was already in place. One of the other owners must have been hauling groceries also.

When she got inside her home, she went directly through the living room to the kitchen. As she set the bags on the kitchen table, she caught sight of several tiny puddles of water on the floor tiles.

She only had time to see the melted snow, not enough time to comprehend fully its meaning. A gloved hand flapped in front of her face like the wing of a huge black bird and settled roughly on her mouth.

She cried out in astonishment: "Jack, my God—" But the flapping bird wing smothered her words.

Her last conscious thought was that some huge, cruelly hard thing had invaded her body from behind. Her ears pounded in a savage rhythm. Incomprehensible pain. She began to slide down a tunnel through shifting, terrible lights. Then into the void.

KOEPP GOT THE PHONE CALL from Terry DeMoss a few minutes after nine, just as he had finished washing several days' accumulation of dishes. Like Koepp, DeMoss was a sergeant and had the reputation of being one of the best homicide detectives in the county. So Koepp was more than a little surprised when he heard what DeMoss had to say. "Ray, Terry DeMoss. I got a female homicide at the Cambria Condominiums. Know where that is?"

Koepp said he did.

"Woman's about forty," DeMoss continued. "Came in with some groceries. An intruder was hiding in the kitchen and stuck a shiv into her."

"Sounds like a simple B and E," Koepp said, "only she surprised the punk, he panicked, then put a knife into her. You're going to have a long night, Terry."

"So are you."

"Sorry, partner, I'm off duty."

"The woman's tongue has been slashed to ribbons. God, I've never seen anything like it." DeMoss's voice cracked with emotion, something Koepp had never heard from him before.

"I'll be there in half an hour, maybe more on account of the roads."

"Don't rush. We're not going anywhere."

By the time Koepp arrived, the entire condominium complex was ablaze, which was not surprising; people tended to turn on lights when a serious crime had been committed next door, or across the street. On the street in front of the corner condo were three county squad cars, at least two unmarked vehicles belonging to the detectives' pool, a meat wagon from the medical examiner's office, and, not surprisingly, Lieutenant Tarrish's dark-green sedan. The second shift obviously thought this was day-shift business.

Koepp showed his gold shield to the uniformed cop in the

downstairs hall and climbed the stairs to the second floor. He waved his I.D. in front of a second officer and entered the apartment. The scene in the living room was as familiar to him as a stage set was to a theater director. He knew most of the actors by name. Russ Kalmbach was dusting a closed desk for prints. A police photographer named Rusty something was moving slowly about the room following the snout of his video camera. Tom Sturmer, a county pathologist, droned a summary of his preliminary findings to Detective Milt Farmer, who was writing furiously in an open notebook. The two caretakers of the meat wagon stood in a corner of the room, doing what they spent most of their lives doing—waiting. Neither the lieutenant nor DeMoss was in the living room. He went to the kitchen and poked his head in. DeMoss was kneeling on the floor next to the victim, chalking an outline of her body. She was still wearing high leather boots and her overcoat. The place smelled of urine and human blood. Koepp glanced around the narrow room, saw the blood on the floor and on the white cabinets beneath the sink. Two paper bags of groceries were on the kitchen table. There was blood on the table as well.

He reconstructed the woman's entry through the doorway in which he was now standing. He assumed the intruder surprised her from the back, which was perfectly plausible he discovered when he circled around the refrigerator next to his right elbow. On the side of the appliance opposite the door was a space about two feet wide where a person could comfortably stand, screened from the view of anyone entering the kitchen. From the hiding place it was only about three or four steps to the kitchen table. He stood in the space looking at the body.

DeMoss noticed him and nodded. "Yeah, that's how I figure it. He was waiting right there."

"Have they dusted this area for prints—fridge, walls, the countertop?"

"Yeah, Russ went through there first," DeMoss said, standing up. He was a tall, good-looking man with dark, curly hair and olive skin, who only recently had started to get a little paunchy. He was very defensive about his weight, and blamed it on the superb cooking of his second wife, to whom he had been married less than three months.

"Where's the lieutenant?" Koepp asked.

"In the apartment below talking to the president of the condo owners' association."

"How about filling me in," Koepp said, pulling a small notebook and a ballpoint pen from the pocket of his overcoat. As if on cue, DeMoss took out his notebook also. Both men laughed.

"Victim's name is Joanne Whalen. Forty-one, according to her driver's license. Single, career woman. The guy downstairs says she had a high-powered job with an auditing firm in the city. Just made partner, or something, not long ago." DeMoss paused, trying to decipher his notes. "Oh, yeah, she had a boyfriend who visited her pretty often. They didn't go out much, so the guy downstairs—Rademacher is his name— thinks her visitor was married."

"Does Rademacher know the boyfriend's name?"

"No," DeMoss said. "Wounds look like a hunting knife, according to the M.E. Nobody in this end of the building saw or heard anything unusual."

"Who discovered the body?"

"The dispatcher took an anonymous phone call about eight-thirty. Probably the boyfriend. I figure he came over here for a piece of ass, found her, and called it in on 911."

"Maybe he killed her first," Koepp suggested. "Then called it in." All incoming phone calls on the emergency line were taped as a matter of policy, so Koepp would be able to listen to the actual call later. That would be helpful not only to determine the caller's identity, but to assess his state of mind at the time of the call. He made a mental note to have Margaret listen to it as well; though she suppressed her own emotions, she had a knack for reading other people's emotional state.

"Maybe he did," DeMoss said. "Then again, maybe she was killed by her maiden aunt from Poughkeepsie. It's a good thing the county has a bunch of smart detectives around to figure it out, eh?''

"Killer leave anything behind?"

"Just some water." He enjoyed Koepp's puzzled expression for a few seconds, then added, "Killer must have stashed his boots or overshoes in the hall closet. We found a puddle of water on a plastic mat."

Koepp nodded. "I better go check in with the scoutmaster," he said.

"Yeah, he wants to see you," DeMoss told him.

The door to Rademacher's condo was partially ajar, so Koepp rapped on it once and went in uninvited. Tarrish was seated on a print sofa in the middle of the living room talking to a stocky, red-faced man of about forty-five years and a woman in blue jeans and a checkered shirt. Tarrish's brisk introductions confirmed that she was Rademacher's wife. Koepp sat next to the lieutenant, who nodded at the man, encouraging him to resume his narrative.

"Like I said, I didn't notice anything unusual at all until these two college girls came to the door and asked to use the phone," Rademacher said. He sounded cautious and tentative, the way witnesses often did after the first flush of excitement wore off, and they began to consider the consequences of being a witness in a major crime. "It didn't have anything to do with—" He jerked his head back, meaning to direct their attention to Joanne Whalen's apartment. The motion called Koepp's attention to his stiff, premature gray hair; it reminded Koepp of steel wool. "Their car slid on the ice at the intersection and rammed the side of his Accord. It was really a mess. That's the trouble with those Jap cars—no protection.

"Anyway, they said nobody was hurt. I let them use the phone. The Chinese girl actually reported it to the cops."

"They came very quickly," Mrs. Rademacher said in a soft voice. "In fact, while they were investigating the car accident they got a call on their police radio to check out Joanne's place.

"Well, we got a set of keys for it, so I got the keys and

took them right up. I asked 'em what it was all about, but they wouldn't tell me.''

"Did you go inside?'' Tarrish asked.

"No, they told us to stay out in the hall,'' Rademacher answered. "God, they had guns out and everything. I'm glad I didn't go in. It must have been awful.''

"She's really dead?'' Mrs. Rademacher asked.

Tarrish brusquely confirmed the fact, then he extracted as much information as he could from them about the Chinese girl. They didn't know her name, but they thought she shared one of the condos at the end of the cul-de-sac with her mother. "You saw nobody else, you heard nothing from upstairs?''

Rademacher said a little defensively they had not. He rose, walked to a cherrywood cabinet and took out some papers. He handed them to Tarrish. "That's a layout of the whole development and a list of the current owners.'' Maybe he was trying to atone for having seen or heard nothing useful, Koepp thought.

The detectives thanked them and started to leave. "Oh, Lieutenant,'' Mrs. Rademacher said, "the other girl—the friend of the Chinese girl, I mean—talked to me while her friend was reporting the accident. She was very aggravated because she said another driver saw the accident but just drove away. She wanted to be able to call him as a witness—somebody to prove they weren't going fast, that it was just the ice.''

"And?'' Tarrish prompted.

"He just drove off, she told me. Wouldn't help. I suppose he didn't want to get involved.''

Tarrish just nodded, thanked them again and closed the door gently. Once they were alone, he said to Koepp, "You as curious about the uncooperative driver as I am?''

"Indubitably, Holmes.''

Finding the Chinese girl was easier than they had expected. She was standing in the hallway of the last building, talking to six or seven other residents, when Tarrish and Koepp ducked in out of the storm. At least Koepp thought they had found her. There were two Orientals in the group, both female, one young, one middle-aged. Tarrish spoke to the younger woman. "We're looking for someone who had a fender bender at the corner."

"That's me, Amy Shue," the girl said, turning to face the lieutenant squarely. She was a pretty girl and rather tall for an Oriental, maybe five seven or five eight. She glanced at Koepp for a moment, decided he was irrelevant, then turned her attention back to Tarrish. She watched him warily.

"We'd like to talk to you privately," Tarrish said. His voice took on the mellifluous quality which he always reserved for conversations with pretty women.

"Sure." The girl said something to the other Chinese woman in a foreign dialect and led the two detectives up the stairs to the second floor.

Her apartment was tastefully decorated in strong contrasting colors and furnished with a large, white modern sofa and chairs. Koepp didn't notice anything Oriental in the living room. He could tell at a glance that the layout of the unit was the same as that of the murder victim. For some reason the girl didn't sit down, nor did she invite them to do so. They stood uneasily in the center of the room while Tarrish solicited basic information, such as name and phone number, circumstances of her departure earlier in the evening, the name and address of her friend.

"Mrs. Rademacher said that another motorist was following you and saw your accident," he said. "Is that right?"

"Yes." She volunteered nothing else.

"Do you have his name and address?"

"No."

"Didn't you try to find out? It seems like he might have been a useful witness."

She assayed her informational nugget for a moment before passing it to Tarrish. "We tried to stop him, but he just drove off." She paused, again weighing the consequences of what she was going to say. "My friend Debbie got part of his license plate."

"Part?" Koepp asked.

"Yes, she remembered 6XL."

Koepp again: "Beginning or ending numbers?"

The girl shrugged apologetically. "She doesn't remember where it was on the plate, but she did memorize that sequence—first three, last three, she doesn't know."

"What kind of a car?" Tarrish asked. He sounded as if he was getting impatient, which amused Koepp, because it betrayed the fact that Tarrish didn't interrogate many witnesses anymore.

"A station wagon, dark, but I didn't recognize the model. I'm not good on automobiles. I'm always losing mine at shopping malls and things."

"I have the same problem," Koepp said sympathetically. "Did you see anyone else around?"

"Yes, a man who lives in our building. He was unloading the trunk of his car." She laughed softly. "His trunk's a mess."

"What time was that?" Koepp asked.

"Between seven-fifteen and seven-thirty, I think."

Later, as they trudged back through the snow to the scene of the crime, Tarrish asked, "Think DMV can do anything with those three digits to get a make on the vehicle? The driver of the station wagon could be our man."

"I'll try it out on them in the morning. I think it'll be tough, but you never know."

"She had her tongue slashed," Tarrish said. "So it looks like the same one who got what's her name—"

"Nancy Sorgel."

"So I'm making it your case. You can have Margaret full-time. I'll get you as much help as I can. The media will be all over this one. I'll try to keep them off your neck, but you gotta keep me briefed. About *everything*."

They arrived at the corner condo in time to see the pair from

the meat wagon bringing Joanne Whalen out the front door in
a body bag. Snowflakes flecked the dark bag, then swirled off
in the next gust of wind, as if anxious not to remain.

"Sturmer doing the autopsy?" Koepp asked.

"Yeah, at County General. He said he'd do it right away.
You better get over there."

"I plan to."

At the foot of the walkway to the building, Tarrish turned
toward Koepp and said, "Ray, that kid that was following Dr.
Robbins. Just for the hell of it, find out where he was tonight
at seven o'clock. We might get lucky."

"I doubt it. There are two problems. Dr. Robbins's patient
drives a van, not a station wagon. And his license number
doesn't have the sequence 6XL in it. It starts with a six, but
I'm pretty sure it doesn't have an X or L in it."

"Check out his alibi anyway," Tarrish said.

UNLESS HE HAD a compelling excuse, the senior investigating
officer on a homicide case was required by department policy
to witness the autopsy of the victim. It was one of the most
distasteful assignments a cop could get, and most of the detectives honored the directive only in the technical sense; they
were in the operating room with the pathologist, but usually as
far removed from the body as they could get. And most didn't
watch any more than they had to.

Koepp had disciplined himself not only to watch, but had
also schooled himself with textbooks on the basic anatomy of
the human body. He was sitting on a plastic chair in the anti-
septic operating room which the county used now only for
autopsies and during overflow emergencies. In addition to the
bank of lights above the operating table, a microphone hung
down from the ceiling.

The nude body of Joanne Whalen lay directly beneath the
microphone. Often in similar circumstances in the past Koepp
had found the juxtaposition of live mike and dead body wildly
irreverent. It was as if the mysterious, green-gowned medical

powers wanted to be ready in case the deceased had any parting wisdom to share.

Even at a distance Koepp could see that Joanne Whalen had possessed a well-formed body, one that had been cared for rigorously by dieting and exercise. She confirmed his thesis that the rich and successful, who could best afford self-indulgence and gluttony, were thinner and more muscular than poor people. America: winner take all.

He wondered if she had been killed out of love, like so many of the other murder victims he encountered. Despite all his years on the force, he was still amazed how often love, in its many distorted forms, resulted in a woman or child being stretched out on an operating table like this. The poets were right: love and madness weren't far apart.

Tom Sturmer and a med student assistant, dressed in green "scrubs," appeared after a while and began rearranging the scalpels, syringes, and assorted tools of their grisly profession. Sturmer nodded briefly in his direction, pulled the microphone down to accommodate his five-foot eight-inch stature and proceeded to make a Y-shaped incision, cutting from each shoulder to the pit of the stomach, then in a straight line down to the pubic bone. In a flat monotone he began to record the mayhem that had been visited on the once-lovely body of Joanne Whalen, auditor. "Nine centimeter incision approximately in the middle of the descending colon, three to four centimeter laceration of the liver lobe about three centimeters above the gallbladder, nine to ten centimeter incision in the transverse colon above the kidney, transverse laceration of the renal vein, diagonal laceration of the celiac trunk, one, no, two perforations of the left ventricle…"

Koepp listened not to the descriptions of the wounds but to the tone of Sturmer's voice. What he was describing was consistent with multiple knife wounds inflicted by an attacker facing the victim, and so was of little interest. If Sturmer's inflections changed, Koepp would know the balding pathologist had discovered something he didn't expect. From time to time

Sturmer stopped, flicked off the mike by pushing a switch on the side of the operating table, and discussed some medical point with the student. He heard the medical terms applied with monotonous dispassion to the hideous wounds around the victim's mouth. *My God,* Koepp thought, *how could anyone cut up someone's tongue like that?*

The two pathologists turned the body over after more than an hour of investigation of the stomach and chest wounds. They would make an incision across the back of the head next; in most cases the two incisions could be sewn up after the autopsy so neatly they would not be evident to mourners at the mortuary. But Joanne Whalen's wake would have to be a closed casket affair; nobody could fix the damage to her face. Sturmer was about to make the incision when he stopped suddenly and called Koepp's name.

Koepp went to the table and stood next to the pathologist, who was in the process of cleaning the woman's lower back with a sponge. A discolored area surrounded a single perforation in the ash-colored skin. "One stab wound in the back, then a whole mess in the front," he said. "Also nothing under her nails, like skin or hair. She was jumped from behind, got this wound first, then turned to face her attacker. And she was collapsing while he jabbed her in the chest and stomach. That may account for the slicing nature of some of the wounds."

"As she fell, her body turned stabs into slices, is that what you mean?"

"Yes. Also, the attacker was right-handed." For a moment Sturmer watched him expectantly, as if weighing whether to tell Koepp something obvious or wait for him to figure it out for himself. Koepp knew the look; he had seen Sturmer use it on countless medical students. But he didn't grasp whatever it was Sturmer wanted him to see.

A little lamely Koepp asked if there was any evidence of sexual activity. Because the body had been fully clothed the question might have seemed stupid, but Koepp had seen enough sexual aberration to know it wasn't.

"No." Sturmer finally lost his patience. "Ray, remember those two autopsies you showed me at the time of the Sorgel homicide—the cases in Chicago and Michigan—"

"Indiana," Koepp corrected him.

"Wherever. Same M.O. for all three. All had their tongues slashed."

"Yeah, just like this one," Koepp said.

"What else?"

Then Koepp realized what Sturmer was trying to tell him. "Okay, I see. No back wounds on the other two. They tried to fight off their attacker."

"Right, lacerations on their arms. Particles of the killer's hair under their nails."

"Okay, this one is different. I don't know if it's significant, but thanks for pointing it out. What about time of death?"

"We can be fairly precise because we got there so soon. Between six-thirty and seven."

Sturmer turned back to his youthful assistant. "Let's get going, lad. I didn't get any supper and I'm getting hungry."

EIGHT

THE DAY-SHIFT DETECTIVES assigned to the Whalen murder gathered in one of the conference rooms the next morning. In addition to Margaret Loftus, who had been pulled off community relations until further notice, their number included homicide detectives Bill Wendt and Jerome "Jack" Jackowski, as well as Sergeant Cathy Andrews and Detective Cal Friedel, both on temporary loan from narcotics. All of them had been picked by Ray Koepp, who was to head up the investigation.

At nine o'clock Tarrish and Koepp joined the others for a briefing. They began by distributing a summary of the scene-of-the-crime investigation conducted by DeMoss and Farmer. Also in the packet each cop received were the preliminary report from the medical examiner on Whalen's autopsy, maps of the condominium complex, a roster of residents of Cambria Village, names, addresses, and phone numbers of friends, neighbors, business acquaintances, which had been collected by second-shift investigators during interrogations of Whalen's neighbors. The investigation was less than a day old, yet the paperwork was already daunting. At least it was to Koepp, who thought of himself as a street cop, not an administrator.

Tarrish didn't give them a chance to study the case. Instead, he provided a verbal summary, which lasted about twenty minutes. Then he invited questions.

Predictably, Margaret asked the first one. "Do we regard last night's homicide as a serial killing or not? It looks like the same M.O. as the Sorgel case, but you didn't emphasize the connection."

"Ray thinks it's the same assailant. And ties into cases in Illinois and Indiana. It certainly looks that way."

"What do *you* think?" Bill Wendt asked. Then he added

sheepishly, "Meaning no disrespect to Sergeant Koepp." Everyone laughed.

"It doesn't *look* like a copycat situation," Tarrish answered in a measured, deliberate manner. "Security about the tongue-slashing signature was good in both Indiana and Chicago. Ray is probably right, but don't spend all your time trying to force a connection with Sorgel. Solve this case."

Cal Friedel, chewing gum furiously in his latest frenetic effort to find a cigarette substitute, asked about fingerprints. Tarrish looked expectantly at Koepp.

"We've got an I.D. on some latent prints on the knob of a storage closet," Koepp said. "They belong to a salesman named Nick Panetti who lives at Cambria Village. I left word on his message recorder. Margaret and I will talk to him."

"Forensics got anything?" Wendt asked.

"Not yet," Koepp answered. "They're sorting through the stuff the vacuum picked up. I'll circulate whatever they have as soon as I get their report. Any other questions?"

There were none.

"I've put your initials next to the people I'd like each of you to call," Koepp told them. "If you get leads that look promising, let me know. If I'm not around, brief the lieutenant right away. The next thirty-six hours are critical. Let's not blow it because we didn't share information."

They dispersed and returned to their respective desks in the squad room to begin making phone calls. This would be frustrating and time-consuming because nearly everyone would be at work. When they did reach their assigned contacts, the ensuing conversations were apt to be very unpleasant. In many cases the person called would be learning for the first time that Joanne Whalen not only was dead but that she had been murdered. This news would be greeted with incredulity, which would be superseded by shock and outrage. The detective would have to explain what happened, answer questions, then cope with that peculiar resentment which people had when they realized they were being questioned about murder suspects. At this stage of the conversation the person on the other end of the line would be saying aloud, or at least thinking: Why are the stupid cops calling me? What the hell do I have to do with it? Why aren't they out trying to find the guy who did it?

Koepp's first two calls, to residents of the Cambria Village who had not been interviewed the previous evening, followed the usual pattern. Neither was able to offer any constructive line for further inquiry. While he waited for a secretary at Whalen's business office to find a general partner named Morganthaler, he eavesdropped on Margaret's phone call. She was commiserating with someone about how people weren't safe anywhere these days. He heard her say that was why the police needed the person's help.

"Morganthaler," said an authoritative voice on his line. A voice used to command.

Koepp explained again who he was.

"Yes, I've been expecting a call from someone, Sergeant Koepp. It's a terrible shock, terrible." Koepp was impressed that the man had comprehended his name; most people didn't even hear it in these circumstances. "How can I help you?"

"We'd like to meet with you today at your convenience," Koepp said. "And while we're there, we'd like to search her office." Too late, Koepp realized he had put it badly.

"Search her office! My God, what for?"

"It's just routine, Mr. Morganthaler. We're trying to find a motive, a reason why someone would do this to her."

"I thought the police *had* a motive. I heard on the radio coming to work this morning that she surprised a prowler and he killed her. What's that got to do with the firm?"

"A prowler is one possibility, of course," Koepp said. "But we can't be certain of that at this stage. We have to check out other possibilities."

Morganthaler's tone was altered slightly by a filter of sarcasm. "I can't imagine what you'd find here. We're an auditing firm, not drug dealers."

"I realize that. When would it be convenient for us to come to your office?"

"You'll need a warrant," Morganthaler said.

"Not if I have your cooperation." Koepp could have told him he didn't need a warrant to go through a victim's effects, but that would put them in a confrontational relationship. This way he forced Morganthaler to decide whether he wanted to be "cooperative" or "uncooperative." He waited in a cocoon of smugness for Morganthaler's capitulation.

"Around two o'clock would be best," the man said at last.

As Koepp hung up, he saw Margaret pointing at his phone while she talked on hers. He interpreted that to mean she had picked up one of his incoming calls while he was on the line with Morganthaler. He heard her say, "Yes, Mr. Panetti, we can see you here in half an hour. Thank you for your cooperation."

As she placed the phone back in its cradle she said, "The ex-boyfriend," emphasizing the "ex" ever so slightly. She smiled at Koepp, thinking the same thing as he was: on the table of probable murder suspects, an ex-boyfriend rated a lot higher than the head of an auditing firm or somebody who lived two condos up the street from the deceased. Not as good as an ex-husband, or better yet a jealous husband, but still a genuine suspect.

Panetti didn't disappoint them when they met him in the interrogation room on the ground floor. He was a little taller than Koepp, maybe six two, but more massive by far in the upper torso and neck, suggesting that he worked out with weights. He had jet-black wavy hair, a straight, aquiline nose, and rather thick lips, which formed the kind of mouth some women thought of as sensual. He had a mustache, which was very black, but had flecks of gray in it. Koepp glanced at Margaret to judge her reaction, but her face was blank. Nonetheless, Koepp marked Nick Panetti down as attractive to women. Sensual.

Margaret explained briefly the circumstances of Joanne

Whalen's murder. That's the way they usually worked, Margaret taking the lead in the questioning, Koepp observing the physical mannerisms of the witness or the suspect. It was part of the department mythology that Koepp had a sixth sense when it came to discerning lies. Some detectives said it was this quality which had enabled him to break a few of the toughest cases which fell into the county's jurisdiction. In Koepp's mind his success was more likely the result of having Margaret Loftus as his regular partner, but he did seem to be able to tell when someone was lying. It was the little things which gave people away, such as stammering or stumbling over words. Liars' voices often rose in pitch when they departed from the truth, and some prevaricators grew distant, using few hand motions or descriptive phrases. He tried to fix in his mind what was normal for Panetti as he responded to Margaret's introductory questions about where he lived and worked. Koepp would compare this unstressed behavior with Panetti's reactions when he had to answer the crucial questions.

When he told Margaret the name of the medical equipment manufacturer he worked for, she commented that she was familiar with their building on Collins Avenue and complimented him on how nice it looked.

"They do keep it looking good," he said, smiling tentatively. "That's important to our company because we're always trying to project the appropriate image."

"Oh," she said, paying him back with a smile of her own. "How do you mean?"

He warmed to his topic. "Well, we're not selling mufflers or bowling alleys. We sell strictly to health-care professionals, people with postgraduate degrees in many cases, and they aren't going to buy from us if they see our headquarters is a warehouse in some industrial development."

"What sort of products do you sell?" Margaret asked him. It was part of her "loosening up" exercise; people too reticent to discuss the weather would talk about their job.

"It's pretty technical," Panetti said, looking at Koepp warily.

"I would like to know," Margaret told him. "I'm sure it's really interesting."

"Well, our most exciting product line right now is called Nurse Mate. It consists of a small computer terminal mounted next to a hospital patient's bed, a PC—personal computer—at the nurses' station, a printer, a processor, and the system software which my company developed. Basically, all of a nurse's note-taking and record-keeping is done on the computer. All the data on a patient is entered in the computer at bedside—diagnosis, special treatments, medication, the whole nine yards. Saves up to an hour per shift for a nurse in doing her paperwork."

"That's fabulous. It's the kind of product you can really take pride in selling," Margaret said.

"Yeah, it's a good feeling to see the improvement in the hospital's efficiency. A lot of people think you can't get more efficiency in a service job. That's simply not—"

"Where were you at seven o'clock last night, Mr. Panetti?" She was still smiling when she asked the question.

She had succeeded in taking him by surprise, but he recovered with an alacrity that impressed Koepp.

"I was coming back from Chicago, driving through the damned sleet," Panetti said. "It was a mess. Trucks jackknifed all over the interstate."

"What time did you get home?"

"Seven-thirty, quarter of eight. Somewhere in there."

"Was anyone with you?"

"No. There never is." He switched his attention from Margaret to Koepp. "Look, do you have some idea I'm a suspect? That's ridiculous. Who told you about me anyway?" How like a businessman, Koepp thought, to assume that his inconvenience was caused by a conspirator. Koepp had encountered the same tendency in politicians and lawyers.

After dictating his rights to Panetti, Koepp said, "We found your prints on a storage closet door. Mind telling us how they got there?''

Panetti could have told him to suck wind and he wouldn't have been able to do anything about it. But the salesman answered casually that ''I used to spend time there. My prints are all over the place, including the bed.'' That little braggadocio might cost him dearly; like most women, Margaret was contemptuous of men who publicized their conquests.

Margaret's eyes narrowed ever so slightly, but the rest of her mobile face remained sympathetic. ''Do you travel in Chicago very much?'' she inquired.

''At least one week a month. Sometimes more. Chicago is a medical center, so most of my major accounts are there. I used to live there, until last March.''

''Where?''

''Orland Park.'' He gave her a street address, which she wrote down in her notebook.

''How long did you live in Chicago?'' Koepp asked.

''Five and a half years.''

''That's a long time for a salesman,'' Koepp commented. He didn't know whether it was or not, but he wanted to keep Panetti talking about Chicago.

''Yeah, it was, I guess,'' Panetti said. ''I changed jobs there. I'd been selling drugs.'' Then he smiled knowingly. ''That's how you got my prints, right, because I was a drug salesman?''

Neither detective commented on his speculation; letting a suspect ask questions permitted him to collect his thoughts, which in turn facilitated lying. ''How big was your territory?'' Margaret asked him. ''What were the boundaries?''

''Indiana, Illinois, and parts of Ohio—Dayton and Cincinnati.''

''Did you have any accounts in Elkhart, Indiana?'' Koepp asked.

''Now, or when I was with the drug wholesaler?''

''Both.''

''I didn't have drug accounts. I call on a hospital there now.

I do more business by far in South Bend, which is right next door." Panetti shifted awkwardly in his chair. The chair creaked under his considerable weight. His face was beginning to darken with anger. "Say, what is this anyway?"

"South Bend is crowded sometimes during the football season," Margaret pointed out. "When that happens, do you stay over in Elkhart?"

"Sometimes."

"Just during the football season?"

"No, other times, too. I like the Holiday Inn there. I'm used to it. When you spend so much time on the road you get lonely. So you tend to go back to the same places, where somebody knows you. All salesmen do it. Lots of times, though, I'd hit northern Indiana on the way home. Then I'd usually just drive into Chicago. It only takes two hours."

Margaret looked at Koepp expectantly. When he didn't ask any follow-up questions, she switched to another topic. She was able to determine that Panetti was a good friend of Joanne Whalen, that the two of them had occasionally gone to Vail together to ski and that Whalen stored his ski equipment for him because his own closets were filled with demonstration medical devices and instruments. Without much effort, she elicited that Panetti had sex with Whalen from time to time, but that they never lived together. "We even had separate rooms at the ski lodge, because she was afraid she might run into a client and she didn't want anybody to know she was shacking up with anybody."

"Did that offend you?" Koepp asked.

"You mean, not sharing the same room? Nah, this wasn't *Wuthering Heights* or anything like that. We liked each other. We had fun getting it on once in awhile, that's all. It stopped a few months ago, though. I haven't seen her much lately."

"What happened?" Koepp asked.

"She met some guy. Said she was in love with him. Said she hoped I'd understand."

Koepp again: "Did you?"

"Sure, I told her, no problem. We stayed friends. She even asked me to take out her girlfriend from college when she was visiting from New Hampshire. Joanne's boyfriend was married, so she didn't see him very often. He came back from a business trip early, and Joanne wanted to get rid of the college chum for the evening."

"Did you help her out?" Koepp asked.

"Sure, why not? Her name was Rachel something. We had dinner, went out to a jazz dive on Regency street, then I took her back to my place."

"Did she spend the night at your apartment?" Margaret asked in a flat, unemotional voice. Koepp couldn't imagine why she wanted to know except to satisfy her curiosity.

"Sure, that was the whole point," Panetti said. "Joanne sure as hell didn't want me bringing Rachel home while she was entertaining her boyfriend."

"How did you know Rachel would spend the night?" Margaret asked. She reminded Koepp of a teenager sneaking a look at *Penthouse* magazine in a bookstore.

"It was their idea, the girls', I mean. Rachel told Joanne she wanted to get laid. She was going through a divorce and was pretty horny." He grinned at Koepp in conspiratorial fashion. "What was I gonna do? She was kinda cute, had a great body, so I said, 'Sure, why not?'"

"How was she?" Margaret asked with carefully masked malice.

"A ten, the first day or two—she moved out of Joanne's place and into mine for almost a week—but then she started to get on my nerves. Too frenetic, if you know what I mean. She talked all the time, never bothered to listen. She was one of those women who go without sex for a long time, then go crazy because they can't get enough. I had to haul her to the airport myself and put her on the plane to get rid of her. Joanne thought it was hysterical."

They interrogated Panetti for another fifteen minutes, until a lull developed, during which Margaret looked at Koepp questioningly. When the suspect saw Koepp shrug, he asked if he could go.

Margaret let a smile of unaffected admiration flood over him. "Sure, why not?"

PHILIP HAD GONE to a drugstore in his neighborhood as soon as it opened to get a copy of the morning newspaper. The ten o'clock news the night before on Channel 7 had mentioned the homicide at Cambria Village, but gave few details. As he sat in the kitchen of his apartment, thumbing through the paper, he had trouble concentrating. His mind kept reconstructing the scene with the two girls who were in the fender bender, trying to see it from their perspective, trying to imagine how visible his license tags had been to them in the darkness and snow. Nobody else saw him, of that he was certain. Because the weather had been so terrible, he was sure that She didn't notice that he was behind her on the freeway. The guy in the parking lot hadn't looked his way, either. So the only problem was the two girls. If the cop made his van, he was in deep shit. He'd need an alibi and a story about his van being stolen. His mother would say that he was with her. She had done it before. But how to explain the presence of the van in Cambria Village? His best—his only—idea was to drive it to a mall, abandon it, and say it was stolen. When they asked him why he hadn't reported it until this morning, he would say that he stayed over at his mother's house. That would explain the time lapse. But then everything depended on his mother. She would have to back up the whole story. And she wouldn't let him forget what she did. God, it would be unbearable.

He made up his mind. If there were no report about his van in the paper, then he was going to take a chance that he hadn't been identified. There would be no need for an alibi, no need for a stolen vehicle report, no dependence on his mother.

At last he found the story buried on an inside page. It was only six paragraphs long. There was nothing about the van or the two girls in the auto accident. His momentary relief was supplanted almost at once by renewed anxiety. Even though nothing was on the news, they might still have the license number, might even now be coming to interrogate him. No, it was too risky. He had to dump the van, go to his mother's and call in a report. And tell her what to do. He put on his jacket, felt for the keys in the front right-hand pocket and went downstairs to the parking lot. It had warmed up during the night so he had no trouble starting the vehicle. He backed the van down the driveway which ran between his apartment building and the one next to it.

As he approached the street, a dark sedan turned off into his driveway. At once, in panic, he recognized the two detectives who had been to his apartment. There was no place to go. The man was driving. He saw Philip and honked his horn.

For a second or two Philip thought about making a run for it, but he realized how futile that would be. He pulled his vehicle next to a mound of freshly plowed snow and waited. *Stay calm,* he told himself, *and find out what they know. Even if they put him at the scene, they haven't got a motive or evidence. See what they've got before you say anything.*

The woman detective was rapping with a gloved hand on the window of his vehicle. She beckoned with her finger. Philip shut off the engine, climbed out of his van and got into the backseat of the police car. The woman, back in the front seat again, swiveled to face him. The man adjusted the rearview mirror so that he could look at Philip as well. He could see the cop's eyes. They loomed gray and impassive, like the eyes of a cat.

But the woman's eyes were bright and cheerful as she smiled at him. For some absurd reason she asked him how he was doing.

"Fine, I'm doing fine," Philip said, trying to match her bouncy enthusiasm. "Why did you stop me? I've got a license. Do you want to see it?"

"We don't want to see your license," the woman said. She looked at him expectantly, as if she were waiting for him to say something else. She obviously wasn't ready to answer his first question. A long, uncomfortable silence ensued, but Philip was able to keep from saying anything. He stared back at the woman.

"What have you been doing with yourself, Philip?" she asked.

"Nothing much."

"What did you do last night?"

"I went to a movie early, then I went home after that."

"Did anyone see you come in?"

"Yeah, the woman who lives downstairs in my building." This part was true. "Her name is McLeod. I met her about nine-fifteen or nine-thirty in the hall outside her apartment. She was taking out some trash."

"How long were you at the movie?"

"Till around nine," Philip said. "It started about seven."

"What was the movie?" she asked.

"*Pretty Woman.*"

"Any good?"

"No."

"Anybody go with you?"

"No." He resisted the urge to say anything else, and let the silence settle on them again.

"We had a report that you were parked outside Dr. Robbins's house last night."

Having prepared himself for that question, he was able to respond immediately. "That's a lie," he said, letting her see his anger for the first time. He was becoming more confident. No matter what she said, he was going to deny it.

But she surprised him by saying, "Well, thanks for stopping, Philip. We appreciate your cooperation."

He got out of the car and walked back to his van, trying to look unhurried, a little irritated. But inside his belly he was weak with relief. The two stupid girls hadn't identified him. There was nothing to tie him to Cambria Village!

THE SOUND OF THE SHOWER awakened Lisa, who rolled over and peered at the alarm clock. She saw with relief that she hadn't overslept; in fact, she was awake fifteen minutes early. She shut off the alarm, put on a wool bathrobe and went to Kevin's room. She peeked in to make sure he was asleep and safe, then went to the kitchen. A welcome smell of brewing coffee greeted her, which meant that Jack had risen early and filled the machine. She hadn't remembered to do it the night before because of his unexpected, late arrival. She put two slices of bread into the toaster and turned the radio on softly, a habit she inherited from her parents and one that annoyed her husband.

After a batch of commercials the news came on with an update on the latest partisan wrangling about the budget deficit and more threats from Iraq's mad dictator. She recalled then her amazement as an adolescent that the world could be so cursed as to have men like Hitler and Stalin in control of countries. Only later, after she had begun to study psychology seriously, did she conclude that many men were capable of being a Hitler. It wasn't bad luck at all; it was human nature. Given sufficient power, maybe a Philip Schroeder was capable of such depravity.

The timer signaled that the coffee was ready. She poured herself a cup, buttered the toast and sat down. In a few minutes Jack came in, wearing a robe and toweling his dark hair. He kissed her perfunctorily, poured coffee for himself and settled across from her. He looked haggard and his face was ashen, the same color it had been when he returned the night before.

"My dryer is on the blink," he said. "Can I use yours?"

"Sure." She told him in which cabinet drawer to look for it. Then, seeing the pained expression starting to settle on his features, she switched off the radio. He didn't thank her or seem to pay any notice, but she observed that the set of his jaw had softened. They talked of his trip for a few moments, after his morning gloom had dissipated, and she described her adventures on her day off. He pretended to listen, but she could tell that his attention was elsewhere. Something bad had occurred, she decided, something related to his work, because that was the only part of his life that caused him substantial concern; problems at work were calamitous, while problems at home were annoyances. With a resurgence of bitterness Lisa realized it wasn't that way with her. Although she worked as many hours as he did and made more money, she could never subjugate family concerns to her career.

Jack, on the other hand, easily rationalized family affairs. He had even assimilated the fact of Philip Schroeder following her into the fabric of his domestic life; it was another annoying distraction, like Kevin's asthma attacks, the occasional unreliability of the sump pump, and entertaining his in-laws.

To prove he had heard at least some of what she said, Jack asked, "Did the police do anything?"

"They talked to him, but it hasn't made any difference. He's still following me."

"It's time I talked to him," Jack said, suddenly grim and determined.

"No." The word, etched with fear, had burst from her. She tried to recover at least a semblance of calm so that he wouldn't become even more concerned. "I think I can deal with it in therapy. I just can't risk your talking to him. He'll feel threatened, which will destroy whatever trust he has in me. I can't help him if he doesn't trust me."

He greeted this outburst in silence.

"Promise me, Jack, please. He won't dare do anything because he knows the police are aware of what he's up to."

"All right, but if he keeps it up much longer, we'll have to do something."

Jack got dressed and sat down at the kitchen table again while Kevin ate his breakfast.

The boy was in a buoyant mood because he had been awakened by his father, whom he had not been expecting. For a six-year-old he had a well-developed sense of time, defining its passage with precision on the basis not of days and hours, but on when his father's trips began and ended. Having Jack home a day early was like removing twenty-four hours from his life. He had watched a science documentary on television the evening before about Easter Island and now proceeded to tell his father about it in surprisingly coherent detail. "They cut those big stone faces out of the rocks, then they slid them down the side of the hills," he said earnestly. "The people there were making some new ones when all of a sudden they stopped. They just stopped. Nobody knows why they stopped." He paused to see how his father was following all this, because he was old enough to realize that adults frequently didn't listen to children even when they pretended to. Satisfied, he went on. "They had an epidermic—"

"That's *epidemic*," his father told him.

Kevin nodded. "They had an epidermic and everybody died. Now, almost nobody lives there."

"How did the people get there in the first place?" Jack asked. "It's so remote—so far from everywhere else."

"They came in canoes from China."

"From China?"

"Yes, China," Kevin said emphatically.

He had been studying the globe in the den one day while Rose dusted and had been attracted by the size of China. After Rose explained what its name was, every unknown and faraway place became China. The boy began to eat his oatmeal with the same serious concentration he had been lavishing on Easter Island.

The conversational break gave Lisa a chance to ask her husband to take Rose to the garage.

"Is she having that car serviced again? She just had it in."

"Something's wrong with it. I think they're putting in a new battery."

"She didn't have a car last night?"

"No, she—"

"Can I have some more milk, Mama?" Kevin asked. "It's too dry."

She opened the refrigerator and handed a carton of milk to Jack, who proceeded to pour infinitesimal amounts on Kevin's cereal. He made a game of it, inviting Kevin to form his oatmeal into a mound that resembled Easter Island. Then he made a big production of adding the ocean—the milk. Lisa was both amused and dismayed at how easily Jack could slip into a shared boyhood with Kevin. What had Wylie said once? "All men are nine years old functionally. Once you understand that, you can begin to deal with their repressions."

Lisa tried to recall, as she studied Jack's handsome, craggy features, what he had been like when they first met. That he expected to succeed had been manifest in his easy confidence and his effortless dominance of both men and women. Until recently those qualities had propelled him gradually but inexorably toward the pinnacle of his professional career. Then his persona of success had mysteriously shattered. He no longer assumed he would be a success, which was the precursor of failure. Was it before or after that failure of nerve that he began having an affair? Which was cause, which effect?

Jack at last shifted his attention from his son back to her. His eyes didn't glow with affection as they had after they made love in the early days of their marriage, but they weren't dead, disinterested, as they had been lately. His searching expression hinted at questions, but he didn't ask them. She saw something else there. Fear? Loathing?

She rose, kissed him lightly on the mouth, clumsily embraced her uncooperative son and escaped to work.

She found the atmosphere at the clinic to be frenetic and yet somehow satisfying. Having a lot of patients clamoring for attention did more than anything else to affirm her usefulness. She immersed herself in the professional stream.

In mid-morning Lisa was astonished when Philip Schroeder turned sideways on Wylie's leather couch and grinned at her. It was incredible that she hadn't remembered his regular appointment. Perhaps, she thought, he had become such a ubiquitous presence in her personal life that she had all but obliterated him from her professional milieu. A defense mechanism?

He didn't wait for any exchange of pleasantries. "The cops questioned me this morning," Philip said. He meant to sound cocky, but she knew him well enough to discern his underlying fear.

"What happened?" she asked.

"What happened?" With the meticulous recall which psychopathic personalities were sometimes able to summon, he reviewed in detail his interrogation by Koepp and Loftus. His recital, which treated both important and insignificant facts with equal weight, at first unsettled Lisa, then shocked her as he calmly revealed the murder of a woman named Joanne Whalen in someplace called the Cambria Condominiums. Almost at once she felt dismay at how quickly the police had searched out Philip Schroeder. Yet she was relieved also; she had never wanted to be sole custodian of the knowledge about Philip's frightening tendencies.

Despite her conflicting emotions, Lisa was able to concentrate on his description of the confrontation with the police, hoping to learn that something of the experience would dissuade him from following her. But if Philip could be believed, the police were not in possession of any evidence linking him to the crime.

When he finally concluded his sentence-by-sentence recounting, she blurted, "I want you to stop following me." Verbalized, the demand sounded hysterical. An hysterical woman. The mode she dreaded most.

He grinned for a long time, then leaned toward her. "I'm not following you." The arrogance with which he invested the lie chilled her more than the falsehood itself. She felt a frightening compulsion to smash something in his face, which subsided as soon as her brain recognized the urge. She actually flushed with embarrassment. Lisa had never lost control with a patient before, and it surprised her that she could do so now. The id unchained?

"That's not true. You followed my mother and me to the garage and the shopping mall yesterday."

"No, I didn't."

"If you are not going to be truthful with me, there is nothing I can do for you, Philip. I believe it's best for you to see another clinician. I think Dr. Luchow—"

"Piss on Dr. Luchow. You're my shrink. If I say it, that's how it will be."

"Not if I choose not to treat you."

"But you won't. If you try to dump me, I'll tell the cops what I know."

"And what's that, Philip?" she asked, suddenly weary and enervated.

"I'll tell them you killed that woman."

NINE

AT RAY KOEPP'S REQUEST, the county's consulting psychologist, Larry Kimble, joined the mid-afternoon briefing of the Whalen homicide investigating team. He wore a doeskin jacket with patches at the elbows over a raspberry-colored, checkered sport shirt. The effect was decidedly academia and drew an expression of vague contempt from Jack Jackowski. Like most narcs, Jackowski came from a working-class background where suspicion of college boys, and their instructors, was deeply ingrained.

Kimble ignored him. His full attention was on Margaret.

She gave brief summaries of the interrogations of two of their better suspects, Panetti and Philip Schroeder, hoping that one of the other detectives might have come up with something relating to the pair. Cal Friedel picked on the salesman. "Yeah, Panetti used to sleep with her, according to the neighbors," he said. "They think he probably had a key to her condo at one time. She let him store skis and his hunting gear there."

"Bill, did you call Panetti's two employers about his whereabouts on the Zeto and Holloway killings?" Koepp asked.

Wendt flipped past several pages of his notebook, stared at his infamously bad handwriting and grunted. "Haven't heard back from the drug company yet," he said. "They have to go dig in some old files. The place he works now said he was in town last June sixth."

"That's the night of the Sorgel homicide," Koepp said for the benefit of the others.

Wendt nodded confirmation.

"Panetti does have an alibi for the time of Joanne Whalen's murder," Cathy pointed out. She rummaged through the investigation reports in front of her. "According to this Amy

Shue, she and the other college girl met him in the parking lot. She said that he had just gotten there and was unpacking his trunk.''

"His alibi is soft," Margaret said. "They didn't actually see him drive in. They *assumed* he just got there."

Koepp listened in silence as each detective in turn contributed isolated facts and observations gleaned from their phone calls. No one reported anything significant; mostly they were just letting him know they had carried out their assignments. He began to feel unsure of himself because the moment would soon arrive when the team would look to him to focus the investigation.

During Cathy's summation, a red-haired uniformed officer stuck her head through the doorway and told Wendt that his call from the drug company had come through. The detective left to answer his phone.

"I'd still like to know if we're treating this as another serial killing," Cal Friedel said. "The tongue-slashing—"

"It's possible," Koepp said.

"Possible?" Friedel said. His eyebrows, thick and bushy, raised a little.

"This one is different," Koepp told them. "The killer struck the victim in the back first. In the other slasher cases he was facing the victim." He waited for their reaction, but nobody said anything, presumably because none of them felt it was a significant difference.

"A couple of neighbors heard the car crash," Friedel said. "One guy looked out his window, concluded nobody got hurt and went back to his TV set."

"Nobody noticed a stranger in the hall or the parking lot?" Koepp suggested.

Several heads shook glumly.

"It's a transient neighborhood anytime," Cathy said. "They aren't close-knit. In fact, it's not even a neighborhood." Cathy had majored in sociology.

"What about the possibility it was an interrupted break-in," Kimble asked. "Nobody seems to be considering that."

Koepp looked at Margaret, who had done an inventory of the apartment that morning. "We compared the condo's contents with the insurance company policy on the household effects," she said. "Nothing of value was removed. Not even her wristwatch, which she was wearing."

Bill Wendt reappeared and sat down. His face was impassive, but the tense way he carried his arms and shoulders suggested to Koepp he had something substantial to tell them.

Koepp looked at him encouragingly.

"Guess who was staying overnight in Indianapolis when Jane Holloway was killed?" Wendt asked.

Margaret and Kimble said the name simultaneously. "Panetti!"

"Bull's-eye," Wendt said. "That's where his expense report said he was. The accountant I talked to said his folio from the hotel is attached to the expense report. I told him to fax me a copy and lock up the original."

"How far is Indianapolis from Elkhart?" Koepp asked.

"A hundred and sixty miles, give or take," Wendt informed him. "He could drive it in three or four hours, cut up Holloway and get back to his hotel for breakfast. She was killed at two in the morning."

"I'd like to go through that guy's place," Friedel said.

"We don't have enough for a search warrant," Wendt replied unhappily.

"But the Indiana cops have a blood sample of Holloway's killer," Koepp said. "They found blood on her wristwatch that wasn't hers."

"DNA match?" Cathy asked.

"Takes a warrant," Wendt reminded all of them. He was grindingly methodical on matters of procedure in collecting evidence. His failure some years earlier to Mirandize a young drug runner accused of homicide had resulted in an acquittal. Wendt never forgot his lesson. Part of squad-room lore held that Wendt Mirandized his mother in Poughkeepsie when he telephoned to wish her a happy birthday.

"Panetti will let us do a blood test voluntarily," Koepp said. "We won't need a warrant."

"How can you be certain of that?" Kimble wanted to know.

"Margaret will ask him," Koepp explained.

ALTHOUGH KOEPP'S ADMIRATION for the persuasive powers of his partner was considerable, he hoped that she would be unsuccessful in getting Panetti to agree to a blood test. His refusal would be more indicative of guilt than compliance. It had been Koepp's experience that most innocent suspects cooperated fully when it was suggested to them that a requested test would exonerate them. Operating from this premise saved a lot of time. If Panetti submitted to the test, they could attempt a DNA match without any judicial red tape. If he refused, they had more incentive to build enough circumstantial evidence to obtain a warrant.

Once they were back in the squad room, Margaret sat down at her desk, which faced and abutted Koepp's, and started placing phone calls to contact Panetti. He heard her ask someone for the salesman's car phone number. Then he punched up the messages on his phone recorder and began phoning each of the callers. He smiled ruefully when his first two calls were greeted with recorded messages inviting him to leave a message. It seemed to him lately that the more devices that were invented to facilitate communication, the harder it was to reach a live human being. He hesitated about making the third call, because the caller was Assistant District Attorney Tom Styles, which meant that the Whalen case had probably been assigned to him. Styles was acerbic and impatient with almost everyone who could not advance his career, but he was a competent prosecutor. He had never tried any of Koepp's cases without getting a conviction.

Styles sounded out of breath when he came on the line, as

if he had been climbing stairs. Forsaking any greeting, he asked for a status report on the Whalen stabbing.

Koepp gave him a succinct account of what they knew so far, holding his temper in check when he heard the sighs of exasperation from the young attorney. He concluded his summary and waited in silence for a sarcastic response. But Styles surprised him by asking in a mild tone if they had any suspects.

"Not a good one. We've questioned a former boyfriend who lives in the same condo complex. His name is Panetti."

Styles muttered something Koepp couldn't decipher.

Koepp went on. "If Panetti agrees, we're going to try for a DNA match with some blood found on a murder victim in Elkhart, Indiana."

"The tongue-slasher?"

"Right," Koepp said. "It could be we have a serial killer."

"Whatd'ya mean 'could be'? Looks like an identical M.O."

"Not quite. The previous victims were attacked in the front and put up a defense. Joanne Whalen got it in the back."

Styles weighted this information in silence. "What about a warrant?"

"We're trying to get him to take the blood test voluntarily. We wouldn't get a warrant on what we've got."

"Keep me posted."

Koepp promised he would.

As he put the phone back in its cradle, Margaret said to him with a trace of smugness, "Panetti will stop by the M.E.'s office on his way home tonight."

Keopp grinned at her, then dialed DMV and asked for Wendy. When she came on the line, he identified himself and asked about her youngster in day care.

"He's stopped making a fuss, but he still doesn't like it. What did you really call about?"

"I asked for a check of license numbers with the number six and letters X and L. You know about that?"

"Yeah, Adrian is working on it," she said. "How come your witnesses never memorize the whole plate?"

"Tell me about it." He could hear her yelling at someone, then she came back on the line. "You're looking for all tags with those digits, but not necessarily in that order, right?"

"That's right, you can't depend on witnesses—"

More yelling. Then Wendy lowered her voice and said, "Adrian figures he's got four or five hundred, maybe more."

"Can he purge everything except registrations in the county?"

"Yeah, he can do that," the girl said confidently.

"And just give me station wagons?"

"Can't do that. Make, okay, car style, no way."

"Okay, give us what you can. When can we pick up a hard copy?"

"Dunno. Don't call us, we'll call you."

Wendy did call back two hours later and Koepp sent a uniformed officer to the motor vehicle department to pick up the list. When she returned with it half an hour later, both Koepp and Margaret searched through the printout, looking for either a name or address that might relate somehow to Joanne Whalen or one of the suspects. Halfway through the list, Margaret suddenly sat back in her chair and stared at Koepp for a few seconds.

"Do you have Philip Schroeder's license number?" she asked.

Koepp rummaged through the papers on his desk, found his notebook and thumbed through it. "65D, space, 4L7," he read aloud. Then he added, "Also, it's not a station wagon. It's a van."

"It's got a 6 and an L," she said lightly.

"Nice try," Koepp replied.

PHILIP HAD SPENT most of the afternoon at the New Messianic Church putting new names into the list of potential contributors, printing labels and stuffing envelopes. He liked doing this kind of work because it didn't require much concentration, so he was free to think about Her. More and more he found him-

self fantasizing about Her. Mental images of different scenes
and situations impressed themselves on his mind in graphic
detail, then melted away immediately, much as the ripples dissipated after a pebble was dropped into a still pond. But each
fantasy, though different than the one that preceded it, contained two unvarying ingredients: her body was always a part
of the scene, even though her face changed sometimes, and she
experienced humiliation. He imagined her in various stages of
undress, supplicating, cringing, being dominated as he had been
dominated.

These dreamlike reveries pleased him greatly. Only one
thing bothered him; why did her face keep changing? Was it
because he couldn't remember what she looked like? Did it
mean anything? He wished that he could ask her to explain
what the changing faces meant.

At five o'clock he excused himself and drove to the clinic.
Now, knowing that she was always aware of him, he parked
boldly across from the parking lot entrance and waited for the
Volvo to appear. When it did, he followed her toward her home
at a close distance. But he didn't go directly to her house.
Instead, he circled around to the south and parked on a street
which paralleled hers. He pulled the van into the curb so that
he had an arc of vision between two houses that encompassed
the rear of the Robbins home. He saw light emanating through
the drawn drapery which must have hung in the living room.
Once he saw a shadow move behind the drape. For the first
time he noticed a second window on the west side, this one to
the rear of the one he saw so easily from the front. Two thick
evergreens, spruces, he thought, shielded the window from ob-
servation from the other direction. Interestingly, because the
yard had a pronounced downward slope on the west side, the
window was too high for anyone to see into. So no drape was
in evidence.

But if someone climbed about eight or ten feet up the spruce
closest to the house he would be level with the rear window.

It had to be a bedroom window. Possibly Her bedroom window.

Philip got out of the car, then walked between the two houses that faced his van. A single room was lighted in one house, on the end of the building opposite his path; the second house was completely dark. Slipping and sliding on the icy slope, he made his way to a low hedge at the rear of the Robbinses' property, threaded through the brushy barrier and walked slowly to the larger spruce tree. His heart pounded with excitement.

The tips of the tree branches were so dense with foliage that he could barely penetrate them. Branches scraped his face and tugged at his coat and trousers as he tried to get through to the trunk. He was enveloped with the pungent, pleasant smell of pitch. Once he bypassed the tips of the branches, he could feel bare limbs. It was impossible to see anything in the black interior, but he felt above him for two stout limbs and used them to lift himself off the ground. Slowly, with painful contortions, he snaked up the tree until the limbs became so close together that further progress was barred. Then he clumsily rotated his body until he faced the house. He reached out with a gloved hand and pushed a branch aside to discover that he was directly opposite and slightly above the bedroom window. He could see the foot of a single bed in the middle of the room and a mahogany highboy against a wall. No one was in the room.

For fifteen or twenty minutes Philip stayed perfectly still, waiting. Then a small boy appeared from the left and threw himself on top of the bed. In his hand was a model airplane which he zoomed about above his head. The boy turned over so he was on his hands and knees and began to make motions which suggested the plane was circling the bed. Then he "landed" the plane on the field of the blue spread. He produced a toy pistol next and began firing at imaginary interlopers, then hopped off the bed and disappeared from Philip's view. Philip momentarily felt guilty about watching someone who didn't know he was being observed. People acted differently when they thought no one was looking. He knew that from his own behavior. It was not right for him to watch the little boy, Her son, this way. As he was about to climb down, a woman came into view in the bedroom, and appeared to speak to the boy. This must be his grandmother.

The boy reappeared, still holding the toy pistol, and submitted to a hug from the woman. Then both of them disappeared from view. Philip immediately felt better. It was not a violation of privacy when two people were together. It was all right to watch then.

He had liked that, the warm moment, the hug. He tried to remember a scene like that when he was little. But he couldn't think of one. He wasn't the kind of person anyone wanted to hug, now or back then.

As he climbed down the tree, he imagined what it would have been like if the bedroom had turned out to be Hers and She had been undressing. That's what he hoped he would see. He wondered if he would have felt guilty watching Her. He decided he would not. He imagined Her preening in front of the mirror, admiring Her own delicious body. It would be all right to watch, because that was what women wanted, to be admired. They undressed to get control of men. It was all right to watch something like that.

Inside his head, the body, lissome and pale with nakedness, remained, but the face changed until she looked like a small boy. And blood began to drip down her from the slashes on her breast and her belly.

MOST MURDER INVESTIGATIONS reached their climax within the first twenty-four hours after the discovery of the victim's body, unless the corpse had been undiscovered for weeks or months. The usual result was an arrest and conviction, a fact which often surprised private citizens, who tended to confuse the severity of the crime with the reality of detection. The conviction success rate for murder was higher than for any other felony.

Murder was usually a crime of passion, committed by an

amateur and almost always for a specific motive. None of these three ingredients was characteristic of burglary, for instance, a crime that generated a very low rate of successful apprehension and conviction. While a murderer kills a specific person for a specific reason, a burglar chooses victims at random and commits the crime for the most universal of reasons: to acquire wealth.

But there was an exception, a certain kind of homicide that resembled burglary more than it did other homicides; a psychopath killed at random and without a specific grievance against his victim. That's what made serial killers so successful: their motive was generic, difficult to divine.

More and more, Koepp's investigative team was coming to the conclusion that Joanne Whalen's murder was the work of a serial killer. They didn't come right out and say it, but Koepp could tell from their comments that they felt that way. Part of the reason they did could be attributed to frustration. Despite an impressive amount of phone calling and legwork, they didn't turn up anything that resembled a clue to a motive. Without a specific motive, the obvious conclusion was that the killer had a generic one: kill any woman who was somehow involved with caregiving.

Because his frustration level was the highest of anyone's, he probably overreacted to the one anomaly that came across his desk on the fourth day of the investigation. Bill Wendt had managed to track down Debbie Kohlmayer, the young woman who had been riding with Amy Shue when they collided with a vehicle outside the Cambria Condominiums.

In his report, Wendt had uncovered one fact which he had encircled with a red pencil: *witness said unidentified vehicle was a minivan—NOT A STATION WAGON.* He was referring to the vehicle whose driver had not stopped to render assistance or volunteer to be a witness. Amy Shue had described the third vehicle as a station wagon.

Margaret's subsequent phone conversation with the Chinese girl confirmed that it might indeed have been a minivan. As she readily admitted, she tended to think of "those boxy things with the sliding doors on the sides" as station wagons. Margaret couldn't be certain, but she thought the girl called pickup trucks station wagons, too. "It's kind of a general term, I think," Margaret informed him. She smiled wanly, knowing that they both were thinking the same thing: Philip Schroeder drove a minivan. Two digits out of three which Debbie had remembered formed part of Schroeder's license tag.

"We could see if the girls can identify the van," Margaret suggested.

"What do you think the chances of that are?"

"Not great. It also won't get us anywhere in building a case. In court his attorney will show that there are ten zillion vehicles just like it in the metropolitan area. Then he'll defy us to prove the one the girls saw was Schroeder's." She grinned sheepishly. "Forget I even suggested it."

"How about the tape from the 911 call?" Koepp asked. "Did you listen to it?"

"Yes. A man. Educated. Sounded composed. A little out of breath like they always are. Didn't sound like anyone we've talked to."

"Where is it?"

"In the lab. Want to hear it?"

"Yes," Koepp answered. "But let's have our favorite psychologist listen to it at the same time."

"Larry Kimble?"

"No, let's hear what Dr. Lisa Robbins makes of it. I'll call her for an appointment while you get the tape."

LISA'S FINAL APPOINTMENT of the day turned out to be a "no show," which permitted her to join the two detectives in the clinic's conference room shortly after five. They had been there for some time, but neither the man nor the woman showed any signs of frustration or impatience. Having spent so much time waiting to talk to people, they were probably inured to delays, she thought. The woman, Margaret, was wearing a stone-washed denim skirt with a white blouse and a dark-brown suede vest, which accentuated her slimness. She also appeared fresh, as if she had just come on duty, not as if she had been working at an active, grueling job all day. Lisa, by contrast, did nothing more strenuous than walk from one consulting room to another, yet she was certain that she looked more care-worn than the detective. It bothered her because she was sure Koepp noticed the difference between them.

She felt his gaze settle on her as she sat down at the table across from them. His hair was in some disarray and a little tuft stood up defiantly at the back of his head, mocking in a way his long, sad, monastic face. He was the kind of man whom women felt compelled to mother.

Were they lovers? she wondered. They seemed to be very comfortable with each other, but they never betrayed by gesture or eye contact that they were anything more than friends. She envied them anyway because friendship was what she and Jack had lost in the last few months.

"As I explained on the phone," Koepp was saying, "we have this tape of the phone call to the emergency number."

"And this is the person who reported the Joanne Whalen murder?"

"Yes." He stood a portable tape recorder on one end be-tween Lisa and himself and pushed the control button.

For several seconds all she heard was a faint hissing sound. Then the voice, surprisingly clear, not as upset as one would have expected: "Get the police. A woman has been stabbed. In the Cambria Condominiums. Her name is Whalen." There was a pause, as if the phone caller were trying to catch his breath. "She's dead." The sound of the phone disconnect prompted Koepp to reach out and push up the control switch.

"Do you want to hear it again?"

Despite her astonishment Lisa answered affirmatively. Hear-ing the voice, the words, a second time gave her a chance to recover her composure. It also helped confirm the reality of what she had been listening to; if the voice was the same the second time, then she wasn't hallucinating.

It was. She was aware that both of the policemen were watching her intently. Surely they had noticed the effect the tape had on her. She waited in terror for the first, the inevitable question. But neither of them asked it. Instead, Koepp said softly, "Any impressions you have of the caller, or the state of his mind, would be helpful. Anything. The first thing that pops into your mind."

She tried to recover by talking, because then her features would be mobile, less easy to decipher. "He's surprisingly calm, given the circumstances."

"But what *are* the circumstances?" the woman detective asked.

"What do you mean?"

"We could be listening to the person who found the body, or to the murderer."

"Why would the murderer report it?" Lisa demanded incredulously. "He'd want to get away. Why would he run the risk of having someone identify his voice?"

"Because he might want to be apprehended," Koepp suggested. "Or it might be a way to taunt the police. Maybe it gives him a thrill to take a risk like that—to expose his voice."

"You're starting to sound like a forensic psychologist," she muttered. She had intended the silly comment as a distraction, a means of breaking the oppressive inquisitional mood that had begun to coil around her. But Koepp responded to it with only a puzzled expression.

"He portrays real emotion," she said. "He sounds real. And there is nothing on that tape to suggest that he's taunting anyone. That's not the way the murderer would sound. Did he identify himself?"

It was apparent that the caller had not revealed his name, but Lisa couldn't help asking the question. What if they knew? Then what was the point of this whole grisly exercise?

Koepp ignored her question. "How might the killer sound?"

"If that man had killed the woman—Whalen, right?—he wouldn't call 911 just to get someone to come and get the body. He'd have another motive, which would be evident from what he said. Your theory about taunting the police, for instance. If that were his purpose, where is the taunt? If he wants to be caught, where does he betray that desire?"

"You're applying rational analysis," the woman detective said. She spoke in a reflective manner, as if she had arrived at the same conclusions that Lisa had expressed, but wanted something more. "Violent people often do very deliberate things for reasons that make no sense. Not even to themselves."

"Even the deranged are trying to satisfy some need when they engage in what we regard as eccentric behavior," Lisa said. She regretted it almost at once. It sounded like the conclusion of a first-year psychology student.

Koepp must have felt the same way. He ignored the statement. "Might this caller be a clever murderer who knows that we'll track him down because he has a motive, and he'll use this phone call as a means of diverting suspicion?" When she didn't respond, he added, "You said it yourself, a murderer wouldn't take the risk of exposing his voice. Maybe that's how this guy figured it."

Lisa weighed that possibility in silence.

Koepp signified that the conference was at an end by sliding the recorder into the pocket of his sports jacket and standing up. Detective Loftus rose also.

Lisa accompanied them to the clinic's rear entrance and held the metal door open for them as they went into the cold night. Koepp paused for a moment just outside and said, "If you think of anything you haven't told us, call us. I assume you still have my card?"

She nodded stiffly, then shut the door.

As she walked slowly back to her office, she realized that she was alone in the clinic. Bereft of human habitation, the building reasserted its own peculiar sounds, the sounds of electrical appliances buzzing faintly, of creaking structural joints. She began to consider the possible consequences of her lie. Sooner or later it would come out, she was sure of that, but the lie would give her time. Time to think what to do. Time to assimilate what she had heard.

She knew the voice, she thought with a strange, dead resignation. From the moment when she had heard the first words, she knew her life would never be the same.

MARGARET DROVE the county car back to the Safety Building, which allowed Koepp to slouch down in the passenger seat and stare out at the twinkling city lights and snow-covered slopes cradling the freeway. The snow shimmered in a faint wash of light from a gibbous moon.

One of the many reasons Koepp preferred Margaret as a partner was because she genuinely enjoyed the challenges of driving in heavy traffic. Koepp, tentative by nature, did not. But riding as a passenger also was a liberating experience, sometimes enabling him to synthesize a mass of seemingly unrelated facts into a comprehensive pattern. That's what was missing in this case. A series of crimes appeared to be the work of one demented mind, making it likely that some strain tied the slashing homicides together. But Joanne Whalen's murder was different. She had been stabbed in the back first, ambushed. It didn't fit.

He said it out loud. "It doesn't fit."

Margaret knew what he meant without an explanation. Another reason he liked her. "Maybe this time it was just more convenient for him to stab her in the back. Could be she was more trusting than the others, made it easy for him, and he took advantage of the opportunity."

"Where's the thrill? He'd want to see the look in her eyes. He wants her to know she's powerless before him." Margaret didn't say anything, probably because she was so familiar with Koepp's conviction that repeat offenders committed crimes to compensate for their helplessness. Seeing a victim quail before the only power that rivaled God's, the power to terminate life, was what seduced a man to commit murder. The interaction of the victim provided the gratification. This line of thought led Koepp to one of the curious aphorisms for which he was noted in the squad room "bull" sessions—that is, that serial killers didn't hate the people they killed.

He smiled in the darkness when he recalled that Margaret had never disagreed with his theory, nor had she attempted to refute it. A good partner knows when to leave an issue alone.

He realized she was talking to him.

"Huh," he said inadvertently.

"I said, if you're right, then we don't have a serial killer at all. We have a copycat."

"A copycat who knew a lot," Koepp said. "I asked Friedel to find out from the guys who headed the investigations of the Zeto and Holloway murders if the press carried anything on the tongue-slashing. Both of them said no. And for the same reason that we didn't talk about it after the Sorgel murder."

Margaret glanced sideways at him. "That's how they screened out the weirdos who came in to confess?"

"Exactly," Koepp said. One of the more macabre aspects of investigating a murder was the appearance, following the first media revelations, of innocent but unstable characters claiming to be the murderer. To assist in the process of winnowing out the not guilty, cops withheld a unique but vital piece of evidence to use as a litmus test for anyone who confessed to the crime.

"That leads to some interesting speculations," Margaret said as she swerved to the left to pass an eighteen wheeler.

"Doesn't it? I'll go through their names. Larry Kimble had the Sorgel file. He gave it to Dr. Robbins. That's two, plus all the cops involved in the Sorgel investigation. And what about Philip Schroeder? Maybe Robbins got into that with him, trying to play detective."

Margaret chuckled. "She'd say 'Why not, you try to play psychologist.'"

"Who else might have access to the file?"

"Anyone in Robbins's office or home could have come across it."

"That's almost as farfetched as believing Robbins or Kimble did it," Koepp said. He was trying to get Margaret's intuition started. He wasn't having much success.

But then she surprised him. "You can probably eliminate Robbins, but I wouldn't necessarily assume that Kimble is incapable of killing someone."

"Motive?"

"Your motive. He wants to experience the ultimate power trip. Does he have an alibi for the Whalen killing?"

"I don't know," Koepp said glumly. "Probably not."

Margaret didn't pursue it. She knew as well as he did that most innocent people don't have alibis which will stand up in court. A bromide among experienced homicide cops held that only the guilty established alibis because they were the only people who knew they would need one.

One of the green signs spanning the highway informed them that Hillsdale Boulevard was the next exit. He sat up straight. "Partner, have you got a heavy date tonight?"

"Depends what you have in mind—partner."

"I'd like to take another look at the murdered woman's condo," Koepp told her. "I've got a key."

"You're insidious." But she turned onto the exit ramp, slowing the car to a crawl to maintain traction on the treacherously slippery incline. Despite her caution, the car fishtailed as she neared the intersection of the exit ramp and Hillsdale; Koepp felt his stomach muscles contract. Margaret seemed not to notice the vehicle's instability. Her mind was on the case. "Ray, I don't know what you think we can find there," she said, "but tell me how I can help."

"I want to walk through it, do everything the murderer did, then everything Whalen did—as near as we can reconstruct it."

Yellow police streamers warning people away were still on the door of Joanne Whalen's condo. Koepp peeled them back carefully and unlocked the door. With Margaret behind him, he moved through the entry hallway to the kitchen, switching on lights as he went. He took his time, stopping often to study the surroundings closely. Already the place had an abandoned feeling to it, even though all of the woman's possessions were untouched; rooms without active inhabitants regressed in character toward hostility.

The only specific reason which Koepp had for returning to the crime scene was to consider where fingerprints might have been left which were undetected by the lab team. He knew that light switches and doorknobs, notoriously poor sources for usable prints, had been checked, as had the edges of doors and jambs. The refrigerator, stove, and all the counter surfaces had been dusted. What had they missed?

In the kitchen they walked through the sequence of assumed movements of both the victim and the attacker, with Margaret in the role of the victim and Koepp acting as the murderer. They had to conclude that it must have happened the way the investigating team had assumed.

"Let's reverse the roles," Margaret said. "You be Joanne and I'll be X."

Koepp agreed. He walked out the door, turned around and came back inside the kitchen, pretending to carry two shopping bags in his arms. But Margaret hadn't taken up the killer's hiding place behind the refrigerator. Instead, she was standing next to the now-empty table, staring at it fixedly. At length, she asked, "Two shopping bags on the table, right?"

"Yep."

"Was anything taken out of the bags—you know, lying on the table?"

Koepp tried to reconstruct the picture of the kitchen in his mind. "I don't think so. We could look at the photos to be sure. Why does it matter?"

"It probably doesn't," Margaret said. "I was just thinking what a woman would do who had just put two grocery bags on the table. Most times I start to pull some of the stuff out of the top that's bulky and always put in last so it won't get crushed. Like loaves of bread.''

"I don't remember seeing any bread loaves on the table or sticking out the tops. But again, we can be sure by looking at the photos.''

"Did they find the sales slip with the items purchased on it?''

"Yeah, the lab boys found it at the bottom of one of the bags. The lab has the bags and their contents.''

Margaret walked to the appliance and opened the door. For a few moments she studied the contents of the refrigerator, then she closed the door and opened the smaller, vertical freezer door. She withdrew two frosted packages of meat and studied their labels for several moments. "The first thing you would put away would be frozen foods," she said. "I wonder if any of this stuff was put in here the night Whalen got it.''

"There are dates on meat labels," Koepp told her.

"True," Margaret said, then laughed softly. "But you apparently don't read them. They tell you how long the store has to sell a fresh item. But frozen foods don't have any dates on them.'' She held a package of cod fillets in front of Koepp's nose. There was no date.

"She wouldn't have been able to put anything in the fridge," he said. "As soon as she turned to face it, she would have seen the killer standing next to it.''

"If our assumptions about where he was standing are correct.''

"Do you see any other options?'' Koepp asked.

Margaret returned to the table and moved back and forth along its edges, surveying the doorway to the kitchen continuously. It was obvious that she was trying to decide if the killer had followed his victim into the room. Koepp backed out of the kitchen and reappeared in the doorway several times to help Margaret evaluate this possibility. "I guess not," she said, sighing. "Whalen would have seen him out of the corner of her eye.''

They spent another half hour in the place, looking for evidence of relationships with someone other than the people they had already talked to, or for physical evidence that might have been overlooked. They left the crime scene in a dispirited mood. Their failure to develop some new line of inquiry, even a tenuous one, from their visit to Whalen's home, convinced Koepp that his investigation was in trouble. He could usually tell if a crime was going to be solved by whether the physical evidence was increasing or decreasing. In the Whalen investigation the number of promising leads was declining day by day. Not surprisingly, the media had begun to exploit the terror of a serial killer on the loose and a police department which was floundering. The *Morning Dispatch's* page-one story was headlined: *Sorgel, Whalen Homicides Linked? May Be Work of Serial Killer*. That started it. All three TV channels piled on with taped interviews of a detective in Elkhart and an assistant DA in Illinois, who talked about the murders of Jane Holloway and Dorine Zeto respectively.

He had been depending on Margaret for one of her inspired insights, but all she had been capable of were inquiries about the contents of the victim's shopping bags. He couldn't imagine that anything substantial would come of that. She must have known she had let him down because she was uncharacteristically silent during the drive back to the Safety Building.

To ward off his depression more than for any other reason, Koepp suggested they do a "suspect walk-through" as they called it, which meant they would consider one suspect at a time and review everything they knew about him.

Although they had been through this exercise several times, Margaret agreed to try again. "Start with Panetti," she said. "Not only is his alibi suspect, he's the only one who has any connection with Elkhart and Chicago. He also knew the last victim and was even her lover for a time. She jilted him, so he has a motive."

"How about his motive for the other killings?"

Margaret paused for a moment, then said in a musing tone,

"Maybe he knew them and they jilted him also. Maybe he kills any woman who looks cross-eyed at him. We've also got a set of prints at the murder scene. He's my first choice."

If pressed, Koepp would have put Panetti at the top of his own suspect list, but he was not comfortable with such a choice.

"Fortunately, the lab analysis will tell us if it's Panetti," Koepp said. "So all we can do in his case is wait." Despite the fact that a successful DNA match would get him off the hook, Koepp felt the old resentment against faceless technicians with their arcane sciences who unmasked and convicted criminals simply by juggling a few chemicals. Someday the world would be divided not into "haves" and "have nots," but into those comfortable with technology and those who were not. He was bound to end his days in the impoverished segment.

"Even if the DNA proves negative for the Holloway murder, it still leaves him as the chief suspect for Joanne Whalen," Margaret said. "He might not have done the other three but he certainly knew about them. And it's possible that he picked up on the tongue-slashing M.O. somewhere. He tried to copy it to throw us off." She fell silent as she carefully negotiated another treacherous off ramp. "Who's your best suspect?"

"It was that kid Schroeder, just because Dr. Robbins was so concerned about him. But nothing ties him to any of it."

"He doesn't have any alibi for the time of the Whalen homicide," Margaret pointed out.

"It's too pat. I feel about him the way the Trojans should have felt about the horse. I get nervous when a murder suspect gets delivered with no effort by us."

"Next is the voice on the phone," Margaret said. "So far nobody has recognized him. We've tried the neighbors—"

"Yeah, I know, Bill and Cathy have been playing it for everyone they talk to. So have Farmer and DeMoss on the second shift. The guy could tell us a lot, but did he do it? I don't think so. It's absurd that a guy would kill someone, then report it when he must know the call will be recorded."

"You're assuming that he's rational," Margaret said. "Serial killers often call up radio stations, newspapers, the police."

"This guy didn't sound like that. You heard the tape. He wasn't taunting anyone." But he had to concede that she had a point.

Koepp, in effect, admitted that he didn't have any more suspects by saying in a tired voice, "Right now we need something real lucky to happen."

TEN

FOR THREE MORE WEEKS the investigation of Joanne Whalen's homicide continued to spiral in on itself, then the "lucky" event which Koepp had been hoping for occurred. The thunderclap of good fortune came in the form of a fax from a private medical research lab in Chicago. Margaret brought it up from the communications center and placed it in the center of Koepp's orderly desk. Her expressive eyes glistened with anticipation.

Koepp picked up the lab report and began scanning it quickly to get to the conclusion paragraphs. He found it halfway down the opening page. The DNA in the blood identified as that of Nick Panetti matched the DNA of the blood found on the wristwatch of Jane Holloway of Elkhart, Indiana, murder victim number two. A match. Panetti had killed Holloway; almost certainly he had killed the other three women as well.

Koepp shook his head in disbelief. "Let's get a warrant and pick him up," he said. "Better fill in the lieutenant first, though."

They went to Tarrish's office together and closed the door of his cubicle behind them. The watch commander frowned as they settled themselves on the chairs directly in front of his desk. He looked as if he wanted to be someplace else. "I told you Maggie was off the drug ed detail, so that can't be it. I hope you're here to tell me you've cracked the Whalen killing."

"We are," Margaret told him laconically.

"I'll be damned!"

Margaret launched into a concise summary of the DNA match, then told him they wanted to get a warrant as soon as possible. "We better get this guy off the streets before he kills anyone else."

Tarrish demonstrated his enthusiastic endorsement of that suggestion by banging an open hand on the top of his desk. The framed family portrait danced perilously close to the edge, prompting Margaret to slide it unobtrusively to a more secure location.

Lieutenant Tarrish was fond of aphorisms, office bromides that he drew on during moments of high drama or low comedy. If, for instance, a detective complained to him about a long and tedious investigative assignment, Tarrish would tell him, "If it was easy, I'd do it myself." Now he employed one of his favorites, which Koepp conceded was brutally accurate: "I'd rather be lucky than smart."

Margaret called the regional sales office of Panetti's company, learned that he was making calls in the area and informed Tarrish that they wanted a surveillance team assigned to Panetti's apartment. Tarrish nodded and instructed them to wait in the squad room while he briefed Assistant District Attorney Styles.

Koepp was feeling the inevitable letdown which always accompanied the successful conclusion of a major investigation. To shake off the ennui, he decided to talk to the medical examiner himself. Margaret, understanding his mood, nodded sympathetically and began to busy herself filling out reports.

Koepp walked down to the ground floor of the Safety Building.

Sturmer was sitting in the tiny cubicle in one corner of the large lab which served as his office. For once he was seated at his desk, doing nothing apparently but waiting for Koepp's inevitable visit. *Am I that predictable?* Koepp wondered.

The M.E. grinned at him. "Congratulations on another sterling example of logical deduction," he said, waving at his lone chair. He punctuated the sarcasm with a wheezy laugh. DNA fingerprinting was, in Sturmer's opinion, the greatest crime-fighting discovery since, well, real fingerprints. The new science had nothing to do with actual fingerprints, of course, but the phrase "DNA Fingerprinting" had caught on because a person's DNA composition was also unique and therefore a means of making a positive identification.

Koepp understood the technique in general terms, but he was unfamiliar with the laboratory process. He asked Sturmer to give him a short course on the technology involved. The pathologist grinned evilly because he often made fun of Koepp's mistrust of scientific inquiry; the Panetti case was going to provide good sport for weeks to come.

"You know what DNA is?" Sturmer began.

"Not exactly. It's the double helix thing, right, made of atoms or molecules?"

"DNA refers to various acids in cell nuclei. It forms the molecular basis for heredity. The double helix you always see in science journals is the shape that occurs as the carbon and hydrogen and oxygen et cetera bond together. Our DNA composition is unique to each of us."

"And the courts recognize that—uniqueness."

"Absolutely. The courts recognize it as valid, scientific evidence. Of course, the lab work is still being refined."

"What does that mean?" Koepp asked.

"There have been some cases in which the DNA evidence was tossed out because of sloppy lab results." Sturmer added quickly, "But the principle of DNA identification has not been discredited."

"How do you do it?"

Sturmer sighed; they had been through these detailed explanations of evidence gathering before and he was not a patient man in dealing with laymen. Then his frown of annoyance lifted. "Ah, there is a nice, simple explanation in one of these magazines." He stood up, walked to a rickety bookcase and began thumbing through medical journals. After a minute or so, he found what he was looking for and spread the open magazine on his desk so that Koepp could read it. In a box at the top of the page a diagram showed the various steps in comparing DNA samples.

Sturmer put a stubby finger next to each numerical step as he explained them. "First you chop up the DNA from the suspect—in this case, Mr. Panetti, I believe his name is—and from the victim's wristwatch. They use restrictive enzymes to do that and they place it in lanes in a gel substance. Then they electrify the gel to separate the fragments." He paused to let Koepp absorb the diagram.

The second illustration showed the DNA fragments bonding to a nylon membrane. "Next, the membrane is subjected to radioactively labeled probes that bind to specific areas on the DNA fragments. After washing, the membrane is placed next to an x-ray film, which shows where the probes are attached to the fragments.

"See, in the last illustration," Sturmer said. His finger punched into the magazine. "If both DNA samples come from the same person, the bands match. That's what the lab discovered when they compared Panetti's blood with the sample from the woman's wristwatch." He studied Koepp for a minute, then asked, "Got it?"

"No, but I've got a general idea. What is that x-ray film called?"

"Autoradiograph. To find out if two DNA samples came from the same person, you just compare the autoradiographs— see if the bands match. If they do, you're in business."

"What can the defense do to challenge results?" Koepp asked.

"Cast doubt on the lab's proficiency. It's been done. But the process is accepted."

"So you said," Koepp reminded him.

By the time Koepp returned to the squad room, Tarrish had arranged for surveillance of Nick Panetti's apartment, and contacted the Elkhart PD. In less than an hour the stakeout team called in a report that the suspect had returned. Koepp and Margaret drove to the salesman's home to make the arrest.

Panetti offered no resistance, listened to Margaret's reading of his rights with an incredulous expression on his face and asked about calling a lawyer. Koepp wrote in his notebook that this was the second time they had Mirandized him.

"As soon as we get to the Safety Building, you can use a phone there," Koepp told him.

"You people are making a big mistake," Panetti told them. "I didn't kill Joanne."

"You're not being charged with her murder. You're being charged with killing Jane Holloway in Elkhart, Indiana." Koepp had told him that earlier, but apparently it hadn't made any impression.

"That's crazy. I didn't kill anybody. I *screw* women, I don't kill them." Then he seemed to remember the blood sample which he had supplied voluntarily. "It's that DNA sample, isn't it?"

When neither Koepp nor Margaret answered him, he added angrily, "Your tests are wrong. Somebody messed it up. You got the wrong guy."

At the Safety Building Panetti called a lawyer named Wertz, who advised him to make no statements until somebody from the law firm counseled him in the morning. After a uniformed sergeant led the suspect downstairs to the lockup, Margaret called Dr. Robbins's home to tell her they had the serial killer in custody.

Koepp paid little attention to his partner while she was on the phone, but when she hung up, her face was white. She stared at Koepp with eyes dulled by shock.

"What happened?" Koepp asked, suddenly alarmed.

"Dr. Robbins wasn't in. I talked to her husband."

"And?"

"You're not going to believe me," Margaret said. She tilted back in her chair and stared at the ceiling.

"I won't if you don't tell me." Margaret could be irritating.

"Ray, it's him—the man who called in the 911 on Joanne Whalen. *It's Lisa Robbins's husband!*"

LISA EMERGED from the bathroom just in time to see Jack putting the telephone receiver back in its cradle. To anyone else, her husband's handsome, impassive face would not have revealed any inner turmoil, but Lisa realized at once that the phone call had upset him. The tic which betrayed him was subtle but unmistakable; he rubbed his fingers rapidly against the ball of his thumb. Jack was unaware of this mannerism, and Lisa had never called it to his attention, even though she often felt guilty about not telling him. Maybe his business associates had noticed the tic also and were taking advantage of it. She hoped not, but that concern was outweighed by her desire to maintain for herself a psychological edge in their deteriorating marriage.

She walked to the large closet to search for a dress, determined not to inquire about the phone call. If he wanted to tell her, that was one thing, but she wasn't going to press him. She realized, as she pushed hangers of clothes back and forth, that she was wearing a black slip, which had served early in their marriage as a symbol of their lovemaking. Wearing black lingerie in front of him had been her way of signaling her physical need. Now, she thought bitterly, he wasn't aware of what she had on.

To her surprise, he decided to tell her about the phone call. "That was a message for you from a woman who said she was a police officer. Detective Loftus?"

"Yes, I've met her. I'm a consultant on a case the police are working on."

"You are? Since when?"

"Just a week or so." She understood suddenly what it was that disturbed him so. He was thinking that the detective might have recognized his voice as the same one recorded on the 911 phone call reporting Joanne Whalen's murder. From what she had observed of Margaret Loftus, Lisa felt sure his fear was justified. She had been expecting this development ever since she recognized his voice on the tape at police headquarters. Now, inevitably, the corruption of Joanne Whalen would seep into her own home, her own family. God, what a fool Jack had been.

She managed to keep her composure enough to ask what the message was.

Jack blinked at her, uncomprehending.

"What message did she give you for me?"

"Oh, she said that a man—they think they've arrested a serial killer—somebody who killed several women."

"What was the name, Jack? What was the suspect's name."

For an uncomfortable moment she feared that he didn't remember. But he answered after a moment. "Panetti. The guy's name was Panetti." She could tell that he was feverishly assessing the implications of this intelligence, just as she was, and it gave her some bleak satisfaction to know that he was way behind her. She tried to put herself into the common mind of Koepp and Loftus. If they had what they thought was the serial killer, did it follow that they believed they had Joanne Whalen's killer as well? Even if they did, how could they reconcile the fact that Jack had made the 911 call? The logical answer was that Joanne Whalen was Jack's mistress, but that she had been killed by Panetti. Jack, entering her home for an assignation, found her body and did the decent thing—called for help. The only thing casting doubt on this scenario was the unlikely coincidence that the victim was the mistress of the husband of the consulting psychologist on the case. The coincidence was ludicrous, absurd.

She found the navy-blue dress she wanted, stripped it off the hanger and fluffed it out in front of her as she faced the full-length mirror on the inside of the closet door. It would do, she thought. What difference did it make what she wore?

Jack had put on a shirt and was on his hands and knees searching for his shoes underneath his bed. She watched him silently, beset by a panoply of emotions: resentment, contempt, anger, even hatred. Through his stupidity, he had involved all of them in the sordid death of Joanne Whalen. Suppose the police had to release Panetti because of insufficient evidence?

They would have to focus on her family. The coincidence would be too pervasive to ignore. She remembered with relief Larry Kimble's comment that Sergeant Koepp had a reputation for building a thorough case before he charged anyone. His arrest of Panetti meant he had compelling physical evidence against the man. They had a serial killer. Whalen had been killed and mutilated in the same grisly fashion as the others. Therefore, she also had been killed by Panetti.

The coincidence would gnaw at Koepp, but in the end it wouldn't make any difference. It was an extraneous oddity, unconnected with the process of judicial conviction.

Everything hinged now on Panetti being found guilty.

Quite unexpectedly and incongruously Jack remembered it was Tuesday, the night when he had to haul the trash barrels from the back of the garage to the sidewalk so that the city's sanitation crew could empty them in the morning. Anticipating his exasperation, Lisa decided to help him collect the waste-baskets. She picked up one in Kevin's room and another in the study and carried them to the kitchen. The door to the garage was open, and she heard one of the lids fall to the concrete floor. In a moment Jack appeared in the doorway and took the two wastebaskets from her outstretched hands. She noticed that his features were ashen and subtly contorted, and that he avoided any eye contact. He departed wordlessly.

Her annoyance about being late for their dinner party grew when Jack did not return for several minutes, prompting her to walk into the garage to see what had happened to him. He wasn't there. She went to the open doorway and peered into the street. The trash barrels stood next to the curb, but her husband was nowhere in sight. Suddenly, she heard his foot-falls in the crusty snow and looked toward the corner of the house just in time to see him emerge from the side yard.

"What are you doing?" she demanded.

"I noticed some indentations in the snow back by the spruce tree, so I went to take a look."

"Indentations?"

"Well, footprints. Somebody came in from the back and must have climbed the tree. Looks like it might have been a day or two ago. Probably just some kid."

"It wasn't any of the neighborhood kids," Lisa said in a strained, strident voice. "It was him. The little bastard was trying to peek through the windows."

As Jack entered the garage where the light was better, she saw that his color had returned and that his jaw was clamped, another tic, a sure indication of intense anger. "This time he's gone too far," Jack said. "He's on our property. That's trespassing, that's a criminal offense." He made it sound as if Philip Schroeder had committed armed robbery or aggravated assault. "I'm going to make a formal complaint to those detective friends of yours in the morning."

She recognized his true intent immediately, with a certainty born of considerable experience with deceitful patients. The footprints, real or contrived, provided him with an excuse to confront the police. She could envision his meeting with Koepp and Loftus. He would complain about Schroeder all right, but he'd also be giving the woman detective a chance to confront him with the fact that his voice matched the man's who reported Joanne Whalen's death. If she didn't recognize him, he knew he was safe. If she did, he would make his case directly that while he might have been Whalen's lover, he was not her murderer. How like Jack to get the issue resolved as soon as possible. It wasn't his nature to allow disaster to overtake him; he had to turn and face it. It was a trait she had admired greatly during most of their married lives. Now, conditioned to the idea that he preferred another woman's bed, she saw it as additional evidence of his lack of control.

Still, she decided with cool detachment, his impulsive confrontation with the police might be the best course under the circumstances. Sincerity clung to Jack as tightly as a periderm. If he succeeded in convincing them of his innocence, the police might not direct any attention on the Robbins family.

But it all depended on one thing: they had to believe that Nick Panetti was the killer.

PHILIP MISSED his appointment with Dr. Robbins during the second week of March. He had no excuse. He just didn't want to go. When the secretary at the clinic called him afterward, he told her he had the flu. When he didn't go to the next appointment, either, nobody at the clinic called him. On the thirty-first his mother sent him a check for a thousand dollars with no explanation. Accustomed as he was to her wily forms of bribery, he waited for several days before he cashed it, even though he was desperately short of money. He wanted to find out what she expected in return for this maternal impulse before he spent any of the cash.

He hadn't tried to find a job although he did read the want ads every day. He identified several possibilities if he got desperate enough. In the meantime the thousand dollars would keep his landlord off his neck for another month or so. By then the church would put him on as a regular paid employee; they would have to because all their bookkeeping entries were on the system he had set up and they couldn't get along without him. It seemed to him sometimes that they were stalling deliberately, but the business manager always said that he had to get board approval before they could hire any more management staff. Still, he had stopped volunteering his time, reasoning that they wouldn't hire him as long as his services were free.

He had consciously made a decision to stop following Lisa Robbins because he wanted her to think that he wouldn't be around anymore. This was part of his new plan to make her feel more secure so that it would be easier for him to do something that he had been thinking about constantly since the night he had climbed the tree outside her house.

He was going to get inside.

A woman like her would have drawers full of lingerie—slips, bras, slinky negligees, teddies, the female trappings of sexual indulgence. He wanted it all. Just thinking about it made his hands shake and sent rivulets of sweat running down his body from his underarms. He recognized the impulse, coiled up and dangerous inside his mind, because he had experienced similar obsessions. For now, though, viperine desire, although it squirmed, was held in check; he could plan, consider the possibilities, anticipate the pleasure of violating her at will.

He was in the van again, driving on a north-south boulevard outside the city limits. In Koepp's jurisdiction. The thought made him smile. He did his best thinking in the van because here he felt safe; nobody could get at him as long as he stayed within the speed limit. The red eye of his mother was powerless against him when he was on the move. When he got to 109th Street, he turned into a large shopping mall and parked his van outside a Sears store. Then he went inside to the central concourse and sat down on a bench that faced a water fountain. Light emanated from the base of the central fountain column through a slowly revolving ring of colored filters, which had the effect of changing the color of the descending water. It was a restful experience, watching the colorful falling water, except when the red filter passed his side of the fountain. He hated red. He hoped he would never see red again.

He glanced upward at the skylights in the dome of the rotunda and saw with satisfaction that the light was beginning to fade rapidly. In half an hour, maybe less, it would be dark, dark enough for him to go to her house. Dark enough to open the back of the van and take out the burlap sack which lay on the vehicle's floor.

What a jolt that was going to give her when she came out to get the newspaper in the morning and found the sack, and looked inside. She wouldn't even know for sure that he was the one who had left it, because he hadn't followed her for almost a week. It would pay her back for those devious questions about if and when he was out of town, and what did he think was the reason that a man who murdered women cut off their tongues. That had been a bad therapy session, the worst of all, because he had seen her in the role of inquisitor. That was the means by which women castrated men, by asking question after question.

It would give her something to think about all right.

He waited for almost an hour, until long after it was dark enough. Then, giddy with excitement, he drove to her street and parked the van. As he opened the sliding door of the vehicle and withdrew the bundle, he felt a surge of power through his body, a sensation like an electrical shock which generated itself from inside his spine and suffused his arms and legs.

He felt he was in control.

He arranged the blood-sopped bag in front of the door.

IT HAD BEEN a bad morning, starting with one of those ugly incidents that undermined Koepp's belief that the law would prevail in the end. An all-night self-serve gas station at 106th and Crescent had been robbed in the early-morning hours. The attendant, a nineteen-year-old black college student, was shot to death inside his glass enclosure. He was found at seven o'clock by his relief.

There were no witnesses.

When the station manager arrived, he ran a printout for the investigating officers of the digital instruments on the pumps. "Jesus Christ," he said. "Three people came in here after it happened. None of them paid. The bastards didn't report it!" The manager, a Mr. Broghammer, kept turning around inside the glass cubicle like a lion trying to find his way out of a cage. "They didn't report it," he said again and again. Koepp felt a weary empathy for the man; the bestiality of one criminal was less threatening than the callous indifference of three anonymous citizens.

"They didn't pay, either," Broghammer said once more. He stared uncomprehendingly at the two detectives. Civilians, as Margaret called them, didn't understand each other's natures very well.

When they got back to the Safety Building, the desk sergeant

told them that Jack Robbins was waiting, had been waiting for
close to an hour for them. The man looked up as the detectives
entered the conference room, the same one in which they had
interviewed his wife several weeks ago. He was older than
Koepp had expected, but he gave off an aura of virility that
modified the age difference. He was a good-looking devil,
Koepp thought, very distinguished. He glanced at Margaret to
evaluate her reaction, but her face was impassive as she shook
hands with their visitor.

Following brusque introductions, Robbins blurted, "You
have to do something about this Schroeder kid. He's stalking
my wife—my whole family, for all I know." He paused to
give them a chance to reply (or, Koepp thought, to identify him
as the man who had reported Joanne Whalen's murder).

Margaret chose to let him wonder awhile longer by asking
for specifics about Schroeder's behavior.

"This morning," Robbins began, "when I went out to get
the newspaper off the front steps, I discovered a burlap sack.
Inside it was the head of a dog."

"The head of a real dog?" Margaret asked. When she saw
his shock and confusion, she quickly added. "I mean it wasn't
from a toy, a stuffed animal—"

"A dog's head. It was appalling. The stench was horrible."

"How do you know Schroeder left it?" Margaret asked him.

"Who else would do something like that?"

"You tell me," Margaret said flippantly. "Somebody you
owe money to, a prankster, business enemy, a cuckold, somebody wanting revenge—" Her face was a study in benign innocence. "Where is this dog's head, by the way?"

"In the trunk of my car," Robbins said angrily.

"Did Dr. Robbins see it?"

"Of course," he replied hotly. "Also, my six-year-old son."
He took out a handkerchief and blew his nose. "We know
Schroeder came on our property at least once before. He
climbed a tree to peep into our son's bedroom."

"What did your wife say about the dog's head?" Koepp

asked. He realized immediately how bizarre the question must have sounded to Robbins, and would not have been surprised if the man had answered that his wife actually favored sheep's heads with dried watercress.

But Robbins had grasped the intent of his question fortunately. "That it was not unusual for a patient like Schroeder to do things to animals. Those kinds of people—someone with his disorder—are likely to torture animals. What are you going to do about it?"

"Did anyone see him put the bag on your front steps?" Margaret asked.

"No, but—"

"Did anyone see him trespassing on your property?"

"No."

"Mr. Robbins, we've warned Schroeder about harassing your wife," Margaret said. "But without evidence that he's broken the law, we can't charge him. And we don't have the personnel to watch your house and your wife continuously."

"Then what do you expect us to do?"

"You might consider hiring a private security firm to—"

"Not on your life. We're entitled to protection. That's why I pay exorbitant property taxes in this county. But I'll take that up with my county supervisor. Maybe he'll see things differently than you do, Detective."

Policemen often heard implied threats of political power being brought to bear. Experience had taught Koepp that few citizens had the political clout they thought they had. Robbins's threat could be ignored.

Margaret, with that deft timing touch that he had come to admire, chose this moment to regain the initiative. "Mr. Robbins, we know you discovered the body of Joanne Whalen. We'd like you to explain the circumstances." Before he could respond, she held up an elegant hand and crisply explained his rights to him.

Robbins didn't deny that he had made the call. In a mechanical tone of voice, as if he had rehearsed himself carefully, he admitted that he was having an affair with Whalen and that it had been going on for several months. His manner oscillated between arrogance and condescension as he related what he found when he arrived at Whalen's condominium; he was a patrician bestowing cooperation on lower-class civil functionaries.

It was a bad attitude to take with Margaret Loftus, as he would discover sooner or later.

"We know when you called the 911 number," Koepp told him. "How long before that did you discover her body?"

"Twenty minutes. Half an hour maybe."

"You didn't call from her flat?" Koepp asked.

"No. I got out of there as soon as I was sure she was dead. Naturally, I was frightened—not thinking."

"But you hung around long enough to clean out the place of evidence that you were shacking up with her." Margaret had put the charge in the form of a statement deliberately so he would not know if they had evidence or were guessing.

Robbins looked surprised, but he didn't respond.

Pressing her advantage, Margaret asked, "What did you take with you?" When he didn't answer immediately, Margaret said to him in a measured tone, "The murder weapon wasn't there—"

"Some pictures," he blurted. "I took a couple of snapshots out of her dresser drawer. That's all. I didn't see a knife."

Touché, partner, Koepp thought.

"What did you do with the evidence?" Margaret asked.

"What evidence? All I did was take some personal photographs—"

"You removed physical evidence from the crime scene. Photographs can establish a relationship to the victim. They're obviously very important in an investigation of a felony. What did you do with them?" Her voice was coarse with controlled menace.

"I'm going to call my lawyer before—"

"Can you produce them?"

Robbins was silent. He glanced at Koepp, probably hoping for some relief. Koepp shifted his eyes to the wall behind him and began to study the crack that was shaped like the state of Florida.

Margaret had bent over the table and was writing rapidly in her notebook.

Robbins watched her for a few moments, then answered, "I burned them when I got home and flushed the ashes down the toilet." Margaret continued to write energetically.

"Start from the beginning—when you arrived at the air-port—and tell us everything that happened," Koepp instructed him.

The man responded in a voice that now conveyed neither condescension nor arrogance. Koepp listened carefully to everything Robbins had to say, waiting for a subtle change in the chronological order of his recitation. But he was consistent throughout.

Nevertheless, the coincidence in the Whalen case mocked him: Dr. Robbins wonders if her patient might be a serial killer; then, a few days later, her husband turns out to be the lover of one of the victims of a serial killer. To attribute this just to an accident of fate was absurd, almost laughable. Panetti might be guilty of killing Jane Holloway, and possibly two other women, but he didn't kill Joanne Whalen, of that Koepp was certain. That one belonged to the Robbins family. He had outlined his hypothesis for Margaret that morning: Jack and Lisa Robbins decided to kill Joanne Whalen because she was threatening them somehow. Jack killed her, after Lisa had set up Philip Schroeder as the prime suspect by calling attention to his dark tendencies. To make sure the police jumped to the desired con-clusion, they had made the homicide look like the work of a serial killer.

Margaret had dashed his theory against the cold stone of her common sense. "I have a problem with that," she had told him. "If you're worried about coincidences, consider this. As-suming that Panetti killed one or all three of the other women, you're prepared to say he didn't kill Joanne Whalen? He knew her. He had a key to her apartment for God's sake! Talk about coincidence—''

Random incidents occurring at the same time which appeared to be connected but weren't happened every day. Yet in Koepp's experience coincidence in a murder investigation was almost always a sign pointing toward conclusive evidence.

This time two signs pointed in opposite directions.

ELEVEN

PHILIP SCHROEDER HAD CHOSEN to sit on one of the high-backed benches in the rear of the courtroom so he could get out without calling attention to himself, but his distance from the judge's podium made it difficult to follow the technical presentations of the lawyers. He could hear the judge because the old man made his infrequent comments into a microphone. Mostly he leaned back in his chair with his eyes half closed, looking bored. Philip didn't blame him; the lawyers and their witnesses were talking about some of the dullest stuff he had ever listened to.

Particularly the attorney who was representing Nicholas Panetti, the man accused of killing some social worker named Jane Holloway. The lawyer was a big woman with washed-out brown hair pulled back severely around her long head, which reminded Philip of a mane and had the effect of accentuating the horsey aspect of her face. Almost all her questions for the past half hour had dealt with the esoteric procedures used in a laboratory to match DNA samples; both questions and answers were replete with scientific terms which no layman comprehended. But Philip could pick up enough from watching the increasingly harried expression on the face of the witness, a Dr. George Ryder, to know the state attorney had some problems. Ryder had supervised the experiment to determine if Panetti's blood was on the victim's wristwatch. As the chief expert witness for the state, he had testified that it was, unmistakably. Panetti's attorney contended that it wasn't. The issue turned on a phenomenon called "band shifting."

"We need to go over this once more, Doctor, because it's so critical," the defense attorney said. "You chop up the DNA sample with a restrictive enzyme into tiny fragments."

"That's correct," the witness answered, nodding his head slowly. "The DNA is cut in sequences, which are different in each individual."

"And because the sequences are unique to an individual, you can then discriminate between individuals."

"Yes, the pattern of fragments provides you with markers, so to speak."

"How do you discern the pattern of these DNA fragments?"

"First, the fragments are placed in a gel, then an electric field is applied to separate them. The fragments are transferred from a gel to a membrane to which they permanently bond."

"What do you do with the membrane?"

"Wash it with a radioactively labeled probe that bonds to a specific sequence of bases in the DNA. Then you see where the probe attached by putting the membrane next to an x-ray film."

"Which is called?"

Dr. Ryder shifted forward in his chair and eyed the attorney with a baleful expression. "An autoradiograph."

"That's a big word, isn't it?" she said, but then she repeated it flawlessly, proving that it wasn't too big. "Is that the end of the process?"

"No, you'd have to do multiple autoradiographs."

"Which you would do how?"

Without rising, the state's attorney, a thin, stooped man with sandy hair, objected that the witness had explained all of this in previous testimony.

"It bears repeating, Counselor, and will do nothing to diminish the court's comprehension," the judge told him. "Overruled."

The defense attorney repeated her question.

"You'd chemically remove the first probe and use another that binds to a different sequence of bases. Then you'd compare the two autoradiographs to find out if both samples come from the same person."

"When you were comparing the DNA sample from the victim's wristwatch and from Mr. Panetti's blood sample, how many probes did you use?''

"Well, we had four different probes that produced identical results. From that we deduced that the DNA samples were a match.''

"The developed film, the autoradiograph, shows bands where the probes are attached to the DNA fragments, is that correct?''

"Yes, it is,'' the scientist said.

"But the bands didn't actually line up, did they?''

"The pattern was the same, but the bands were displaced in one direction. It would be similar to badly hung wallpaper.''

"You encountered what is called band shifting? And you testified that this occurred because the DNA from Mr. Panetti's blood ran faster along the gel than the blood sample from the victim's wristwatch?''

"Yes. Band shifting isn't that unusual. It occurs in about thirty percent of the cases we examine.''

"How did you correct for it?''

"One way is to use a probe that attaches to a fragment of DNA that's the same in every person,'' Ryder explained. "It's called a monomorphic probe.''

"Did you do that in this case?''

"Of course. We used a probe that attaches to a constant fragment on the X chromosome. From the displacement we calculated that the size of the fragments on the victim's watch should be corrected about 3.15 percent to account for the band-shifting phenomenon. The differences between the two samples all fell within the threshold required to declare a match. Both samples came from the same person.''

"So you say, Doctor, but that's not what Mr. Landermann, who also works for your company, discovered.''

Ryder watched warily while the defense attorney walked to her desk and picked up a sheaf of papers. His jaw muscles flexed and unflexed and a tiny stream of sweat began to trickle down his left temple.

"You're familiar with Mr. Landermann?" she asked in an obscenely cheerful tone of voice. "Are you aware that he did a second probe of the samples?"

Knowing what was coming had at least given the witness a chance to decide whether or not to lie. He said "yes" with all possible haste.

"Is it not true that Mr. Landermann used a second mono-morphic probe that attaches to a constant fragment on the Y chromosome?" She didn't wait for him to answer. "And is it not true that he discovered that his calculation showed a much smaller correction was appropriate?"

Philip couldn't hear the respondent's answer, but he judged from the triumphant look on the woman attorney's face that it had been a "yes."

"Is it not true that if you use Mr. Landermann's data, as many as three out of seven of the bands were different by more than the threshold required to declare a match?"

This time there was no answer immediately. But it didn't matter. The preliminary hearing wound down in acrimonious debate for another hour, then the judge ruled with grim exasperation that the DNA specimens could not be used as evidence. He directed that Nick Panetti be released from custody immediately.

By finding him innocent of the murder of Jane Holloway, the judge in effect removed him from the suspect list for the murder of Joanne Whalen as well. That meant that the police back home would reopen the Whalen murder case with a vengeance.

Philip wasn't surprised; he knew Nick Panetti hadn't killed Joanne Whalen.

KOEPP LEARNED that Panetti had been released by the Indiana authorities as soon as he turned on the ten o'clock news on Channel 7. The coverage included a brief interview with a distinctly uncomfortable Assistant District Attorney Tom Styles, maliciously juxtaposed between snippets of interviews with

Tarrish and the chief of detectives. Both policemen said they were certain that Holloway and Whalen had been killed by the same man.

As he was accustomed to do during moments of stress, Koepp addressed the television set aloud. "Ring up another loss for the men in blue, made to look stupid by a television crew." He was not surprised by the failure of the DNA samples to match. In fact, he felt a curious euphoria because the news confirmed that crime detection wasn't pure science, but rather an art form. Technology had not rendered him obsolete yet.

Equally satisfying was the knowledge that now he could stalk the coincidence of Jack Robbins finding the body soon after his wife had called attention to a potential serial killer. He felt about coincidence the way some people felt about unpaid bills; he could never be comfortable until it was dispensed with.

Margaret, ever vigilant, called him just as he was rising to pour himself a second, or maybe a third, Scotch.

"Did you hear the news?" she asked without any preliminaries.

"Yeah," he answered. He swirled the ice cube remnants in his glass and experienced a moment of regret that he had not grabbed the bottle from the kitchen counter on his way to the phone. He realized that she hadn't said anything else, which concentrated his attention; a silent woman was a cue for a man to say something. But what? Panic began to course through his arteries because he didn't want to disappoint her, but he was afraid he was going to.

To gain time, he asked, "Where are you?"

"O'Malley's," she answered.

Only fifteen minutes away, he thought. *That's it.* "Why don't you come over?" he blurted. "We can talk about it."

It took her almost half an hour because, as he discovered when he opened the door, she had stopped for a bottle of wine en route. He took the Chablis into the kitchen while she hung up her overcoat in the hall closet. She perched on one of the

high counter stools and watched him impassively as he poured
her wine into a glass and refilled his tumbler with Scotch and
fresh ice cubes. He knew she thought he drank too much, but
she never spoke openly about it. Like most women, she cen-
sured most effectively in silence. A wondrous quality women
had, he thought resentfully, to be able to communicate so well
by what they didn't say.

"So Panetti is out," he said, hiking himself onto the stool
next to hers. "Who's in?"

"I owe you at least the acknowledgement that you told me
so," she said, raising her glass in a mock toast.

"Your total self-abnegation is gleefully accepted," he said.

She laughed. "I mean it. You were right about Panetti."

"Don't overdo it, partner. I was perfectly willing to let them
put Panetti away and drop Whalen's murder in the closed file."

"Yes, but your instincts were right—again. This has been
very instructive to me." She looked completely serious. "But
I want to make up for my doubts by helping you get the real
slasher."

"I'm going to help *you*," he said lamely. He was embarrassed by what she had said, but could not understand why.

"It's got to be somebody in the Robbins household, doesn't
it?" She sipped delicately from the wineglass, set it on the
countertop and massaged the stem of the glass thoughtfully.
Before he could respond, she continued. "I mean it has to be.
You pointed out that Whalen had a back wound—unlike all
the others. That's point one. It could mean that somebody
stabbed her, then tried to make it look like the work of the
slasher by mutilating her tongue. The only people who would
know about the mutilation were cops and civilians who had
access to the investigation file—"

"Sure, we discussed those we know about," Koepp said.

"Right, Dr. Kimble for one, but he doesn't seem to have
had any connection with Whalen. He loaned the file to Dr.
Robbins, who took it home. So it's conceivable that her hus-

band and maybe her mother-in-law saw the contents. It's got to be one of the Robbinses.''

"What about Philip Schroeder? Dr. Robbins admits she quizzed him about the two earlier murders. Maybe she let it slip.''

"How did he get into the apartment?'' Margaret asked.

"How did Dr. Robbins's husband get in?''

"Easy,'' Margaret said, then took a generous swallow of the wine. "Mr. Robbins had a key. The victim knew him, presumably trusted him, so he had the best chance of stabbing her in the back. He also had a motive. She might have been hounding him to get a divorce. Or extorting money out of him. Mistresses offer lots of reasons for murder. But the clincher is opportunity. We know he was *there.* He killed her, knew he'd be suspected, and made the phone call to report the crime. That was just what we suggested, a bit of reverse psychology to throw us off.''

"Sounds solid, Detective Loftus. Nice theory. Now, perhaps you'll show the court your physical evidence.''

"Zip.''

Koepp watched her animated profile with amusement. She possessed the faculty to generate her own enthusiasm by listening to her arguments. Often her impulses were deadly accurate, but he had to guard against letting her stampede him into a premature conclusion. She understood her own tendencies as well as he did; she occasionally chided him if he didn't challenge her.

"Why not the good doctor herself?'' he asked. "She has the best motive of all.''

"How did *she* get into Whalen's apartment?''

"She could have found Whalen's key when she was washing her hubby's blue jeans.''

Margaret chuckled. "I hate to disillusion a chauvinist like yourself, but I doubt if Dr. Robbins washes blue jeans—or anything else. But he wouldn't leave that particular key in his pocket. He'd hide it someplace.''

"And the mother-in-law?"

"No key either, plus no strong motive. I mean, if she knew her son was playing around, she might not have approved. But would she kill because Junior was a naughty boy?"

"I admit it's a stretch—trying to find a motive for either Kimble or Mrs. Robbins, but not having a key is a problem for Kimble. It's not a problem for either of the Robbins women."

"It's a problem for Kimble *and* Schroeder," Margaret said. "You saw how careful Joanne Whalen was. She had two expensive locks on the door. She wouldn't have let anyone in she didn't know, especially not a man. But I agree with you about the two women. Once either of the Robbins women had identified herself, Whalen would have buzzed the downstairs door and let her come up. She really wouldn't have had much choice."

"That takes care of the key problem for both of the Robbins women," Koepp said. "Only it doesn't, does it?"

He suspected that her mind was working ahead, and she confirmed it. "If the killer called on the intercom from downstairs, Whalen would have had time to take off her coat. But she was still wearing it. Also, why would she have taken her uninvited guest into the kitchen? Then turned her back on him—or her?"

"Try this," Koepp said. "Dr. Robbins waits for her to come home, demands to talk to her, goes upstairs with her, and stabs her in the back."

Margaret nodded immediately. "That's one possibility. On the other hand, she could have discovered that her husband had keys to Whalen's place. She may have made some duplicates so she could get in and ambush her," she said.

"You haven't said anything about Panetti." Koepp regretted immediately that the name had popped out of his mouth. The salesman would probably hold a press conference and bellyache about "false arrest" as soon as he got back in town. Unless he admitted to multiple murders in the town square they'd never get an arrest warrant for him now. But Margaret wasn't worried about lawsuits or public relations.

"I'd like to hang him with it," she said, "but the DNA mismatch in Indiana makes it impossible for him to be the serial killer. Yet the serial killer did his slashing M.O. on Whalen—"

"Motive?"

"A tried and true one: If I can't have her, nobody else can have her, either." She swiveled to look at him directly. "You men are very possessive."

"I'm not."

"No, you're still a Capuchin. You don't want to possess anything."

"I wasn't a Capuchin. I was a parish associate pastor."

"But you have the soul of a monk." She looked embarrassed then, and turned back to face the counter. She finished her drink with a couple of quick swallows and slid off the stool. Koepp climbed down as well and followed her to the front door. If he invited her to stay, would she?

But he said nothing.

"So, what's next, coach?" she asked in her old saucy manner.

"First thing in the morning, get the contents list of what was in those grocery bags from the lab. Also a copy of the checkout tabulation from the supermarket," he told her. "I'll try to get Dr. Robbins to go with us to Whalen's place. I'd like to see her reactions to the crime scene. And she might offer some psychological insights."

Margaret looked at him skeptically, but didn't make any comment. She said good night abruptly and left.

Her scent lingered in Koepp's apartment even after he closed the door. That annoyed him because it felt like a reproach. But a reproach for what transgression? They had come to an agreement almost two years before that their exceptional compatibility in their police work would be jeopardized if they developed a romantic attachment for each other. Margaret herself, who often resorted to flippancy when the emotional air become close, had summarized their relationship: "We're terrific partners. We might be lousy lovers. Why risk it?"

But there had been too many shared triumphs and disappointments, too many times when they had nobody to depend on but each other, too many long periods of isolated intimacy on stakeouts, for them to be just partners. They had become friends to the point where they fit Aristotle's definition of the word: one soul inhabiting two bodies. But they had never slept together, which Koepp regarded as the touchstone of their relationship; as long as they didn't violate that taboo, they could remain partners.

He was certain that Margaret felt the same way. So why did her reproach hang in the air?

LISA ROBBINS MANAGED to clear her schedule and promised to meet Koepp and Margaret at the Cambria Condominiums at one-thirty. During the phone conversation Koepp told her that Panetti's DNA specimen didn't match the blood from the Holloway woman's wristwatch. He added that this meant they had an active murder case again.

When Koepp and Margaret arrived at the condominiums, they parked in the lot behind the building. As Koepp was getting out of the car on the passenger side, he noticed the Chinese girl Amy Shue exiting from the lot at the opposite end. She saw him, too, and nodded slightly in recognition. Her arms were full of textbooks.

Lisa Robbins was only about fifteen minutes late, which seemed to Koepp, considering her profession, a form of punctuality. They had left the door to Whalen's place open, but the psychiatrist paused just outside it, as if an invisible barrier stood in her way. Fortunately, Margaret saw her and encouraged her to come in. Observing her timidity, Koepp wondered whether she expected to find the murdered woman's body stretched out on the floor. He helped her take off her coat and hung it next to Margaret's and his in the closet near the front door.

The woman's blue eyes rolled inquisitively from side to side as she crossed the living room, as if she were looking for something she had misplaced. As they had planned, Margaret reconstructed what might have happened the night Joanne Whalen came home to a violent death, while Koepp studied their visitor's reactions. There was little to observe except for a rapt expression that never changed from the time they left the hall until they all stood shoulder to shoulder in the kitchen. It was clear that Lisa Robbins was completely engrossed in the experience of absorbing the crime scene, but she did nothing to betray that she might have been there before. Koepp knew instinctively that she was imagining what had happened here, but whether she was thinking about an assailant knifing a victim or her husband kissing another woman, Koepp had no idea.

Margaret's comparison of the inventory of groceries found in the shopping bags and the items on the supermarket checkout tape had turned up one interesting fact. They had agreed they would share it with Dr. Robbins to see if she had any particular insights to offer.

Margaret introduced the subject of her discovery in answer to one of Dr. Robbins's questions. "No, the groceries were still in the bags," she said laconically. "Except for the frozen foods, which had been stored in the freezer compartment." Both of them waited for Lisa to reply.

At first she said nothing, but she glanced at the refrigerator out of the corner of her eye, then looked at the kitchen table.

"That's very odd, don't you think?" She directed the question specifically at Margaret. Women talk.

"How so?" Margaret said blankly.

"You said she was wearing her overcoat when she was stabbed," Lisa said. "It strikes me that she would have removed her coat before she started to store groceries. It's awfully clumsy trying to put things on shelves or in bins with overcoat sleeves dragging into everything. She would have taken her coat off.''

Margaret shrugged but said nothing.

Lisa turned to the freezer compartment door, opened it, looked in and shut it again. ''It doesn't make sense,'' she said with conviction. ''You're sure that some of what she bought was put in the freezer right away?''

Margaret produced her notebook from her purse and read off a list she had made. ''Everything on the checkout tape was in the two grocery bags, except for four items. Three of those were marked ''mt'' meaning meat and were for $4.68. $4.31, and $2.05. Inside the freezer were a package with two chicken breasts for $4.68, pork tenderloin patties for $4.31, and some cod fillets for $2.05.''

''Did you find the fourth item?'' Lisa asked.

''The register slip said ''gr'' for groceries next to the figure of $2.59. There was a carton of linguini with shrimp—you know, the low cal kind—marked with that price in the freezer. We're *sure* all four items were put away.'' Margaret snapped her notebook shut, underscoring the incontestability of her conclusion.

Lisa allowed herself a quick, tight smile. ''The Whalen woman couldn't have put the frozen food away. She would have seen her attacker next to the freezer.''

''What are you suggesting?'' Margaret asked.

''The killer put the frozen food away!'' She made a sound like a laugh as soon as she had said it.

Neither of the detectives said anything for several seconds, letting silence act as their surrogate inquisitor. But Lisa didn't say anything, either, derailing their aspirations.

''The same thought occurred to us,'' Koepp told her, ''although there's another explanation. She came into the apartment with her killer. She put away the frozen food, then the killer attacked.''

''That still doesn't explain why she was wearing a coat. She would have taken off her coat first. Wouldn't you?'' she asked Margaret.

"Yes, I suppose I would have."

Perhaps because she suspected that Margaret was humoring her, she made motions with her arms above the table to approximate the process of lifting groceries out of a bag. "Reaching into a bag with the loose sleeves of an overcoat around your arms is ridiculously awkward." She moved her elbows in short arcs to buttress her contention. Koepp found her quite convincing.

"Okay," he said. "If you're right about the coat, then we have to assume the killer put the frozen foods away. After stabbing somebody a dozen times. Does that sound likely?"

"Some compulsions are very ingrained, very strong. It's entirely possible."

"But is it likely?" Koepp persisted.

"It's not unlikely if the personality of the killer is compulsive."

"What does that mean?" Margaret demanded with more asperity than she probably intended.

"Tell me if the killer is compulsive and I'll tell you whether or not it's likely." Their frustration was plain enough, so Lisa asked, "Do you know of anything else the killer did while he was here? Anything, no matter how trivial?"

Margaret had begun to shake her head from side to side when it hit Koepp. The overshoes, or street shoes. He had forgotten completely. Something in his expression had alerted the two women, both of whom were now staring at him expectantly.

"DeMoss found a puddle of water on a plastic mat inside the hall closet," he said. "Since the victim was still wearing her boots, the puddle was caused by the killer's shoes or boots. So you're right, Doctor, the killer didn't come upstairs with Whalen. He was here before she was."

Margaret's sheepish grin indicated she had also forgotten about the puddle. To her credit, it only took Lisa a moment longer for her to make the connection. "Ah, I see," she said, "if the killer had come in with her, he wouldn't have time to put away his boots."

"Or a reason to," Margaret added. "He killed her before she could take off her coat, so he would not have taken off his overshoes or rubbers. Why bother?"

Koepp and Margaret were now talking for their own benefit. "On the other hand," he said, "if the killer was waiting here, he couldn't wear his boots in without leaving wet impressions on the carpet, which would give him away. So he had a problem of where to hide the overshoes. He solved it by leaving them in the closet with a lot of other footwear."

"Yes, but how could he know the Whalen woman wouldn't stop to put away her boots and notice the strange overshoes?" Lisa protested.

"You have a point," Margaret admitted. "Maybe there's an explanation." They moved as one back to the hall with Margaret in the lead. She collapsed the folding door to her left and peered into the closet. At first all of them were confused at not seeing the plastic mat. Margaret pushed some of the clothes to one side, which exposed a long shelf in the back of the closet. She kept pushing the hanging clothes until they could see that the shelf extended along the entire width of the closet. It was piled high with shoes, boots, umbrellas, and vacuum cleaner hoses and attachments.

"No problem," Margaret concluded with a tone of finality. "You could stash a body back there and nobody would notice it for a week."

Lisa agreed with a nod of her head.

The two detectives glanced at each other then, comparing mental notes. By prearrangement they had agreed to wait until they had gained Lisa's insights and impressions about the murder scene before they brought up the subject of her husband. Koepp lifted his eyebrows slightly, which was all Margaret needed to detonate the emotional bomb. "Was your husband wearing overshoes that night, Dr. Robbins?" she asked quietly.

The psychiatrist's expression never changed. No doubt she had been expecting something like that from the moment she received Koepp's phone call earlier that day. "No. He hates overshoes. Most men don't wear them. But a man may have put his street shoes in the closet."

"Boots, shoes—it doesn't matter," Margaret said impatiently. "What matters is your husband found the body. You knew that as soon as you heard the 911 tape."

"Of course." An edge of defiance had crept into her tone.

"Have you discussed it with him?"

"No." Somehow she had managed to invest the one word with sardonic overtones. "Isn't it about time for you to read me my rights?"

"If you like," Margaret said. She could do sardonic as well as anybody. She recited the Miranda warning in a mellifluous voice, as if she were reading a commendation for excellence.

When she finished, Koepp asked, "Did you know that Joanne Whalen was your husband's mistress?"

"No."

"But you did know your husband had a lover?"

"Yes, but I didn't know who. Who didn't matter. People like me get divorced, we don't kill someone."

"Were you planning to get a divorce?" Margaret asked. Koepp liked it when his partner did the dirty work.

"I hadn't decided. Probably not. A lot of husbands have affairs. Women, too, for that matter. Life goes on." She swept back a wisp of hair from her forehead and looked at Koepp. "Is there anything else?"

"Why do you think your husband called the 911 number to report Whalen's homicide?" Koepp asked. "We might not have connected him with her except for that."

"I wondered about that as well," Lisa said. "It seemed very stupid to me, what he did. Maybe he just couldn't live with himself knowing her body was lying there—just lying there unattended."

Her coolly detached, analytical speculation about her husband's motivations struck Koepp as remarkable; it was as if she were discussing the aberrations of one of her patients with a group of medical students.

"Is there anything else about this crime that you'd care to comment on?" Koepp asked. He sounded more formal than he had intended.

"No," Lisa said quickly. "You should treat the killer's compulsion as important. It takes a certain kind of person to kill, then put groceries in the freezer."

"We intend to," Koepp answered.

They locked up the apartment and walked together back to the parking lot. Just outside the door Amy Shue was leaning against a white Celica, obviously waiting for them to reappear. She grinned at Koepp in conspiratorial fashion. "Do you want to see the station—the van that drove away the night that woman was killed?"

"Yes, I would."

"Follow me, my man," she said gaily. Koepp fell into step next to her as she walked toward the main access street on the south side of Joanne Whalen's building. At the side of the building she stopped, looked at Koepp and crooked her finger to suggest that he should look around the corner. Koepp edged ahead and peered out toward the street. A minivan was parked on the opposite side of the street, its blunt nose pointed in Koepp's direction. He recognized Philip Schroeder's vehicle at once.

He pulled back out of view and asked the girl, "How do you know it's the same one?"

"I just do. It's just—it's nothing specific, but I know that's the van."

"You're sure?"

"Definitely. Did you get the license number?"

"I don't need it. I know who owns the vehicle."

"You do?" For a moment she appeared to be confused, before asking, "Do you know what he's doing here?"

"Yes." That was true enough. Undoubtedly, Schroeder had

simply followed Lisa Robbins. What was far more interesting and puzzling was the question of what Schroeder had been doing there the night Joanne Whalen was killed. *If* he was there. Suddenly they had a surfeit of suspects.

The girl left them standing next to Lisa's car. Koepp told the two women about Schroeder, neither of whom showed much surprise. After a pause, Lisa said that she had not seen his vehicle when she drove from the clinic, adding unnecessarily that his tailing techniques might be improving.

"Did you see Schroeder when you were here before?" Koepp asked casually.

He wasn't casual enough because Lisa laughed before she answered. "I wasn't here before, but nice try, Sergeant." She made a point of opening the door to her car. "If there is nothing else, I really need to get back to work."

Margaret told her she was free to leave.

Koepp checked in with the dispatcher and was assigned to provide backup for two county detectives who were staging a raid on an automobile "chop shop." En route to the garage on Quincy Avenue, they reviewed the Whalen murder case again. "Suppose the girl is right, suppose Philip Schroeder was there the night Whalen was killed," Margaret was saying.

"I wouldn't get carried away with that," Koepp said. "This is the witness who described a van as a station wagon."

"I can see her making a terminology mistake like that. But she was so positive that it was the same vehicle—never mind what you call it."

"Maybe."

"You don't want to believe Schroeder was there because it makes a bigger mess of everything," Margaret said, displaying once more her depressing insight into his character.

"Have you noticed that the longer this case goes on, the more suspects there are?"

She laughed outright at that. "Yeah, I know. It's supposed to be the other way around: the longer the investigation goes on, the more suspects we eliminate. But we're getting close, don't you think? Suppose Schroeder was at the Cambria Condominium that night like Amy Shue said. How could that happen unless he had followed Dr. Robbins there? If he wound up there, she had to have been there. If she was there, she's our killer.''

Koepp didn't answer right away. He had been thinking the same thing as Margaret, but he was vaguely unhappy with his conclusions. One of the aspects of criminal investigation that he feared the most was what he called the "red herring syndrome''; sometimes a false line of inquiry seems so obvious that you fail to follow up on other leads.

Amy Shue had been persuasive when she identified Schroeder's van as the vehicle that had sped away the night of her accident. After awhile you developed a sixth sense about whether a witness had her story correct or not. Assuming she was right, was there any explanation for his presence on the scene other than Margaret's?

He couldn't think of one, not even a farfetched one.

Finally, he said, "Okay, if Schroeder was there, it was only because Dr. Robbins was there. But that doesn't mean she killed Whalen.''

"Well, it sure—''

"Look, she comes here to tell Whalen to stay away from her husband. They have a nasty argument in the parking lot. She leaves. Young Schroeder, figuring out what's going on, follows Whalen to her apartment and kills her.''

"How does he get in?''

"He's right behind her. When she lets the door slam shut, it doesn't, because he's inserted his gloved hand inside the jamb.''

"Of course, he stops en route to put away his snowy shoes in the hall closet—''

"Shit!'' Koepp said.

She grinned, as she usually did whenever one of his rare lapses into vulgarity occurred. "She did it, Ray. Face it. Beautiful women can kill. We need to get a warrant and turn her house inside out.''

"What are we going to tell the judge we're looking for?''

"We know the killer got into Whalen's place ahead of her, so the killer had keys. She could have duplicated her husband's keys. We are also looking for the murder weapon, clothes to match any fibers found in Whalen's kitchen—''

"Tarrish will want to check with the assistant D.A. It'll take time.''

"We've got probable cause," Margaret said. "If Styles will push it, he can get the warrant.''

TWELVE

LISA'S HANDS, clamped on the steering wheel, felt as if they were molded from lead. Joanne Whalen, so evil and disruptive in life, threatened in death to finish the destruction of the fragile Robbins family. It gave Lisa no satisfaction that they had not charged either Jack or herself yet, because she was convinced that they would do so before long. Right now they would be sifting through fingerprints from Whalen's apartment, cataloguing fibers and hair vacuumed from her couch and carpeting. It was just a matter of time. Once the police had narrowed the list of suspects sufficiently, they could concentrate all their efforts; they would find something to tie one of them into it.

Until the Chinese girl came forward with the incredible story that Schroeder's van had been there the night of the·murder, Lisa had assumed that only Jack was at risk. Now, of course, she herself was a suspect. If Koepp accepted the Shue girl's testimony as true, the only explanation for Schroeder being there was that he had followed her car.

She glanced up at the rearview mirror and was relieved to see that Schroeder's van was nowhere in sight. She had been growing more and more afraid of him, due to his latent hostility, only now her fears were redoubled because of his direct involvement in the Whalen affair. Now she understood why Schroeder had threatened to tell the police that she had killed Whalen. God, what a mess, she thought bitterly.

She arrived back at the clinic forty minutes later than she had promised, so she wasn't too surprised that patients had begun to stack up. Cathy Jakes, the receptionist, looked up with undisguised relief when she saw Lisa coming in from the parking lot. She rushed forward to intercept her and blurted, ''Pauline Boushard is in your consultation room. And Tom—Dr.

Luchow—is trying to placate Mrs. Meyerhoff in Wylie's office. She's kinda mad.'' She followed Lisa into her office. "So is he.''

"Who is *he?*'' Lisa muttered distractedly.

"Dr. Luchow. Also, a Mrs. Nogare called about Kevin. She says she's his homeroom teacher. Wants you to call her.'' She handed Lisa a message slip with the teacher's phone number on it.

"I asked you to schedule an emergency slot for me,'' Lisa said as she donned her white lab coat. "Did you do it?''

"Yes, from two to two-thirty.''

"Don't fill that one. Just run them in and out as fast as you can. I'll get caught up. I'll call Nogare later. Tell Tom I'm sorry, but if he can handle Mrs. Meyerhoff, I'll be more or less on schedule by two-thirty.''

The girl scurried away to carry out her instructions. She was one of those employees who believed that any catastrophe could be averted, provided she herself received precise directions.

Lisa composed herself with an effort and went to her consulting room to listen to Pauline's latest theory about how she had lost her husband, Robert.

Pauline was sitting in the high-backed chair in which Lisa usually sat during therapy sessions, so Lisa went to the sofa. "If patients play games with you, indulge them,'' Wylie had counseled. "They might be telling you something important.'' Now that they had exchanged places, Lisa waited somewhat impatiently for Wylie's insight to materialize. But her patient was not helpful. Although Pauline made veiled references to suicide, as she had done often in the past, Lisa recognized the suicide talk not as a real threat, but as a bid for sympathy. She responded mechanically, with only part of her attention engaged, as the young woman verbally roamed through the memories of her marriage to the redoubtable Robert. Her reverie was not intended to find answers, Lisa was sure, but simply to provide a diversion from her humdrum existence; Pauline haunted her past the way some people sorted through boxes in an attic; to satisfy curiosity, not to glean insights. The woman was beginning to fall in love with the dissolution of her marriage.

Finally, mercifully, Pauline's session ended.

As was usually the case, the afternoon passed so quickly that she was surprised when there were no more patients. She remembered Mrs. Nogare's call then and dialed the number Cathy had given her. She heard a recorded message and left her home number on the teacher's machine, feeling guilty that she hadn't called during school hours and resentful that she was the one who always had to deal with Kevin's teachers, his orthodontist, his pediatrician, and his friends. She wished that somebody would call Jack just once.

There appeared to be no one else in the clinic, so Lisa made a quick tour of the offices and consultation rooms, shutting off lights. When she switched off the lamp in Tom Luchow's office, she heard a quick, muffled oath from his closet. She switched on the light. Tom backed out of the closet with his overcoat in his hand and an irritated expression on his face.

Lisa apologized. "I thought you'd all gone." She wondered if he was still angry because she had been late with her appointments. They stood in silence, waiting for the other to speak.

Inexplicably, he asked, "Is that kid Schroeder still following you around?"

She should have guessed that everyone in the clinic knew about Schroeder, even though she had not told anyone. "Yes, sometimes," she answered. Confessing it made a small laceration in her professional pride.

"Is he out there now?"

"I haven't looked," Lisa said. She had a feeling that he was.

"Shut off the lights and let's find out."

They went to the north side of the building and looked out the window of Wylie's office. The dark van, its sides white with dried salt, squatted across the street.

"I'll get rid of him," Tom said. "Have you got a hairpin?"

"A hairpin? What's that for?" She dug through her purse and found one after a determined search.

Tom took it wordlessly and slipped out the side door. Moments later she watched him cross the boulevard and crouch down at the front of the van. Schroeder honked his horn savagely several times, but Tom remained hunched over the front tire. The headlights went on and there was more honking as the vehicle lurched away from the curb. The tall figure, standing erect, watched it depart.

When Tom was back inside, she asked, "What did you do?"

She saw a glint of white teeth in the murky gloom. "I started to let the air out of his tire."

Lisa laughed appreciatively. So simple, so effective, she thought. Picturing Philip's outrage at having his precious van attacked gave her a primitive, if transitory, satisfaction. Why couldn't she have thought about letting the air out of his tires? Wylie's answer presented itself immediately: "All men are nine years old." The attacks of nine-year-olds deserved the retaliations of nine-year-olds.

"Do you want me to follow you home?" Tom asked eagerly, caught up now in the male role of her protector.

She assured him that wouldn't be necessary, but she noticed that he remained in the parking lot until he saw her pull safely onto the boulevard. Then he followed her for several blocks. But the dark van did not reappear; soon Tom's car disappeared in traffic.

Finally, Lisa had committed herself to buying groceries, resisting Rose's offer to do the shopping. Now, despite her fatigue, she stopped at a Piggly Wiggly store and began looking for the items on her grocery list. Only it wasn't her list; it was Rose's. Almost every entry had been made in the neat, slightly back-slanted block letters used by her mother-in-law, which underscored again how crucial Rose's contribution was toward their domestic infrastructure. Being unfamiliar with the supermarket, she had more than the usual difficulty finding every-

thing. But she kept searching until she had every item on the
list. Anything less would have been an admission of defeat, a
surrender to Rose's invincibility.

It was past seven when she snuggled the Volvo into the
garage next to Jack's car. Rose, ever alert to her arrival, was
in the kitchen warming up a saucepan of chili. The kitchen
table was set for one, which meant that Jack and Kevin had
eaten. Rose was humming some indistinguishable lullaby softly
as she roamed about the room.

Lisa hung up her coat, went in search of father and son,
whom she found sitting together on the couch, and kissed both
of them. Kevin was reading for his father, or rather, showing
off his reading skills. Lisa listened for a while, then went back
to the kitchen where Rose greeted her with a Manhattan in
hand. "You looked like you could use one of these," she said.

Lisa took the drink gratefully.

"Where's yours?" she asked.

Rose picked a half-empty tumbler off the counter and raised
it to eye level. "Cheers," she said, as their glasses clinked
gently together.

Rose smiled at her. It was a faint smile, as if she held something in reserve; that sort of restraint, Lisa thought, was characteristic of Rose. The woman was unfailingly kind and gentle
to everyone, but Lisa could recall only a few instances when
Rose Robbins displayed any passionate emotions, any deep-
seated conviction.

After Lisa sat down at the place laid out for her at the table,
Rose told her that Kevin's teacher had called about the boy's
authorization to have his measles shot. "Kevin brought the
form home," she explained, "but he forgot to give it to you.
Jack signed it. I put it in the pocket of his blue coat."

"That must have been the reason Mrs. Nogare called me.
Thanks for taking care of it."

"That's what I'm here for," Rose said casually. Almost at
once she looked embarrassed, having judged her remark as an

encroachment on Lisa's turf. Lisa took no offense. She smiled reassuringly at her mother-in-law.

Whether or not Rose was in fact reassured, she chatted amiably about her volunteer service that morning in a Red Cross blood drive. Then she brought the conversation around to Kevin's penchant for outgrowing his clothes and ticked off specific items she thought the boy needed. They agreed to take him shopping during the following Saturday afternoon. After Lisa finished the bowl of chili, she stood up and carried the bag of groceries to the cupboard which contained the canned goods. As she set the bag on the counter, she realized that it was considerably lighter. Peering in the top explained the difference in weight: Rose had placed the frozen foods in the refrigerator earlier, while Lisa was hanging up her coat.

How like Rose to remember about the frozen food. Rose did things like that. Compulsive.

In that instant a cold, terrifying dread, like a night fog, enveloped her.

THIRTEEN

THIS TIME THE COPS had insisted that he come with them to the Safety Building to answer their questions. They were trying to frighten him, which didn't surprise him. As soon as he saw the judge in Indiana throw out the case against that salesman Panetti, Philip knew he would be the most likely target. Also, in the past several days the newspapers and television stations had been very critical of the police because neither the Whalen nor Sorgel homicide had been solved. There was a good deal of speculation about lack of cooperation between jurisdictions, buttressed by charges and countercharges from politicians in both the city and the county. In that kind of environment he wasn't surprised when Loftus and Koepp tracked him down at the New Messianic Church and practically forced him into their car.

This time when they read him his rights, it occurred to him that he should not say anything and that he should talk to his mother about hiring a lawyer. But Philip dismissed the impulse, partly because he didn't want her big red eye looking at him and partly because he thought she might use his request as an excuse to stop giving him money for anything. Better to take his chances, rely on his own wits. Whatever he did, he couldn't let the bitch-cop, Loftus, intimidate him.

They had him cornered in a small interrogation room that smelled of sweat and stale cigarettes and something industrial that he couldn't identify. He could discern the cosmetic scent of the woman cop, too, which made him feel faintly nauseated. Men smelled like their jobs, but all women smelled the same to him. They tried to be unique, but the pathetic odors they used to confuse men didn't work with him; he could always smell their evil despite the olfactory camouflage.

"We have a witness that puts you at the scene of the crime the night Joanne Whalen was killed," the bitch-cop was saying. "That wasn't a coincidence. You know something about the murder."

He had thought about this moment many times and knew what he would answer. Still, he took his time so he could watch them lean forward anxiously, expectantly. They assumed his reply would incriminate him. He knew that's what they wanted—to let the phony doctor go free and lock him up for life as a sex killer.

At last he threw his surprise into their faces. "I followed Dr. Robbins there." He watched the male cop as he said it, assuming he would be the one who least wanted to consider Her a suspect.

The puzzled expression that puckered Koepp's forehead didn't change; he looked as if he had heard this remarkable piece of news before. Disappointment slid down Philip's insides and settled in his belly. They wanted times: when he got there, how long he stayed, when Lisa Robbins left. Cops were big on time; it was as if they thought they invented it. The sergeant kept nodding, which conveyed the impression he was committing Philip's testimony to memory.

"Why didn't you tell us sooner?" Koepp demanded.

"I didn't want to get Dr. Robbins in trouble," he answered quickly.

"That's a lie," the woman said.

Philip ignored her and kept his eyes fixed on Koepp.

"Did you think Dr. Robbins killed Joanne Whalen?" the detective asked.

"When I read about it in the papers, I knew she did it," he said.

"That's a lie," Detective Loftus said again.

She had begun to remind Philip of a baseball umpire calling balls and strikes: lie one, lie two, lie three and you're out. He hated her; they were all alike.

They made him go through the whole thing again, asking

him once more about all the times, trying to catch him in some contradiction. Because they thought he was lying, they expected him to trip himself up sooner or later. But Philip felt supremely confident they wouldn't succeed because he enjoyed the luxury of telling them the truth. The longer they questioned him, the more buoyant he felt. Even the woman cop had become powerless under the onslaught of his precise, articulate truth.

"Did you see where she went when she got inside the building?" Koepp asked.

"I didn't see her go in. I followed her van until I got there, but I turned around at the end of the cul-de-sac and parked on the street. She parked in the lot behind the building."

"And you stayed in the van until she drove out?"

"Yeah." The lie slid easily into the rushing stream of truth.

"Do you know what her husband looks like?"

"Not really. I only saw him at a distance."

"Do you know his car?"

Philip grinned. "Sure. He drives a Cadillac. Kinda gray-green. An old guy's car. An old, rich guy."

"Did you see that car at the Cambria Condominiums that night?" Koepp asked.

"No."

"Sure?"

"Yes."

"He was there later." The woman cop. She made it sound like an accusation.

"If you say so. I didn't see his car."

Another man came into the room and sat down at the end of the table opposite the three of them; he seemed to be making an effort to show that he was only observing and was not going to be an active participant in the interrogation. This one looked like a real cop, not like Koepp and Loftus, who always reminded Philip of social workers. He was older and had a pot belly that hung over his belt and a red, beefy face. Koepp told Philip that he was Lieutenant Tarrish. But he didn't tell the lieutenant who Philip was. He knew they slighted him that way to irritate him; he smiled at the new cop to show them they hadn't succeeded.

"When the Robbins car arrived at the apartment building, did it go straight up the driveway to the parking lot?" Koepp asked.

Philip reconstructed the snowy scene in his mind so that he wouldn't make any misstatement. "As a matter of fact, no," he said. "She stopped for a second or two on the street in front of the front door. I assumed that she was trying to read the street number above the door."

Koepp again: "So, you think she didn't know for sure which building she wanted to go in?"

"That's what I thought then," Philip answered.

"What other explanation is there?" Koepp asked.

"Maybe she had a loss of nerve. Maybe she was trying to decide if she really wanted to go through with it."

Koepp studied him thoughtfully for a few seconds. "Yes, that's a possibility."

Philip was so pleased by this concession from the detective that he decided to follow up his advantage. "She's capable of murder. I spent a lot of time with her. Believe me, she could kill. She's like my mother, just like her."

"But your mother didn't kill anyone, Philip," Koepp told him.

"She killed my father." In the confines of the small room it sounded like a shout.

"Your father wasn't murdered."

"What she did to him was worse than murder."

They sent him back to the church in a patrol car to pick up his van.

LISA LAY ON HER BACK with the calf of her left leg lined up with the edge of the bed. Ever since she could remember, she had avoided being adrift in the vast expanses of the king-size bed; with one leg on the edge she always knew where she was.

Her psychological orientation didn't match her physical coordinates, however; she had never felt as detached from her moorings as she did at this moment. In a way it was worse than the fear of losing Jack to another woman; at this stage in Lisa's life, Rose was more valuable than her son. She provided so much that Jack did not: practical management of their household, love without reservation, loyalty, the nurturing of their son. No, that was unfair, she thought; Jack did love his son. But where he was inclined to be selfish sometimes, Rose was unfailingly considerate; where he was occasionally irritable, she was eternally patient.

She needed Rose badly. Kevin needed Rose. And Rose might be a murderer.

By any measure Rose was morally superior to her son, yet Lisa knew with certainty that while Jack could not kill, Rose could. This paradox put her mind in as much turmoil as the horror of suspecting Rose of such an act. How could Rose be capable of murder? What could drive her to it? How did she manage it? As each question formed itself in her mind, an answer materialized at once with irrefutable logic. She could kill because she was the strong one, the one who had to sustain herself and her son when her husband Jerry abandoned them. Her motive was plain enough. If Jack would not give up Joanne Whalen, Rose felt that her son's marriage would dissolve sooner or later. In a custody battle, Lisa would surely win, cutting Rose's close ties to her grandson.

Rose could have managed it quite easily, the night her car was in the garage, by driving Lisa's car to the Cambria Condominiums on her way home. She had attacked from the rear, from the tiny alcove next to the refrigerator, then, to make it look like the serial killer, she had slashed Joanne Whalen's tongue. It was obvious how she had learned about the slashing. Lisa remembered the day she had found her briefcase in her study with the combination numbers showing; it had contained the dossier on the serial killings that Larry Kimble had given her.

And the compulsion to put the frozen foods away right after she had killed somebody. Only Rose, only Rose among all living creatures, would do that.

Tears, squeezed from her eyes finally by the dreadful certainty of this new, uncomprehended terror, flowed down along her earlobes to the pillow. She felt Jack stir and heard a change in his breathing, and for a moment she thought about waking him; she suddenly wanted him to take her in his arms, to awaken the old passion. And incredibly, she wanted to share her terrible knowledge with him. Some things had to be shared.

But the impulse passed away as quickly as it had come, leaving her spiraling into even greater depression. *Jack, something terrible has happened. I know that your mother killed that vile woman you've been sleeping with.*

Did he know?

She drifted in and out of a fitful sleep until a faint gray light began to filter past the edge of the drapes across the east windows. With it came a new resolve. She knew what sadistic tricks one's subconscious played. It was insane to believe anything that wasn't supported by physical evidence. She had to know for sure.

And there was a way to find out. Rose must have made copies of the two keys to Joanne Whalen's apartment the day she borrowed Jack's spare keys. If Lisa was right, the two keys might still be in Rose's apartment. She might have thrown them away immediately, but maybe, being compulsive as she was, she had kept them as insurance, in case she had to go back to the Whalen apartment for some reason. Rose was a saver, the kind of person who couldn't throw anything away that might be useful.

Lisa began to plan how to search Rose's apartment for the keys.

KOEPP JOINED THE QUEUE of cops lounging on wooden benches in the hallway outside Judge Davis's courtroom on the fifth floor of the county courthouse. It was just after nine, which meant that the Third Superior Court was in session, because Davis prided herself on punctuality. Courthouse lore held that she had once remonstrated a tardy assistant district attorney with the bromide that "justice delayed is justice denied."

Now they would have to wait for a recess to get the judge to sign the search warrant. All because Tom Styles, whose reputation for punctuality was the polar opposite of Davis's, hadn't met him outside her chambers as promised. For some reason Styles insisted that Koepp not present the warrant until he arrived. Koepp silently cursed Styles and all assistant D.A.s.

A detective from narcotics whom he knew, Stan Bukowski, was sitting next to him. Bukowski was a powerful man with massive shoulders and a bull neck, but the rest of his body was starting to run to fat. He fiddled with his mustache for a moment, as if he were going to say something but was stalling for time until he could remember what it was. The rumor in the squad room was that Bukowski was on the take; but most narcs were suspect because of all the money involved in running drugs.

"What case you testifying on?" Bukowski asked.

"None," Koepp replied. "Waiting for Davis to recess so I can get a search warrant signed."

"Shoulda come early. Be awhile now."

"I came early. Styles didn't."

Bukowski glanced sideways at him, registering surprise. "You don't need that little jerk for a warrant."

"I know that. He doesn't."

They spent the next several minutes alternately damning the county legal staff and commiserating about how entangled the criminal justice system was getting. "Got that new form?" Bukowski asked with a crafty smile carved into his lantern jaw. When Koepp nodded, he grunted his approval. "I tried to get her to sign a warrant so we could open up a truck at a warehouse on Quincy. She said we gotta follow procedure—gotta get the right form. By the time we got the warrant, they had the truck inside the building. Then we had to get a warrant for the warehouse.''

Koepp sighed his sympathy. They lapsed into silence until Bukowski was summoned by a bailiff to testify.

''Let the wheels grind,'' Koepp said.

''Right-o.''

After the big detective had departed, Koepp watched the performers warming up in the hallway for Judge Davis's vaudeville show. There were tired-looking but still earnest young female lawyers from the public defender's office conferring with gangling, sullen teenage drug dealers and breaking-and-entering specialists. As the legal field became more overcrowded, more and more women worked as public defenders. It was the kind of exposure which drove many of them out of criminal law after two or three years. Idealistic at first, they soon became depressed by the monotony of street crime; in the third world of the inner city they came to understand Montaigne's depressing truth: if you have lived a day, you have seen everything. The idealism gave way to cynicism, then outright fear, as they came to know how pervasive crime was, how unworthy and vicious their clients were. In the last year or two before they gave up completely, he saw them turn into vigilantes, lawyers who counseled disadvantageous plea bargains just to get sociopaths off the streets.

Cops from all over the city and county waited to go on stage to recite their lines. They seemed less frenetic than the public defenders, more resigned to the process. Like the tough little ebony justice inside and the impassive petty criminals, the cops were secure in the knowledge that they were essential players in the ongoing morality play. Crime, apprehension, punishment: criminal, policeman, judge. Only the lawyers were extraneous, a modern appendage to the ancient process.

Koepp became aware of the appendage to the Whalen murder, Tom Styles, standing in front of him. The cold eyes were studying Koepp's sports jacket and tie with amused contempt.

"You got the warrant?" Styles demanded. Something about the man always made Koepp think of chickens.

To counter the prosecutor's brusqueness, he said pleasantly, "Good morning, Mr. Styles." He took his time extracting the warrant from his jacket pocket and handing it to the attorney.

Styles put on his glasses and studied it critically for a few moments. He shook his head slightly to suggest displeasure about the way the warrant was drawn up. But he said nothing.

Koepp enjoyed the satisfaction of knowing the warrant had been well executed. He was logical and methodical, essential qualities in establishing probable cause.

Margaret, who professed to admire his gift, said his ecclesiastical background had made him a natural bureaucrat.

Styles offered no explanation for his tardiness. Instead, he looked around with some impatience and instructed Koepp to summon him from his office on the first floor when Judge Davis recessed. He handed back the warrant.

But Koepp had anticipated this maneuver. "Not a chance," he said casually. "If you had been here, we could have had the warrant half an hour ago. I'm not going to blow the next recess trying to get you out of a meeting. I go into her chambers at the first opportunity—with or without you. You wanna be there, you do what I do—wait."

He wasn't surprised when Styles sat down next to him.

FOURTEEN

KEVIN, A LIGHT SLEEPER like his grandmother, heard the sound of Lisa adjusting the blind and sat upright. The glow of dawn filtered between the slats and arranged faint rose-colored, horizontal stripes on the boy's forehead. She walked to the side of his bed and sat down next to him. She put a hand on his stippled forehead, which felt no warmer than usual.

She had to be deliberate about this. Her son was no fool, despite his years.

"How do you feel, champ?" she asked.

"Okay, Mama." He sounded unconcerned.

"I heard you coughing," she told him. "Do you remember coughing?"

"No."

"Lie back. I'm going to take your temperature." She got a thermometer from the medicine chest in the main bathroom. She put it in his mouth, then held his wrist, taking his pulse. Although he had recently gotten over a cold, she knew there was nothing wrong with him. But it was necessary that he stay home from school today. That was the essential first step in her plan to get Rose out of her apartment. She shook the thermometer and eyed it critically. "Oh, Kevin, honey, you've got a fever," she lied. She pulled his blanket up to his chin and began to tuck in the edges.

"Mama, I have to go the bathroom," he announced with some urgency.

She made him put on his bathrobe, which was hanging over the footboard. "Then back to bed. No school today, young man."

Lisa waited for a moment to see how he would take it, but no protest came. Instead, he coughed. A forced cough, signaling that he was going to be a willing accomplice. Jack came into the boy's bedroom, yawning and fumbling with the cloth belt on his bathrobe. He stopped Kevin en route to the bathroom long enough to kiss him on the forehead, then looked expectantly at Lisa.

"Daddy, I don't feel good," the boy told his father in what he calculated was a weak, sickly voice. The boy looked at his mother for confirmation.

"His throat is pretty red and he's got a fever," she told her husband.

Jack nodded. "Better call Mom."

Yes, call Mom, Lisa thought. Inveigle her into babysitting for the day so that her daughter-in-law could riffle her apartment in search of a set of keys that would prove that Mom murdered people when she wasn't babysitting.

As Lisa dialed Rose's number, she began to feel the first stabs of betrayal and guilt. What she was thinking was monstrous. How could anyone as caring and compassionate as Rose Robbins harm another human being? She forced herself to imagine Rose in the dead girl's narrow kitchen, stabbing time and time again. Killing. But the images refused to form.

Rose agreed to come. She promised to be there in forty-five minutes.

By the time Lisa had showered, dressed, and fixed her hair, Jack had made coffee and toast. He still wore his bathrobe, hadn't shaved, and was sitting in the breakfast nook in such a way that he could see the part of the street where Philip Schroeder normally parked his van.

"I haven't seen him for a few days," he said. "Maybe he got bored." His eyes peered at her anxiously out of deep, dark cavities; he looked as if he hadn't slept much.

Neither of them had mentioned Joanne Whalen. She assumed Jack was not aware that she knew about his 911 call. That would account for his not bringing up the ugly subject. But why hadn't she confronted him? She had, after all, been advising patients to openly discuss their spouse's infidelity with

them. Clear the air. Find out why he's sleeping with his secretary. Find out if he wants to stay married. Find out if you
want to stay married to him. Find out—

Now, as she mentally flipped through these issues, she realized in a new, visceral way why her patients resisted the
confrontational approach; one might get answers, but not the
answers desired. Better not ask.

She drank in silence the coffee Jack had poured for her. After
a few minutes she saw Rose's car nudge up to the curb. Its
occupant, looking neat and vigorous, picked her way carefully
up the icy driveway. Lisa went to the foyer to intercept her
mother-in-law. Seeing the older woman face-to-face sent a new
spasm of guilt through her. Lisa helped her remove her overcoat and hung it in the closet. Rose was wearing a pink sweater,
one she had knitted herself.

Leaning back against the door for support, Rose removed
her overshoes and placed them on the tiny rug which Lisa had
laid in front of the door. Melting snow from the boots made
dark stains on the rug, reminding Lisa of the melted snow pud-
dling in the closet of Joanne Whalen's home from a murderer's
boots. The same boots?

While Jack showered, the two women discussed Kevin's
condition and appropriate activities for the day. Rose kept re-
assuring her that the boy would be fine, that she was not to
worry.

Lisa escaped as quickly as she could. She drove directly to
her mother-in-law's apartment, but parked in the lot behind an
adjacent building. She took this precaution because some of
Rose's neighbors knew the Volvo and might mention its presence to her. Everything she did—opening the door of the building, climbing the stairs to the second floor, unlocking the apartment door—duplicated the actions of the murderer entering
Joanne Whalen's home. She felt profaned by it, by the suspicions of Rose that had led her here. The place had a chill
already, which was vaguely ominous until she remembered that
Rose always turned her thermostat down to sixty degrees when

she planned to go out for several hours. Waste not, want not. Another compulsion. She checked her wristwatch, saw that it was almost eight-thirty and called her clinic. She instructed Cathy Jakes to cancel her first two appointments and gave her Rose's phone number in case she had to be summoned for an emergency. "And, Cathy," she said firmly, "I mean a *real* emergency. Don't call me unless it's absolutely necessary." She hung up before the receptionist could protest.

The rooms were sparsely but tastefully decorated, the products of an interior decorator whom Rose had engaged reluctantly at the urging of her son. Lisa liked the result. In the living room a dark-blue sofa which had been built into a window seat faced her at an oblique angle. Directly across a tree-stump coffee table from the window sofa were two cushioned wicker chairs on either side of a lush ficus tree. A mahogany entertainment center occupied a nook in the wall which abutted the sofa and chairs; it was the one concession the designer had made in transferring Rose's furniture from the house on Maynard Drive to the apartment. Two matching black and tan rugs, one in the living room, one under the dining-room table, covered most of the hardwood floor. A spiral staircase led to the bedroom and bath in the loft. Because the living-room and dining-room furniture contained so few drawers, she managed to search the two rooms thoroughly in less than twenty minutes.

She turned her attention next to the kitchen, which required a far more painstaking effort. She probed inside each cupboard, felt inside any jars or open cans she came across and even looked inside the refrigerator. Each time she opened a new cupboard or drawer she was impressed again with Rose's neatness and orderliness. The quintessential housekeeper.

By the time she finished the downstairs closets and powder room, she had concluded she wasn't going to find any keys, but she went to the loft anyway and began looking through Rose's dressing table. In the mirror she caught a glimpse of a large print which hung over her mother-in-law's queen-size bed. She studied its reverse image briefly, then went over to the picture for a closer look. It was Winslow Homer's "In Charge of Baby" and depicted several young people playing with an infant on a rather unattractive section of beach. The characters, indistinctly rendered in muted shades, slouched in such a way that they gave the effect of swaying motion. Perhaps it was the artist's intent to mimic the motion of the waves. Whether intended or not, the sense of motion imparted by the figures was effective. Nonetheless, the scene struck Lisa as melancholy, not as a joyous romp, and it made her very uneasy. Throughout the remainder of her search of the loft she avoided looking at it again.

She started when her probing fingers encountered the .32-caliber automatic in the nightstand, as if she had reached for something she had assumed was inanimate, only to feel it squirm in her hand. She recoiled in revulsion and hurriedly closed the drawer.

If Rose did in fact possess keys for Joanne Whalen's doors, they weren't in her apartment. Lisa had hoped not to find them. But now she felt even more dissatisfied than when she arrived. It proved very little that the keys were not there. Rose might have done the obvious, sensible thing—just tossed them off the Collins Avenue bridge. Or she might still have them with her. Then Lisa remembered the lockup in the basement of the apartment building. She went downstairs to take the key for the padlock off a hook in the kitchen. As she started for the door, she realized that she'd be out of earshot of the phone while she was searching the wire cell in the basement. It couldn't be helped, she decided. The light bulb in the lockup was out, which compelled her to return to the apartment again to look for a replacement bulb. Just as she put her hand on the front door, the phone rang.

She went inside and closed the door. The sound of the phone, lonely and insistent, reminded her of Kevin's cries at feeding time just after she had brought him home from the hospital. She had no intention of answering it, even though the caller was probably Cathy. After she finished searching the lockup, she would call the office. It wasn't until the fourth ring that she remembered that Rose had a phone recorder, a Christmas present from Jack which stood on a lamp table next to her bed. In momentary panic, she ran to the bedroom, impelled by some irrational urge to be there physically in order to prevent the caller from leaving a message. But the click of the recorder activating itself and the sound of Cathy's nasal voice started her mind functioning again. The receptionist, sounding more rattled than usual, said: "Dr. Robbins, call me right away please. This *is* an emergency. The police are here with a search warrant."

Lisa heard the click of the disconnect. A few seconds later the recorder shut itself off.

The panic that had washed over her moments before, then receded, rolled over her again like an ocean wave. She could erase the phone conversation. That was no problem. But a search warrant? It meant they suspected her. But nothing at the clinic could incriminate her, tie her to the murder of Joanne Whalen. Then she realized that the office search would be an ancillary invasion. The house. They'd be at the house soon. They might already be there, pawing through her possessions, frightening Kevin and bringing disgrace to her and her family. The humiliation and injustice of it overwhelmed her as tears began running freely down her cheeks. Damn them, she thought, damn them all for what they were doing to her.

Suppose they came here? What excuse could she give? How would she explain it to Rose? Think. Think.

A search of the lockup was forgotten. She rushed across the bedroom and sat down on the edge of the bed to study the phone recorder. It was the same brand as the one she had at home, with controls in the same colors and configuration. She ran the tape back and forth in the section which contained the strained voice of Cathy Jakes until she was satisfied that she knew where to begin her erasure. She ran the machine for about thirty seconds. Again she rewound it to the message before

Cathy's and pushed the button which activated the automatic phone response.

She thought of calling the clinic, but decided there wasn't time. She couldn't stay in Rose's apartment a minute longer. A police search party might be on the way right now. Once she was out of the building she would call Cathy. The strip mall on Ninety-Second Street must have a phone. After she got the message, she'd go home. She wanted to be there when they came. She wanted to see what Rose would do, how she would act.

At that moment an image of Rose, indistinct and furtive, formed in her imagination: Rose was putting the keys to Joanne Whalen's apartment into one of the drawers of her desk in the study. The idea was so preposterous, so ironic that she felt an irrational urge to laugh out loud.

But that mood was consumed at once by suffocating fear.

WHERE WAS SHE? She always got to the clinic by eight-thirty, and it wasn't her day off, so where the hell was she? Philip hadn't planned to stay once she arrived at her office. His intention had been to show her that he was still around. That's why he had come back to her house again, to make her see the futility of trying to resist him.

He couldn't tell if her car was in the garage because the double doors were shut. He decided to wait. Because she didn't go to work, she must still be in the house.

He was parked on her side of the street, two houses down, with the van motor running. He had the engine on because he needed to run the heater continuously. A warm front was moving in; it would be forty degrees by evening. Good. He wanted to feel the sun on his face again.

On the opposite side of the street a big station wagon with two bobbing children in the backseat crept out of a driveway. One of the children, a little girl with a red knit cap, peered at him out of the rear window as the vehicle edged up the slight incline. A teenage girl carrying schoolbooks hurried by his van, headed in the same direction as the station wagon. She was a fat girl who moved carefully on the slick sidewalk. He thought she might glance backward as she climbed the grade to see who was inside the van. But she didn't.

As the girl passed the walkway to the Robbins house, the front door opened. The schoolgirl waved a mittened hand toward the person framed in the doorway. Philip waited, his attention fully engaged by the unexpected appearance of someone at the front door. He was disappointed to see the other woman come out of the house. She was wearing a dark overcoat, unbuttoned, and pulling black gloves onto her hands. A pink sweater was visible under the opened coat. The gloves and coat matched her hair color. She was rather pretty for a grandma, Philip concluded, but he knew the dark hair was a dye job.

For several seconds the woman stood on the concrete pedestal staring at his van. He wondered why she had come out of the house, and concluded she planned to walk to some place in the neighborhood. He watched her as she picked her way down the walk to the sidewalk. As soon as she turned, he knew she was coming to talk to him. He glanced at the lock button on the door opposite him, saw that it was in the up position, and considered locking it. But he didn't want her to think he was afraid to talk to her or to open his door. He didn't do anything.

When she reached the point where she was abreast of the passenger door, she stepped into the terrace snow. Without hesitating, she seized the door's handle and swung it open. For an awful moment he thought she might try to get inside and sit on the bench seat next to him. But she remained outside the van, contemplating him with something akin to curiosity showing in her dark eyes. He saw tiny crow's-feet splaying from the outside corners of her eyes, which gave her an elfin look. Her lips were full and very red. He didn't like them.

The lips said, "What do you want?"

He didn't say anything, just turned his head a little so he didn't have to watch the red lips anymore.

"I'll make a deal with you, Philip," the woman said. Her voice was deep for a woman's and very calm. "Tell me what you want, what it will take for you to stop coming here and following Lisa around." She put her right hand on the bench seat; the other hand, glove and all, was thrust into the slash pocket of her overcoat. He could tell from the contour of her coat that her gloved hand was moving inside the pocket. Maybe she had a gun, he thought. If she threatened him with it, he would ignore her; she would never shoot him in broad daylight while he was sitting in his van.

"I don't want anything from you, you old bitch."

He glanced sideways at her, to see how she reacted to the insult. But she wasn't paying attention. She had bent over and taken her hand off the top of the seat. Both hands were under the seat, out of his line of vision.

"What are you doing?" he demanded.

She laughed. "My sweater got caught on the metal support. There, I've got it." She put both hands back on top of the seat where he could see them. "I know you don't want anything from me, Philip," the woman said. "You want something from Lisa. She's the one you're waiting for."

"Go away. Leave me alone."

"She's not here. She left for the clinic early."

"She's not at the clinic. I was there."

For the briefest of seconds the woman's impassive face showed surprise, but the smirking red lips continued to move independently of the rest of the features.

"Listen carefully, Philip, because you'll like what I'm going to say. The boy and I are here alone. But I'm going to take him to a neighbor's house. We'll go out the back door and cross the yard like you did the night you climbed the tree. He has a day off from school. A teacher's convention. I'll go to have coffee with the neighbor lady. We'll be gone for at least half an hour. I'm going to leave the front door unlocked." She removed both hands from the bench seat and thrust them back into her coat pockets. She backed away a little from his vehicle. "I put some of Lisa's things out on her bed for you. Nice things. Things you can take with you."

"And you'll call the cops the minute I get in the door," he said as derisively as he could. "You must think I'm really stupid."

"All I want is for you to go away and leave us alone. If you promise you'll do that, I have no reason to call the police. We have to trust one another. Lisa won't call them, either, once I explain that we have made a bargain. Wait for just ten minutes, Philip." She raised her arm and put her hand on the van's outside door handle. "They're nice things, Philip, things she wouldn't give you herself." The woman with the full red lips closed the door and went back inside the house.

It was a trap of some kind, that much was obvious. Once they got him inside the house, he was vulnerable to a B and E charge. But the woman might not be as clever as she thought she was. For one thing he wouldn't have to force entry if she did what she said she was going to do, leave the door unlocked. He could go inside on the excuse that he was desperate to see his therapist. Even if they picked him up with some of Lisa's articles, he could explain what happened. It was his word against hers and also a clear case of entrapment; it wouldn't stand up in court.

That was how he figured it, although he wasn't very confident about what constituted illegal entrapment. He just wasn't sure. But he did sense that the woman was telling him the truth when she said all she wanted was for him to go away. He knew that he had been wearing Lisa's nerves raw. All this proved was that they couldn't take it anymore. Maybe Lisa had put her mother-in-law up to the whole thing. That idea pleased him.

Finally, what he planned to take would confuse them. He wouldn't steal anything of real value, like jewels or a fur coat or money, which were probably the items which the foolish red-lipped woman had put out in plain sight.

He waited for precisely ten minutes, then went boldly to the front door and rang the bell several times. When no one came, he tried it. It was unlocked. He went inside and closed the door. He found the stairway to the lower floor and searched there first. When he found no one he returned to the main floor of the house and began to inspect each room and closet, starting with the little boy's. Somehow he knew that the room on the southeast corner of the house was the master bedroom, so he carefully avoided it until he had gone through all the others.

The bedroom door was partially closed. He nudged it open with the toe of his boot, gingerly, unsure of what to expect. What he saw shocked him. Then he emitted a silly giggle. On every horizontal surface in the room, on the king-size bed, on the dresser, on the dressing table, were lingerie articles. It was gross, obscene.

The red-lipped woman knew.

He stood at the entrance surveying the scene, his heart pounding dully, as he looked at the lacy slips, the panties, her bras, a filmy blue thing they called a peignoir. It was a whore's den, a filthy display of a prostitute's working clothes.

It was also a trap. Now he was sure of it. But he couldn't help himself. He grabbed a black slip, a pair of white bikini panties, and two brassieres. It was a trap, but he'd gone before the woman could spring it.

His hands shook as he fumbled with the front door. He felt his legs turning rubbery. He had to get away.

FIFTEEN

KOEPP AND CALVIN FRIEDEL were halfway across the Collins Avenue bridge when they heard the B and E report on the police radio. A squad car in Hillside acknowledged at once. A laconic voice informed the dispatcher that he would be at the scene in three minutes. Friedel glanced at Koepp, who nodded. Friedel pulled their copy of the search warrant out of his coat pocket and studied it for several seconds.

"What was that address again?" he asked.

"It's the same address as the warrant. Robbins."

Friedel picked up the hand mike and called the communications center to inform the dispatcher that they would also respond to the break-in. Then he went back to drumming his fingers relentlessly on the top of the dashboard. Koepp assumed he was trying to quit smoking again.

The patrol car got there ahead of them. It sat empty at the curb in front of the house. Koepp parked across the street from it. A tall, loose-limbed black officer—Koepp thought his name was Mason—must have seen their car pull up; he opened the front door for them. Koepp took a chance and introduced Friedel to Officer Mason.

"I'm John Chandler," the policeman said.

"Oh, sorry."

Chandler seemed unperturbed by the mistake. He passed along what he had learned so far; it wasn't much. "Mrs. Robbins, the homeowner's mother, reported a B and E in progress from a neighbor's house. Said she saw this guy coming in the front door, so she took her grandson out the back. From what she says, the guy had been following her daughter-in-law for days. She says he's a psycho."

"We know about him," Koepp said.

"She said—Mrs. Robbins—said you did. My partner called in an APB on the kid's van. The woman had written down his license number, she says, because she expected trouble sooner or later. Said his name's Philip Schroeder."

"Does she know what he took?"

"She's not sure. She doesn't live here all the time. But you should take a look at the bedroom back there." He jerked a thumb over his massive right shoulder to indicate the direction.

"Show him the warrant, Cal," Koepp instructed his partner. Friedel handed the pink form to the patrolman, who glanced at it for a few moments. He smiled slightly as he handed it back to the detective. To Koepp's surprise, he didn't ask for an explanation, which indicated either admirable restraint or pardonable confusion.

In any case Koepp decided he deserved at least a partial explanation. "It's just coincidence," Koepp told him. "He wasn't looking for the same thing we are."

"I'm sure of that," the patrolman said. "You better take a look."

Underclothes were strewn throughout the master bedroom. Friedel looked questioningly at Koepp, who explained, "He's into women's underwear." He noticed that Friedel and Chandler both grinned at his unfortunate phraseology. Koepp studied the king-size bed, looking for evidence of defecation. Then his attention was attracted to the woman sitting on a corner chair behind the second police officer. She was a pretty dark-haired woman wearing the blank expression common to crime victims. The second police officer was a middle-aged male whose face was familiar to Koepp. But he couldn't remember this man's name, either. Chandler spared him further embarrassment by introducing his partner. His name was Rick Stauffer.

Koepp had read that the key to remembering someone's name was to make an association between the name of the new person being introduced and his physical appearance. He studied Stauffer intently. Stauffer. Stauffer.

Friedel ambled over to the woman in the corner of the room

and introduced himself. Koepp, defeated, trailed along behind him.

The woman gave them a forced smile. "Thank you for coming so quickly," she said.

"Tell us what happened, Mrs. Robbins," Friedel said.

"This man has been parking outside my son's house a lot. He's also been following my daughter-in-law. This morning I saw that he was here again, so I went out to talk to him."

"What about?" Friedel asked. "Tell us what you told him."

She sighed and gripped the armrests of the Windsor chair. It reminded Koepp of the way he held on to the chair when his dentist was getting ready to drill his teeth. "I told him to stop following Lisa—my daughter-in-law—and to go away."

"What did he say?"

"He didn't say anything, so I repeated it several times. Then I came back into the house. Frankly, I was very upset. He's been making our nerves raw—for days."

"Did you lock the doors?" Friedel asked.

The woman hesitated. "Yes, yes, I'm sure I did."

"The front door wasn't forced, Mrs. Robbins," Officer Chandler told her. "It looks like it was unlocked."

"But I could have sworn—I was worried about what I did. I went to the front window and stood behind the drapes, watching to see if he'd go away. Then I saw him get out of the van and start toward the house. I panicked, I guess. Anyway, I ran to get my grandson out of bed, put a robe on him, and both of us went out the back door. I didn't even wait to put on his boots. All he had were slippers. We went to Mrs. Schmitz's house—the backyards connect. Thank God she was home. We called for help."

"Where is the boy?"

"He's still at Mrs. Schmitz's. I can bring him, but he doesn't really know what happened." She made an attempt to laugh. "He must think his grandmother flipped her lid. Do you want me to get him?"

"How old is he?"

"Six."

Friedel looked at Koepp, who shook his head. "One of the officers will go over to Schmitz's house and see that he's okay," Koepp told her. When Stauffer started to leave, Koepp called after him, "Get a statement from Mrs. Schmitz, then see if the neighbors saw anything. Keep checking in with us every half hour or so."

"Me, too?" Chandler asked. Koepp nodded.

When both uniformed policemen had gone, Koepp asked the woman, "Can you tell if anything was taken?"

"Not really," she said, looking around the room with an expression of puzzlement. "He must be a sex pervert or something."

"He was a patient of your daughter's," Koepp told her. "Did you know that?"

"Yes, Lisa told me."

"Have you talked to your son or daughter-in-law yet?" Koepp asked her.

"I called my son's office, but he wasn't there. They're trying to find him. I didn't get a chance to call Lisa."

"I'll call her," Koepp said. "Do you know her number?"

She recited it for him and he repeated it back to her. He made the call from a wall phone in the kitchen. The young woman who answered told him that Dr. Robbins hadn't come in yet.

"Is a woman detective there named Loftus?"

"Just a minute."

In fifteen or twenty seconds Margaret came on the line. She listened in silence as Koepp briefed her on the break-in. When he had finished, he asked about Lisa Robbins.

"She didn't come in at her usual time," Margaret answered. "Nobody here seems sure where she is. They have a phone number, which the receptionist tried, but she didn't get an answer. I called it myself a few minutes ago and didn't get an answer, either."

"Whose phone number is it?"

"At first the receptionist wasn't sure. One of the other doctors suggested that it might be Mrs. Robbins, the doctor's mother-in-law. So we looked up her number. Sure enough."

"The mother-in-law is here," Koepp said. "She called in the report. She's staying with a sick grandson. He's got the flu."

For a few minutes Margaret was silent. Then she said, "What do you think that means?"

"Damned if I know. But Grandma Rose doesn't know the good doctor was at her house. Or is pretending she doesn't."

"You find anything?"

"We never got started," Koepp said with exasperation. "We heard the report of Schroeder's break-in while we were coming here."

"What do you want me to do?"

Koepp considered the question for a few moments. The original plan had been for Margaret and Bill Wendt to search Dr. Robbins's office first, then come with the doctor to her home. The four detectives would then conduct the house search together. He hadn't expected anyone to be home when he and Friedel arrived. They had only intended to watch the place until Margaret got there. Carrying out the original plan still made sense. "Collect Dr. Robbins if and when she arrives, then come here," Koepp said. "If she calls in, send her home and you come right away. If we hear from her, we'll let you know."

Koepp walked back to the bedroom, asked Friedel for the search warrant, then handed it to Mrs. Robbins.

After a moment or two, the woman passed it back to Friedel. She looked at Koepp questioningly. He had no idea how much she knew, so he didn't know where to begin. He decided he'd parcel out the background in little pieces to her, see what she reacted to. "Detective Friedel and myself were coming here to execute this search warrant. On the way we heard about your problem—your visitor. The two have nothing to do with each other. It was just a coincidence." Another damned coincidence, he thought.

"Why are you searching my son's house?"

"It's in connection with the murder of Joanne Whalen. Do you know about that?"

"That's the woman who was stabbed in one of those condominiums on the west side?"

Friedel nodded.

"What's that got to do with my son?"

"He's the one who found the body and reported it to the police," Koepp said. He studied the woman's face, hoping for a forced, inappropriate reaction.

But she gave nothing away as she said in a flat voice bordering on disinterest, "That's impossible. And absurd. You must be at the wrong address."

"No, we're not, Mrs. Robbins. Your son has admitted it to us."

This time she looked surprised, or tried to. Koepp didn't think her expression very convincing.

"This warrant authorizes us to look for the murder weapon and keys to Joanne Whalen's apartment," Koepp explained.

Mrs. Robbins turned her attention to Friedel as if she were seeing him for the first time. "You won't find them here, I assure you. My son is not a killer."

"And your daughter-in-law?"

"She wouldn't hurt a flea."

They requested that she tell them again what had happened. This time Friedel took meticulous notes, interrupting her narrative often to ask for explanations. Midway through the interview the phone rang. Koepp indicated that she should answer it. When she did, she informed the caller only that the police were there and that there had been an intruder. "They also have a search warrant," she said.

Although he was sitting on the bed about five feet from Mrs. Robbins, Koepp could still hear the incomprehensible, squeaky noise through the phone receiver. It was obvious that she was talking to her son and that he was very angry.

"He's coming home," the woman informed Koepp after he had hung up. "He asked me to call Lisa."

"That won't be necessary, Mrs. Robbins," Koepp said. "We have a search team at her office at the clinic. They'll arrange for her to come here."

"This is incredible. My daughter-in-law is a psychiatrist. Do you have any idea what your idiotic search is going to do to her professional reputation?"

"We know how to do this with discretion," Koepp said lamely.

The woman fell silent, but her features sharpened into lines of contempt. For whatever reason, she seemed to hold him accountable for the entire unfortunate process. He thought it best under the circumstances to let Friedel carry on without him in the room. He went outside through the front door. Almost at once Chambers emerged from a two-story colonial house directly across the street and headed toward him.

"Got anything?" Koepp asked. He could tell from the patrolman's brisk manner that he did.

"Corroboration," Chambers said. "Mr. Knoblock works in his office upstairs. He saw the van, Mrs. Robbins talking to the driver, saw the driver go in, saw him leave. Everything checks out."

"How old is he?"

"Forty, forty-five."

"What's he doing home?"

"Vet. Double amputee. He's a CPA. Does all his work at home. His PC networks with the firm's computers downtown. He also has a fancy copier, a—"

"Okay, good work, Chambers. Get his statement, then get the rest of the houses on that side of the street. I'll see if anyone is home on this side." Only one other house was occupied; the occupant, a young housewife, said she saw the van parked at the curb. She didn't see the driver or anyone else around the vehicle.

When Koepp went back inside the Robbins house, Friedel told him that Margaret was on her way.

"What about Dr. Robbins?"

"Her, too. Margaret said she called the clinic."

"When she gets here, don't leave the two women alone together," Koepp told his partner. "I'm going to check in with Tarrish. Maybe he can make some sense out of this."

BY THE TIME Lisa had reached the small shopping mall and found a telephone, her panic had subsided enough so that her mind was functioning again. She listened to Cathy Jakes's disjointed and excited description of the police search without comment. Her calm was threatened momentarily when Cathy told her she was putting Detective Loftus on the phone, but the woman officer only reiterated that a search of her possessions was in progress and urged her to go home as soon as possible. Cathy came back on the line to tell her that she had cancelled the remainder of the morning's appointments. The girl informed her of the cancellations in such a self-assured manner that it bordered on insolence. Still, she probably felt she had no choice. Lisa fought down the impulse to make a caustic remark, and instead asked her to get in touch with her husband.

Then she drove home.

Seeing the patrol car parked in front of her house reignited her anger; it was like a billboard advertising the mendacity of the Robbins family to the whole neighborhood, the whole bloody world. She parked inside the garage and entered the house through the kitchen. Sergeant Koepp opened the inside door for her.

Her pent-up emotion of the last hour and a half exploded in his face. "Why don't you take an ad out in the newspaper," she cried. "What is wrong with you people! First you raid my clinic, then I come home to find a squad car out front. This is my home. Have you considered that, has it crossed your bureaucratic mind that we live here, that we have neighbors?" Her throat was constricted with anger, but she still managed to gasp, "I didn't see a skywriter. Couldn't your pilot get his airplane started?"

Koepp backed away a few steps toward the refrigerator, as if he could fend off her wrath by adding some physical distance between them. "Take it easy, Doctor. You don't know everything that's happened."

"I know enough, more than enough. You're going to hear from my attorney. I mean it. We don't have to stand for this. Damn you!"

She had the arid satisfaction of seeing him back up a few more paces, until he pressed clumsily into the door of the refrigerator. His face was white and contorted with embarrassment.

"I'm going to see my son. If you've upset him—"

"He isn't here."

"Where is he?"

"He's okay. He and Mrs. Robbins are staying with your neighbor. There's been a break-in. Your mother-in-law took him to the neighbor's out back."

"Mrs. Schmitz?"

"Yes. He's okay."

To her surprise she found that she believed him when he said Kevin was all right. For some reason, once she accepted that, she remembered that he had said something about an interloper.

"What break-in? They said you had a search warrant—"

"We were coming here with a warrant. Before we got here, Philip Schroeder broke in. Mrs. Robbins took your son to the neighbor's house so he would be safe."

"My God. Philip? When?"

"About half an hour ago."

"Did you arrest him?"

"Not yet. We will soon. He won't get far."

"Rose. Did he hurt Rose?"

"No, she left with the boy. Nobody was here when he came in."

"But how did he get in?"

"Your mother-in-law apparently forgot to lock the front door. She got rattled—understandably. That's why the police car is out front. The two patrolmen were responding to the B and E call."

Lisa began to feel a little guilty about her outburst. But she was still too upset to apologize. She walked to the hall closet and hung up her coat. Koepp followed her, which reminded her about the search.

"You're still planning to search our home?" she asked in an unnatural voice. She didn't have herself under control yet.

"As soon as Detectives Loftus and Wendt get here," he said. "They've been at your office. They were only permitted to look at your work area. They didn't go through the entire clinic. None of the patients would even know who they were."

"The staff, the other doctors know," she told him bitterly.

"I'm sorry about that, Doctor, but we're investigating a murder case. We have to do things that are distasteful sometimes."

"Distasteful to you perhaps, Sergeant. Humiliating to me."

He nodded and muttered something that sounded like "Yes, ma'am, I understand." He looked very defeated and unhappy, which struck her as a strange reaction in a man who did this sort of thing for a living. She almost felt sorry for him.

Lisa walked into the living room, sat down on the sofa and waved a hand in the general direction of a leather chair, Jack's chair. He correctly interpreted that as an invitation to sit down. As soon as he did, he said, "It looks like your concern about young Schroeder was well founded."

"Oh, in what way?"

"Early on you seemed to be concerned that he was a possible murder suspect—"

"I wouldn't go that far," she said icily.

Unperturbed, he continued. "At any rate, he's not going to be a problem any longer. We have corroboration from the neighbor across the street that he saw someone answering Schroeder's description enter the house just as Mrs. Robbins said. We think he might have taken some of your clothes. Of course we'll need to have you confirm that for us. He's been in trouble for breaking and entering before."

"So he'll go to jail?"

"It looks like it."

"Whatever he did, he's not fully responsible. You know that. He's a very disturbed young man."

"Hopefully, he'll get the treatment he needs," Koepp said without any noticeable conviction.

For the next few minutes Koepp described what had occurred at her home after she and Jack had gone to work. She listened, but she couldn't keep her mind on what he was saying. Inevitably, she wondered whether Rose had planted anything incriminating in the house. Even though she found the idea repugnant, she couldn't get it out of her mind.

When the other detectives arrived, the two patrolmen and their squad car departed and the search began in earnest. After about twenty minutes she heard the phone ring. As she entered the kitchen, so did Koepp. Both of them paused, waiting for the other to pick up the receiver. Just then she heard the garage door open. Jack was here at last. "You answer it," she told him. "It's probably police business anyway."

"Probably," he agreed wryly.

As she waited for Jack, she heard Koepp say, "Yeah, Lieutenant." That was the only thing he said; the caller did all of the talking. Finally, just as Jack entered the kitchen, he said, "Wait a minute. She's right here."

Lisa looked at him expectantly.

"My boss wants to know if you'll come down to the Safety Building right away and try to identify some lingerie."

"My God, he took my lingerie?"

"We have Schroeder in custody. We need you to swear out a complaint for the break-in and to confirm that he had some of your belongings."

"And what about *your* search?"

"We're discontinuing the search, Dr. Robbins. In addition

the lingerie, the arresting officers also confiscated a hunting
nife. We want to make sure it isn't your property.''

"*Not* my property? I don't understand.''

"They probably found what we were looking for here,
Ma'am. The lieutenant thinks the knife is the murder weapon
n the Whalen homicide.''

For the first time, Jack spoke. "Will somebody tell me what
he hell is going on?''

It pushed Lisa to the edge of hysteria to hear that the person
who had brought this disaster down on their heads didn't know
what was happening. She decided at last that it was time to tell
im. "The police have arrested the man who killed your
over.''

SIXTEEN

PHILIP SAT FACING the cracks in the wall, the ones shaped lik
some hideous phallic symbol.

It seemed like hours since the police car had stopped hir
on 143rd Street. He knew right away they were looking fc
him, that they hadn't stopped him because of some traffic vi
olation. There was no time to get rid of her things, no place t
toss them.

The mother-in-law or aunt or whatever she was had lied t
him, entrapped him. He vowed then that he would avenge hin
self on her as soon as he got out of this mess. Which shouldn'
take too long. What they found couldn't be worth more tha
fifty or sixty dollars. The most they could get him on was pett
larceny, a misdemeanor. He'd have to spend a few days in th
county jail, a week at the most.

The cops had searched him outside the van. He knew th
two cops were interested in something other than the underwea
because they thought they had found other evidence in the var
He didn't know what it was, but he could see a marked dif
ference in their attitude after that. They were more carefu
They had treated him with respect, almost as if they had starte
to like him.

Now a female uniformed cop stood by the door, watchin
him out of the corner of her eye. She had been standing ther
motionless for a long time, her short legs spread slightly apa
like an athlete's in a position of readiness. She was shor
plump, and looked like the kind of toy cop you could buy i
a department store. A baby's toy; squeeze her and she'd mak
a chirping sound like a captive bird in your hand before yo
crush the life out of it.

The sad cop came in after a long time and sat down at th

table next to him. He plugged in a tape recorder without speaking to him. Another detective entered who said his name was Friedel. He didn't offer to shake hands with Philip, but sat down across the table from him. The man had a bulbous nose and thinning sandy hair. He slumped in his chair as if all his energy had been drained off, so that his posture reminded Philip of cabdrivers waiting for a fare in the airport taxi queue. Most of the people in the world were tired.

The sad detective, Koepp, read him his rights once more, then tried to convince him again that he should have an attorney.

"I can't afford a lawyer," he told the detective across from him.

"You can have a public defender. You're entitled to counsel. You'd be wise to take advantage of the opportunity. Shall I call the public defender's office?"

"Should you call the public defender?" Philip asked in the rhetorical style that he had perfected in dealing with the woman shrink. "No. I haven't done anything, so I don't need a lawyer."

"That's not true, Philip," Koepp told him. "This is a very serious matter."

"A B and E?" He giggled. "You must be daft, sire." He watched the detective who looked like a cabdriver to see if his kidding around had energized him. The man stared back at him with a blank expression; his eyes were even more listless than the wreck of a body he was lugging around.

Koepp said: "I'm not talking about lingerie. The officers who arrested you found something else in your van. Are you aware of that?"

"Am I aware of that? Well, I might be. Then again, I might not."

"They found a knife."

"If they did, then the cops planted it there. It's not mine."

"The officers didn't plant it. It was in your van when they stopped you."

"Then somebody else planted it."

"The knife is in the forensics lab downstairs. We think it's going to fit the wounds in the body of Joanne Whalen."

Sergeant Koepp sounded almost apologetic when he said these things, as if he regretted that he had to be the one to bear the bad news. But Philip wasn't fooled. There was no knife, at least not from his van. He kept it locked whenever he wasn't in it. They had made up the whole story to trap him.

"Tell us about the knife, Philip," the other cop demanded with surprising vigor. Good cop, bad cop. He had seen it on TV a lot of times. They had tried to hang the Whalen murder on that poor salesman, that schmuck Panetti. When that didn't work, they started looking around for someone else to frame. Apparently they had decided that he would do. It had been obvious to him that Lisa Robbins had done it. But they were trying to protect her, because she was a doctor and had a lot of money. Only they had no evidence against him, no proof. All he had to do was not admit anything and they'd have to let him go.

But they surprised him by returning him to a cell and going away. Half an hour later, an attorney from the public defender's office came. It was a woman. She met Philip in another conference room, a smaller room.

The woman said her name was Rivera. She was short and Hispanic; Philip didn't like her. For one thing she had a tiny fringe of dark hair above her upper lip. And she didn't look at him when she talked to him. Everything that came out of her mouth sounded like she had memorized it from a legal textbook. Her perfume filled up the room, making him a little nauseated with its sweetness. He never answered one question or talked to her. At last she went away, and the other woman, the toy cop that he could have squeezed to death with almost no effort, led him back to the retaining cell.

They gave him some magazines to read, but turned off the lights only about ten minutes later. He went into the little john in the corner of the cell and turned on the light. The wash basin sat on an antique porcelain stand which had a jagged crack down its side, causing the basin to rest at a slight tilt. A green crust encased the snout of the faucet. He closed the toilet lid and sat down to read one of the new magazines, but he found he could not concentrate on the cover story, a summation of the current sorry state of the nation's banking system. After a time he tossed the magazine into the basin, turned so that he could rest an elbow on the toilet tank and stared at a pattern of orange-brown spots on the bathroom wall. He tried to imagine himself as one of the tiny spots, flattened into two dimensions, inert, lifeless.

But the red light inside his brain began to wink relentlessly.

IN THE MORNING, long after he had finished a rather satisfactory breakfast of French toast and bacon, they took him back to the interrogation room. Koepp was there with the woman detective this time, and the woman attorney was back. She said something to him, but he paid no attention.

The woman cop asked him questions again about what he had done at the Robbins house, why he had gone to the apartment of Joanne Whalen, where he was when a woman named Nancy Sorgel was killed. They told him she had been murdered on June sixth.

"Who was she, the Sorgel woman?" he asked them.

"She was a nurse," the woman cop said.

"Is she the one I killed?" he asked.

But the two policemen were very quiet. The Hispanic woman said something. He couldn't comprehend what it was she said. The red light began to blink faster and faster.

"I didn't kill the nurse," he said at last. "It was the other one."

"You killed Joanne Whalen?" Koepp asked him.

"Yes," he answered. But the light kept blinking inside his head. Then the red began to fade and recede into the distance until it was light years away, floating in a cold galaxy of orange-brown stars. And then it was gone, and all that remained

were the star spots plastered on the opaque wall of God's re-
demption. The women had gone away.

PHILIP SCHROEDER'S LANDLADY, a Mrs. Gimlich, stood inside
the door of the apartment. An enormously fat woman, she was
still flushed and panting from the exertion of climbing two
flights of stairs. While Koepp and Margaret studied the disor-
derly apartment, she shifted her attention back and forth between them as if she expected some juicy revelation about her
departed tenant. Mrs. Gimlich's rather childish face, enameled
with lipstick and heavy rouge, was enclosed in a mass of straw-
berry-blond curls, which made Koepp think of the animated,
life-sized characters which performed in department store windows at Christmas. The effect of animated movement was
heightened by her labored walking and gestures.

"Was he a good tenant?" Margaret asked the woman. "Pay
his rent on time?"

Mrs. Gimlich's breathless response informed them that he
often was late with the rent money, but that he kept to himself
and didn't bother the other renters. Pointedly, she glanced at
the living-room walls as if to say: Look for yourself. See what
he was.

The furnishings and decorations were undistinguished, the
kinds of things the apartment manager might have purchased
at warehouse sales of salvage goods, but the debris which was
scattered about the place did indeed paint a picture of a bizarre
inhabitant. Piles of magazines were stacked on the coffee table
in front of a torn plastic sofa, on the sofa itself, and along the
wall facing the two detectives. Tapestries with Oriental designs
hung from the wall in such haphazard fashion that it seemed
they must have been put there for safekeeping rather than for
decoration. A VCR and television monitor, surrounded with
cassette tapes, stood in one corner of the living room on a
cheaply made oak bookcase. The shelves of the bookcase and
the floor around the base were also littered with cassette tapes.
A floor lamp near the sofa had no shade, so the naked light

bulb filled the room with a harsh, stark wash of light that made the place look like a storage closet. That's what it was, a warehouse. He picked up several of the magazines and was not surprised to find that they were periodicals from various fundamental Christian sects. Margaret had begun to examine the cassettes at the same time. She looked questioningly at Koepp.

"Religious magazines," he said.

"Religious TV shows," Margaret said. "TV evangelists like that guy Foreman you see on Channel 39." She put them back where she had found them, carefully, as if she didn't want their owner to discover that she had touched them.

The landlady announced that they should be sure to lock up. Then she waddled back into the hallway and shut the door behind her.

Once she had gone, the two detectives began a systematic search of the small, three-room flat. The place smelled, although Koepp couldn't discern what the offensive odor was, and the living room hadn't been cleaned on a regular basis for a long time. Margaret found a plate with a half-eaten sandwich under a chair in front of the television set. She probed a piece of the bread and made a grunt of distaste when she found it was hard to the touch. Chair rungs were festooned with cobwebs, and dust was thick on every horizontal surface in the room.

"I don't recall that it was this bad when we were here before," Koepp said.

"It wasn't," Margaret agreed. "It wasn't like this."

Their goal was to find something that might tie Philip Schroeder into any of the "slasher" killings, but in that respect the living room had no evidence to yield. They went on to the tiny bathroom and stood side by side in the doorway for a moment. The wash basin and toilet were stained and dirty and the room stank of urine, but at least it was fairly orderly. Because the room was too small to accommodate two people, Margaret went to the bedroom while Koepp opened the medicine cabinet and examined its sparse contents. He found the expected male grooming implements: hairbrush, two combs, shaving cream, mouthwash, tube of toothpaste, deodorant, fingernail and toenail clippers, extra razor blades, a plastic bottle of aspirin. Schroeder's slovenly habits at least did not extend to his personal hygiene.

When Koepp went to the bedroom, he found Margaret rifling through catalogs and a sheaf of pages torn from magazines and newspapers. She handed him several. All showed women modeling undergarments. He could see that the floor was littered with piles of similar advertisements. Koepp felt acutely embarrassed, wondering if all men were indicted now in Margaret's eyes by the aberrations of one man. Margaret didn't think like that, of course, but he felt dirty just the same.

He glanced at his partner, and saw that Margaret's cheeks were flushed.

She felt compelled to explain. "When my mother's brother died, I helped her go through his things. He was a widower—had been for a number of years—that's what this reminds me of. People should never have to look through other people's belongings. You find out things you don't want to know. My uncle had a closet full of porno magazines. My mother was shocked. Now that's how she remembers him, as a dirty old man with an obsession for dirty magazines. And he was a lot more than that. He was a really nice, gentle man. But that's not how my mother remembers him."

She tossed the catalog pages on the unmade bed.

After what they had seen, Koepp should not have been shocked by the condition of the kitchen, but he was. The door of the dishwasher stood open, exposing a washing basket stacked high with unwashed dishes. More dirty dishes were scattered about the countertop. A toaster lay inexplicably on its side atop the kitchen table surrounded by toast crumbs. There were dried orange peels on the floor, intermingled with pieces of a broken light bulb. Margaret's heel made a crunching sound as she backed over broken shards from the light. A carton of milk on a serving cart next to the kitchen table arrested their attention at about the same time. Margaret bent over it, sniffed at the top and made a face of disgust.

"Only a man could live like this," she said in the judgmental tone she adopted when her nerves were on edge. She looked tired to Koepp and rather more depressed than Philip Schroeder's living conditions warranted. One of Margaret's strengths was her emotional equilibrium, her detachment during their almost daily confrontations with human misery, degradation, and viciousness. On the few occasions when her stolid acceptance seemed to desert her, like now, Koepp felt very unsettled; the truth was that he drew strength from her.

They stood for a few seconds in silence, surrounded and overwhelmed by the sad debris of Philip Schroeder's life. Margaret took a tissue out of the handbag which she carried over her left shoulder, blew her nose as discreetly as she could, then looked around for a place to dispose of the tissue. Anywhere would have been satisfactory, given the condition of the place, but she could find no wastepaper basket, so she put it back in her purse. She avoided eye contact with Koepp. To give her some time to regain her composure, he announced that he was going to call Tarrish and report in. He started to move toward the living room.

"There isn't any phone," she said in a barely audible voice.

"I'm sure there's one under the wreckage," he answered with feigned confidence, although he didn't recall seeing one. He revisited first the living room, then the bathroom, but he found no phone. When he got back to the kitchen, she was still standing in the broken glass from the light bulb.

"There's a phone jack behind the table next to the sofa," he told her even though he knew she wasn't interested.

"Who would he call?" she asked in the same small, distant voice. "Who would call him?"

The two questions were rhetorical, but Koepp felt constrained to reply. Only he could think of no answers. She might as well have asked: What is God?

"Loneliness is the reason why the world needs cops, Ray.

How can the world be full of lonely people. Why don't they get together, why don't they comfort each other?"

Again he had no answer. Instead, he shifted the conversation back to their purpose in coming to this dead place. "Remember how Dr. Robbins described a murderer who puts away the canned goods before he—or she—left Whalen's apartment?"

Margaret nodded.

"Does this look like the apartment of the compulsive person she was describing?"

Some things you knew in your guts. But they still had no evidence. Almost at once, as if they had come to some unspoken agreement, they resumed their search.

They didn't find anything that looked like evidence, circumstantial or otherwise, but in the cupboard beneath the sink Margaret discovered the telephone. It was wrapped in its cord. She picked it up and threw it down in the sink. "Who would he call?" she asked.

KEVIN, SWADDLED IN a blue blanket which Lisa could not recall having seen before, watched his mother with an anxious expression. He had been uncharacteristically quiet since returning from Mrs. Schmitz's house, always a sign of inner turmoil or incipient illness. Because he was only sick to the extent she had convinced him he was, she attributed his listlessness to worry about the events of the morning. She wanted to reassure him, but felt constrained by her own ignorance about how much he knew. What had Rose told him while she was sweeping him across the backyard to Mrs. Schmitz's? Did he comprehend that an intruder had entered the only place where he was safe, the family sanctuary? Did he understand the police had searched their family's possessions, including his own?

The boy had given her no clues. He hadn't asked any questions, either, which added fuel to Lisa's anxiety and frustration. Males of all ages were inclined to be vociferous when complaining, but mute when they were frightened.

Jack came into the family room, fully dressed for work, and

bent over Kevin solicitously. He fussed over the boy, adjusting his blanket, plumping the mound of pillows behind his thin shoulders. These ministrations were out of character for Jack, but they provided a diversion, an excuse for not having to make eye contact with Lisa. At no time had Lisa been alone with her husband since blurting out that his mistress's killer had been apprehended, for which Lisa was grateful, because, almost from the moment she had confronted him, she had begun to regret her impetuosity. What could she say to him now? Worse yet, what could he say to her that would dull the pain and anger?

Her life would never be the same again.

The police had gone. Rose had left more than an hour ago. Only Kevin remained as a barrier to the frightening argument, the recriminations, that inevitably would result from her acknowledgement of Jack's unfaithfulness. For the first time she considered her impulse to confront him in the context of his personality. Like most corporation men he hated confrontation. In Jack's world people who failed to keep their hostility masked were "not in control," one of the most heinous of office crimes. Her husband's sensitivity to this deficiency in various colleagues had endowed him with remarkable prescience. When he predicted that "Bates will be gone by Christmas" or "Johnson blew the L.A. promotion," he was invariably right. Was he now thinking that she had blown it, that she'd be gone by Christmas?

Still avoiding eye contact with her, he glanced at his wristwatch and told his son solemnly, "I have a plane to catch." He stuck his finger into Kevin's midriff and laughed. "You have to fly really fast to catch a plane." Kevin giggled, enjoying one of their newer jokes. The boy only recently had become able to see the humor in play on words. Jack rose, bent over to plant a sloppy kiss on his son's forehead and hurried to the foyer. It was the kind of kiss which Lisa would never quite manage. Kevin turned his head and called after his father, "Daddy, you forgot to kiss Mama." Lisa fought down her panic as Jack stalked back to her chair, stony-faced and silent, and kissed her lightly on the forehead.

"Have a nice trip," she muttered for Kevin's benefit.

Her relief at hearing the back door close gave way in a few moments to a sense of abandonment. Was there any more final sound than that of a door being shut? Her conviction that the best cure for depression was activity prompted her to go to the kitchen to make a cup of hot chocolate for Kevin. When it was ready she prodded him to get off the sofa and go to his own room, holding the chocolate out of reach as an incentive to comply. He made a half-hearted, ritualistic protest, then bargained with her for permission to take his Nintendo game to bed with him.

During their negotiations, she got him to surrender the toy pistol which he had been playing with ever since he returned home to find the policemen there. She hated guns anytime, especially today.

Once he had settled in, she began vacuuming the living-room carpet, a diversion she soon abandoned because she couldn't concentrate on housework. Instead, she made herself a cup of decaffeinated coffee and sat at the kitchen table. This was no time to fall apart. She had to calmly assess the situation and plan how to deal with it.

Rose's apartment had been devoid of evidence linking her to the death of Joanne Whalen, and Philip Schroeder had been arrested for that crime. The facts said Rose was innocent. But facts meant nothing when arrayed against intuitive conviction. Her mother-in-law was a murderer. Worse still, a murderer who mutilated her victim.

To aid her concentration, she found a notepad and began to inscribe on it the options she had. If she didn't make known her suspicions of Rose to the police, she'd be guilty of letting an innocent, confused former patient be convicted of the Whalen murder. On the other hand, if she told Sergeant Koepp that her mother-in-law was the murderer, he probably would ascribe her revelation to a family squabble. Even worse, if he took her seriously, Lisa's accusation would destroy her marriage and devastate her own son. "Kevin, you won't ever see your grandmother again because she killed your daddy's lover." First she thought it, then she said it out loud. She wished then that she had someone safe to confide in, someone to share her pain.

She could wrap Kevin in a blanket, pack a suitcase and drive off, leave them all behind. For a few minutes this alternative, even though it differed not at all in its result from accusing Rose, appealed to her, probably because it eliminated the need to confront anyone. But its impracticality fought to the surface of her consciousness. She couldn't go anywhere that she wouldn't quickly be found. She wasn't street smart enough to know how to disguise herself, alter her identity, lose herself in the great human sea of middle America.

Late in the afternoon, as the setting sun bathed the street in front of her house in orange and burnt sienna mottling, she made her decision, the one she had known from the start was inevitable. She would pretend, go on with her life as if nothing had happened. Rose's secret could be kept secure because the woman posed no danger to anyone else. Lisa understood why Rose had done it. She even felt grateful in a guilty, demented way. Rose had concluded that her son's infatuation with Joanne Whalen would sooner or later lead to a divorce. Lisa would get custody of Kevin, which meant that Rose's access to her grandson would be rescinded or greatly diminished. It was an astonishing thing to consider, that a woman killed to prevent separation from a little boy.

As for the conviction of Philip Schroeder, she concluded that sooner or later he would be guilty of violence. Better for society, indeed, better for Philip that he be guilty by reason of insanity—that was certain to be the verdict—and institutionalized.

Then, for the first time, she realized that she would be called upon to testify as to Philip Schroeder's legal insanity. What if the court didn't believe her? What if other psychologists pronounced him sane? She had never forgotten one of the grislier lectures on medical ethics she heard in med school. In the Chimu society a herbalist who was judged responsible for a patient's death was stoned to death and his body connected by a rope to the buried corpse of the patient. Would Philip die in prison? If so, a psychological rope would be connected to her forever.

Lisa's own parents, had they been privy to the decision she had made so painfully, would have raised the metaphysical question of guilt. Despite their celebrated liberalism, they had clung to some of the Calvinistic flotsam that bedeviled their generation. "Rose is guilty," her father would have reminded her sternly, "she has to pay for her crime." Society was entitled to retribution in George Curzon's mind; you sin, you pay the piper.

Lisa's natural skepticism about her father's views on justice had been reinforced by her psychiatric training, with the result that she looked upon antisocial behavior as something to be modified for the safety of both the criminal and his potential victims, not as something that merited punishment. Rose, of course, was not totally harmless. Judging by her act, she posed a threat to anyone she felt would come between herself and her grandson. In that limited sense she was a menace to society. By not reporting her suspicions to the police, Lisa was in effect accepting responsibility for monitoring Rose's obsessive interest in Kevin. She had to be alert that nothing in the future would cause her mother-in-law to resort again to violence.

Also troubling were the rights of the victim. What about Joanne Whalen? Did her transgression merit capital punishment? No. No. But the thing had been done, the woman was past caring about retribution and, in any case, she should not have been having an affair with a married man. If Rose had committed a crime, so had Joanne Whalen, and her crime had precipitated her murder. Lisa didn't dwell on Joanne Whalen very long.

She walked slowly to the bathroom next to the master bedroom, found a book of matches in the vanity drawer, set fire to the piece of paper on which she had been writing and held it by one corner until the flames threatened her fingers, then she dropped it in the toilet while part of it still burned. She flushed the toilet twice to get rid of all the ashes.

SEVENTEEN

THE EXTENSIVE MEDIA COVERAGE of the arrest of Philip
Schroeder for the murder of Joanne Whalen suspended for a
day the community's apprehension about the rapidly acceler-
ating crime rate, as if apprehending one killer not only eliminated one palpable threat but somehow tipped the balance back
in favor of society. Unhappily for Lisa Robbins, her home and
her mother-in-law were both featured prominently in all the
news accounts. The television newscasts were interlaced with
cryptic interviews with Lieutenant Tarrish and District Attorney
Styles. Throughout, it was implied by the TV reporters that this
proved again that crime didn't pay. Except that criminals didn't
identify with other criminals; if they thought of Schroeder's
arrest at all, it would only be with contempt for his stupidity
in carrying physical evidence in his van.

Upon the beleaguered county detectives, however, a miasma
of relief settled. They felt restored to public favor, vindicated
for their efforts, absolved for their puny collective arrest record.
For a little while, until some university professor released a
study on the burgeoning crime rate, or until a politician promised a "restructuring" of the sheriff's department, they could
go about their business unimpeded by active public hostility.
It wouldn't last long. Another major crime, something that
would arouse the media and the public, was never far away.

Koepp's team had disbanded, each of its members going
back to the mounting case load on his or her desk. Bill Wendt
and Jack Jackowski were part of a surveillance operation involving a prominent restaurant owner with rumored connec-
tions to organized crime. Cal Friedel and Cathy Andrews were
working on a series of liquor store holdups. He and Margaret
were investigating five rape cases, a fatal mugging of a night

watchman in the warehouse district near the north-south free-way, and more burglaries than he could count. Officially, there was no time to think about a solved case, such as the murder of Joanne Whalen.

But for Koepp, the Whalen case remained an irritant in his mind, like a small rock in his shoe. Almost always, when he arrested a murder suspect, he knew the person was guilty. He wasn't sure about Philip Schroeder.

Margaret tried to convince him while they munched on tuna-salad sandwiches at a deli a block from the Safety Building. It was the day of Schroeder's arraignment. "He was seen at the scene of the murder, the murder weapon was found in his van, and he has the psychological profile to fit the crime," she reminded him, then took a mouthful of the sandwich before her concluding argument. "And lest we forget, he confessed."

"But he's failed the litmus test so far," Koepp said. "He's never admitted slashing her tongue, even though we probed for , tried to get him to admit it."

"Are you suggesting that absolves him completely?"

"No." They ate in silence for a few minutes. Koepp wondered if she was thinking the same thing he was, that Styles, the assistant DA, didn't believe Schroeder had killed Dorine Neto and Jane Holloway, either, but he had led the press into thinking that by letting it slip that the suspect had no alibi for either of the first two murders. In his way Styles was compensating the sheriff's department for apprehending Schroeder by deflating public hysteria about a serial killer roaming the streets. If it also caused some unfortunate women to let down their guard, he could claim later that he had not stated definitively that Schroeder had committed all three murders. Styles had the instincts needed for higher office.

Koepp rummaged through his jacket pockets until he found the plastic bottle with the antihistamine capsules. He swallowed two with a mouthful of lukewarm water. Margaret watched him with a baleful expression, then shifted her attention toward the diners at the next table. She was embarrassed by seeing him indulge his obsession with medicine in a public place, thinking Koepp assumed, that one of the other cops would notice and spread the word to the rest of the squad room. Margaret was uncaring of others' opinions of herself, but sensitive to what people said about him. A quintessential partner.

"The kid—Schroeder—didn't do it, Margaret," he said at length. He watched her face for some indication of exasperation, but she gazed at him resignedly; she was prepared to listen if not to be convinced. "Let's take it piece by piece," Koepp said. "Finding the knife in his van was rather convenient, don't you think?"

Her mouth formed a tentative smile. "It was, rather," she admitted. "Sometimes it happens that way. Sometimes murderers want to be caught. Sometimes they're stupid."

"Schroeder isn't stupid. Dr. Robbins said his IQ is above average."

"Then he wanted to be caught."

"Or he was framed." Koepp nearly winced when he said it. While the guilty frequently let the innocent stand accused of their crimes, it was rare that working cops ran across a deliberate effort to frame someone. It was just too hard to manage. Even an evidence pro, Tom Sturmer of the medical examiner's office, had once told him he wouldn't attempt to frame someone. "Murder is a messy business," Sturmer had said, "But frame has to be neat to work, so it inevitably looks contrived."

"Framed by whom?" she asked.

"Any of the Robbins family."

"Which one?"

Koepp grinned. "I think we can rule out the little boy," he said. When she smiled obligingly, he continued. "The only way Schroeder could know about Joanne Whalen was because he followed one of the Robbinses."

"As far as we know, he only followed Lisa," Margaret replied. "He had to have followed *her* there."

"Not necessarily. Nobody remembers seeing the Volvo. Maybe he tailed the husband earlier. He could have been wait ing for the husband, knowing sooner or later he would show up again.''

''And he just happened to be hanging around the night Jack Robbins murdered Whalen?''

''Maybe,'' Koepp answered weakly.

Margaret's forced smile segued to a slight frown, which she, the consummate percentage player, used to register disapproval of his episodes of fantasy. ''Then why didn't he say that?'' she asked. ''Instead, he admitted he killed her. He was proud of it. Schroeder's a misogynist—not unlike yourself, Sergeant.''

Koepp ignored the barb. He knew what she was thinking, though, that he liked women in the abstract, but could not trust them individually. She had once told him he made plastic Madonnas of women, then waited for them to fall off the mantelpiece. She would never elaborate on that thesis; meaningful silence was Margaret's second language.

''Schroeder's confession doesn't prove much,'' he said. ''He's so disturbed he'll confess to anything.''

Margaret didn't respond, perhaps because she was remembering the half-eaten sandwich and the broken light bulb on the floor of Philip Schroeder's apartment. And the sad mixture of religious tracts and lingerie advertisements.

''I don't think her husband is a serious suspect,'' Koepp said. ''If he killed her, it would be stupid beyond belief to report it.''

Margaret, obligingly falling into the role of devil's advocate, reminded him that they would have tied Jack Robbins to Joanne Whalen sooner or later.

''Granted, but he didn't have to admit being at the scene of the crime. His 911 call proves he was there the night she died.''

''What about Dr. Robbins?'' Margaret asked. ''I admit she doesn't seem to have the gumption to kill anybody—''

''But she does have the best motive. Hell hath no fury—''

''What about the mother-in-law?'' Margaret suggested.

''What motive? Lots of mothers have sons who play around. They don't kill the lovers.''

Margaret drained her coffee cup and began looking around for their waitress. "Waitresses are like cops," she said irritably. "They're never around when you need one." Koepp didn't laugh because it wasn't expected. It was a cop joke, one they all used. Giving up, she turned back toward him. "You're making this tough," she said. "You keep exonerating your own suspects. The senior Mrs. Robbins has one mark against her. She's the only one so far as we know who got close to the van. Maybe she got close enough to stash the knife."

"I thought of that, but the investigating officer, uh, Chambers—I've read his report a couple of times and nobody he interrogated saw Mrs. Robbins actually get into Schroeder's vehicle."

Margaret pushed her coffee cup aside and clasped both hands on the table. She leaned forward and gazed thoughtfully at him for a few seconds. "This uniform, Chambers, he and the other officer were asking questions about the break-in—whether the witnesses saw Schroeder enter the house, that sort of thing, right?"

Koepp nodded. Despite his best efforts, he had forgotten the name of the second officer.

"They didn't know then about our finding the knife in the kid's van?"

"No."

"Then maybe they didn't ask enough questions."

"Possibly, so I checked the statement the guy across the street gave us. He specifically said Mrs. Robbins didn't get into the vehicle. She stood next to the van when she talked to him." But even as he spoke, Koepp realized that one detail was missing, one piece of information that would be significant only in trying to determine how the murder weapon got into the van: Did Rose Robbins talk to Schroeder through an open window or an open door?

As soon as they arrived back in the squad room, Koepp called Mr. Jason Knoblock, the paraplegic who worked at his house across the street from the Robbins home.

He let the phone ring for a long time, but after the eighth ring, his patience was rewarded. He had Knoblock's statement in front of him, and, after introducing himself, began to read portions of it. Koepp paused after every three or four sentences to ask for verbal confirmation. Although Knoblock sounded a little testy, he reaffirmed what he had told Officer Chambers. Koepp wasn't trying to verify the accuracy of the statement, only to disguise what he really wanted to know; inadvertently, you could lead a witness to say what you wanted him to say. The power of suggestion often gave birth to misleading information.

They arrived at the point where Knoblock had stated that he saw Rose Robbins talking to the young man in the van.

"Where exactly were both people while the conversation was going on?" he asked.

"The driver stayed in the van just like I told the cop the other day." Knoblock sounded more irritable.

"And Mrs. Robbins?"

"You mean the mother-in-law?"

"Yes."

"She stood on the grass between the curb and the sidewalk—well, not the grass, the snow. What do you call that?"

"The terrace."

"The terrace. Makes it sound like something out of an English county manor. It's just a strip of grass for God's sake."

"Yeah, terrace is a pretentious term, all right," Koepp said. "So they talked through the open window on the side opposite you."

"Right. The van was between the woman and me." Knoblock paused for a moment. An interminable pause in Koepp's mind. "What else did you say?"

"They spoke through the window of the van."

"Right. The driver never got out."

"You're sure."

Another paused ensued. Finally, Knoblock said, "Now that

I think about it, the woman—Mrs. Robbins—opened the door on the passenger side. They talked with the door open.''

"Thank you, Mr. Knoblock," Koepp said. He couldn't keep the elation out of his voice.

Knoblock noticed it. "Is that what you were trying to get me to say? I can't believe this. Is that what you're concerned about? Man, no wonder you cops can't catch anybody.''

Koepp felt a slight tremor in his hand as he placed the phone receiver back in its cradle. During his conversation, Margaret had crossed the squad room to talk to Cathy Andrews. He considered joining them so he could share what he had learned with his partner, decided against it and dialed the extension of the property room.

Dave Vanik's squeaky voice began a brief recorded explanation that he was out for the moment but that the caller was welcome to leave a message. Koepp waited impatiently for the audible beep, then explained that he wanted Philip Schroeder's van vacuumed as soon as possible. "Dave, I'm looking for anything in the way of fibers that might be in the metal seat support on the passenger side, or on the floor,'' he said. "Imagine that someone standing outside the vehicle reached in to plant the knife. Also, did you find any prints on it? And check out the area for prints—door, seat, supports— Get back to me ASAP, please.''

As he stood up, he managed to catch Margaret's eye and pointed toward Lieutenant Tarrish's cubicle. She nodded, broke off her conversation and joined him just as he rapped on Tarrish's window. The watch commander, who was on the phone, invited them in with a wave of his hand. Koepp sat in one of the chairs, but Margaret passed the other one and stood in the corner with her elbow on top of a filing cabinet. It was her way of indicating to their superior that she was only a witness, that the initiative for this interview was Koepp's.

It was a long phone conversation, with Tarrish cast mostly in the role of listener. That usually meant the lieutenant was talking to a superior, probably the chief of detectives. He didn't look happy when he hung up, and he didn't greet them. He simply clasped his beefy hands atop his desk, leaned forward and looked at Koepp challengingly.

Sensitive to his mood, Koepp decided it was best to try to shock him if he hoped to get an attentive hearing. "I want to keep the Joanne Whalen homicide open," he said casually. "I need a couple of detectives from the second shift to help Margaret and me tonight."

"That means O.T. You know how I hate overtime." How like Tarrish, Koepp thought, to seize on a minor point while he pondered the larger issue. His beefy face seemed to sag all over, like plaster that had been mixed too loose.

"The knife was planted in Schroeder's van by Rose Robbins. She's—"

"I read your reports, Sergeant," Tarrish said. "I know who she is. There is, of course, the trifling matter of Schroeder's signed confession."

"The kid is all screwed up. He's apt to confess to anything." Koepp half turned in his chair to look at Margaret for confirmation. She ignored Tarrish's questioning glance and stared blankly at Koepp. He realized that he should have prepared her for this ahead of time; she hated it when he took her loyalty for granted.

Tarrish, sensing that they were not going to gang up on him, threw up his barrier of sarcasm. "Let me make sure I can read all the small print here, Sergeant. You want me to authorize more O.T. and try to steal two cops from the second shift so you can unsolve a solved case. One, by the way, which a certain assistant D.A. says is a slam-drunk for a conviction. And this same distinguished barrister also has been telling the members of the Fourth Estate that this individual is probably a serial killer known locally as the 'slasher.' Did I get it about right?" Now it was his turn to look at Margaret, to solicit her appreciation of his wit.

To her credit, she treated him to the same frozen expression she had directed at Koepp earlier. Neutral, right down the line. Not a toady.

"Schroeder said nothing about mutilating the victim," Koepp told him, "even though we gave him lots of chances. Imagine the stink if there's another slasher homicide while we've got him locked up."

Tarrish smiled wanly, as if he were remembering something unpleasant from the distant past. At first he didn't say anything, then he forced Margaret to commit herself. "What say you, Maggie? Have we got the wrong man?"

Because she understood Tarrish's moods so well, she must have realized that he was going to ask that. "It's a real possibility," she answered crisply, without hesitation.

Tarrish settled back in his chair and studied the ceiling as if he were seeing it for the first time. He began to scratch his side with a stubby finger. That tic meant different things at different times. This time it meant it was time to negotiate. "How about two uniforms from the second shift?"

"No," Koepp said. "Detectives. DeMoss and—"

"Bullshit. You'll take whoever you get."

Koepp nodded, appropriately grateful.

"Now tell me why you think we should keep this case alive," Tarrish said.

Koepp described how Mrs. Robbins had talked to Schroeder through the open door of his van, which provided her with an opportunity to plant the murder weapon. "That's why I need more personnel, to interview everyone in the condos again," Koepp explained. "See if anyone remembers seeing the Volvo, or one of the Robbins women." He hesitated for a moment, then added, "I also want Kimble to hypnotize that Chinese girl, Amy Shue. She's the best witness we've got. Maybe she'll remember some detail."

"Try the shrink if you want," the lieutenant said. "But you're still going to need physical evidence. Did they vacuum the kid's van?"

"They're going to do that now," Koepp said. "They weren't going to bother because it looked open and shut."

"If you find any fibers, I don't know what judge will issue a warrant when we got the killer in the lockup."

Margaret entered the conversation at last. "The new guy, Blandine, will go for it. He's still an idealist and doesn't want to see the innocent railroaded."

Admiration flickered in Tarrish's eyes, then went out; he thought Margaret could get a judge to sign a warrant to search the Vatican.

The lieutenant's phone rang, a signal to conclude the conversation. Koepp was satisfied. Tarrish never said yes to anything if he could help it; success meant leaving his office before he said no.

While Margaret tried to track down Dr. Kimble and Amy Shue for a hypnosis session at the university, Koepp called Dr. Robbins at her clinic and set up an appointment to meet her later that afternoon at the county lockup. If she was surprised by his request that she participate in an interview of Philip Schroeder, she betrayed no sign of it. The woman sounded listless and preoccupied but she agreed after a short pause to be there. Koepp was not very surprised; he had been confident that some emotion—curiosity, guilt—would assure her cooperation.

The listless sound of her voice was reflected in her languor when he met her in the basement of the Safety Building later. Her face was drawn and mottled, and her hair showed none of the luster he had remembered from past meetings. Her hand felt warm and clammy when she took his. She didn't look at him after they first made eye contact. Koepp was reminded of people who were recuperating from major surgery, people from whom vital life substances had been partially drained.

Her physical condition stirred his sympathies. "I wouldn't have asked you to do this except that he was your patient and—"

She brushed his apology aside with a languid wave of her

hand, in the manner of someone shooing away a pesky gnat. "It's all right," she said. "Can we see him right away?"

Schroeder was waiting at a table in one of the interrogation rooms in the company of a young, burly male officer. As soon as he saw Lisa, he started to rise, a look of panic embossed on his normally sullen features. The guard took several intimidating steps toward his prisoner and commanded sharply, "Sit." The cop's voice jarred Koepp; it sounded like an exercise at obedience school.

Schroeder sat.

With escape an impossibility, he tried to model his face into a sneer. He studiously ignored the psychiatrist, even when she sat down at the table. Instead, he focused on Koepp.

"Hello, Philip," Lisa said.

No answer.

"We'd like to run over some of your testimony again, Philip," Koepp said. No answer.

The three of them sat in silence for several long minutes until Rivera, the public defender, came into the room and sat in the vacant fourth chair. They exchanged perfunctory greetings, although Schroeder did not acknowledge her directly. Instead, he relegated her to third-person status by telling Koepp, "I don't want her here." Koepp wondered if it was significant that he objected to the presence of his defense attorney but had made no demand for Lisa's removal.

"She has to be here, Philip," Koepp said. "You're entitled to legal counsel whether you want it or not." To avoid a prolonged argument, Koepp changed the subject. "What did you do to her body after you killed her?" Schroeder remained silent with his eyes half shuttered and his mouth pinched to a narrow gash. "Answer the question!"

"Nothing," Schroeder said. "I never touched her. She was revolting."

"May I read his statement?" Lisa asked. Koepp, relieved to relinquish leadership of the interview, readily handed her several typewritten pages.

To his surprise she began to read the statement aloud.

After listening in silence for half a minute or so, Schroeder began to mutter incoherent statements.

Lisa stopped reading. "What do you want to say, Philip?" she asked gently.

"That's shit!"

"What is shit?" she asked.

He mocked her by repeating the question.

"You think something is incorrect in this statement," Lisa said. "What is it?"

"All of it. All of it is shit."

"Be specific."

"Be specific. Okay. That part about my just driving around is bullshit. Why the hell would anyone drive around in a blizzard like that?"

"You mean the night that Joanne Whalen was murdered?"

"Of course."

"You drove there deliberately, is that what you are saying?" Lisa asked. Her hands, holding his signed confession, had begun to shake visibly.

"I didn't know where I was going. All I was doing was following the other car. I never knew where it was going."

When Koepp saw that Lisa was unable or unwilling to go on, he asked the obvious question himself. "Whose car?"

Schroeder grinned. For the first time Koepp thought he looked like a dangerous man. "You cops are so stupid, I can't believe it. I followed *her* car." He pointed dramatically at Lisa.

"You told us that before. But how do you know she was driving the Volvo that night?" Koepp asked.

Schroeder echoed the question, but didn't answer it.

On Koepp's right, in his peripheral vision, he saw Lisa deliberately lay Schroeder's statement down on the table in front of her. He could see enough of her outline without turning his head to recognize her pain; the rigidity of a person's posture often betrayed what facial expression had learned to disguise.

He waited, confidently, almost exultantly, for something to happen.

"I wasn't in my car that night," she said at last. She was talking to Koepp now, not the hapless suspect. Koepp could tell by the inflection in her voice.

Koepp looked at her. "Who was?"

Now that she had made up her mind, the words came out in a quick gush. "Rose. Rose had her car in the garage. I wanted her to stay over, but she insisted on leaving. She must have known—about Jack—she must have gone there."

Suddenly Schroeder cried, "She's lying. A guy came out of the condo. He saw her. Find him. He knows the truth."

"What man? Could you identify him?" Was it possible Schroeder was telling the truth? If so, who was the man? Why hadn't he come forward? When Koepp received no answer he nodded to the guard, who led Schroeder away.

A phone on the wall behind Koepp rang. He slid his chair backward so he could answer it. The caller was Dave Vanik from the lab. He imparted two useful pieces of information. The murder weapon found in Schroeder's van had been wiped clean. No fingerprints. While examining the van, a technician had discovered the pink fibers snagged in the passenger seat support. Koepp remembered, with considerable satisfaction, the pink sweater Rose Robbins had been wearing the day Schroeder broke into the Robbins home.

Rivera, the attorney, also left the room.

"What now?" Lisa asked in a thin, small voice.

"I have to find out which of you killed her."

"Which of us? What do you mean?"

"I know the killer's last name. Robbins. Now I have to put a first name with it."

EIGHTEEN

KOEPP BRIEFED TARRISH and Margaret in the lieutenant's office as soon as Lisa Robbins had left the Safety Building.

The watch commander was grim, but he had listened carefully. That was obvious when he summarized Koepp's arguments aloud to prepare himself for the phone call to the assistant district attorney. "You got a witness that said Rose Robbins talked through an open door of the van, so she had a chance to plant the knife. Vanik's boys found pink fibers in the seat support. Rose Robbins was wearing a pink sweater. Schroeder hasn't bragged about slashing the victim's tongue. And why would Schroeder carefully remove his prints from a knife he carelessly carried in his van? And now Lisa Robbins says Rose had the Volvo that night—the night Schroeder followed it to the victim's apartment building." He waited for Koepp to nod, then he added unnecessarily, "Mr. D.A. Styles is gonna be pissed." He apologized mechanically to Margaret.

She ignored both the vulgarity and his apology. "Maybe Lisa lied about Rose," she said. "Maybe she was driving."

"Maybe," Koepp agreed. "But one of them killed Whalen. Mr. Robbins found the body later and called 911. He had no idea that either his mother or his wife was the killer."

"Because of the way the victim was mutilated," Tarrish said, more for his own benefit than theirs. "He assumed it was a crazy." He reached for his phone.

As the two detectives rose to leave, Margaret said, "I talked to Kimble and Amy Shue. She agreed to the hypnosis. She'll go to the psych department after her biology lab. They'll be ready about six-thirty, the good doctor says."

They spent an hour briefing the two officers from the second shift who had been assigned to conducting interviews at the

Cambria Condominiums, then drove through heavy evening traffic to the university.

Kimble, looking more disheveled than usual, was waiting for them in the deserted corridor outside the psychology department, grading examination papers.

"Did your subject show?" Margaret asked.

"She's in the consultation room, reading some material I gave her to prepare her for the session. She's never been hypnotized, so she's concerned." He stuffed the exams into a briefcase. "That's normal. I'll get her past that," he said. "By the way, I saw the six o'clock news. What's going on?"

Koepp and Margaret exchanged puzzled expressions.

"They're letting that kid Schroeder go, according to the D.A.," Kimble explained. "Some 'new evidence.'"

"Yeah," Koepp answered. "We think maybe Schroeder was set up. That's why this is important. Amy Shue may remember some detail that could unlock the Whalen homicide."

They spent a few minutes briefing Kimble on what kind of information might be helpful, stressing Lisa Robbins's car and the possibility that Amy and her friend might have seen someone else in the condo parking lot the night of the murder. To Koepp's relief, Kimble didn't demand a fuller explanation. Instead, he told them they could both be present when he tried to hypnotize the young woman. "You can ask questions, too," the psychologist said.

Koepp and Margaret followed him into the consulting room, which contained a leather sofa and several stuffed chairs. Amy Shue, wearing a sand-colored skirt and green sweater, was seated in one of the armchairs, looking ill at ease. She barely acknowledged the two police officers, but watched Kimble warily. He sat on the sofa and laid a clipboard on his knees.

For a few minutes he chatted with her about her family, her course schedule for the semester and what she and her friends liked to do when they weren't cracking the books. Koepp thought she had begun to relax.

"I don't know what you've heard about hypnosis," he said,

'but it's probably not what you expect. You're not going to suddenly become a sleepwalker. In fact, you won't be asleep at all. You'll be aware of what is going on around you, and you'll be able to hear the officers talking. You may decide not to answer a question, so don't. Are you with me so far?''

The girl nodded.

Kimble then patiently explained that during the relaxed state of hypnosis a person could often remember things that are stored away in the subconscious mind. He said he felt it was because people were relaxed and not distracted.

"Will I do anything foolish?"

Kimble smiled at her. "Crow like a rooster, you mean? Or bark like a dog?''

"Yes," Amy said in a voice barely above a whisper.

"No. Those tricks stage hypnotists do is not what this is about. You and I are going to relate to each other so we can help the police." He forewarned his subject that nothing dramatic was going to happen. "You won't feel much different than you do right now. You'll just have a relaxed, floating sensation. You should feel good."

When he was satisfied that her nervousness had dissipated, he punched the record button on a small tape recorder on the sofa next to him, announced the time and date and identified everyone in the room. Next he asked Amy to describe what had happened the evening she and her friend were involved in the accident. Koepp listened carefully, but heard nothing that wasn't in the summary of her previous statement.

"Now," Kimble said, "I want you to sit up straight, put both feet on the floor and relax. Imagine that each part of you is being warmed by an electric blanket—your toes, the soles of your feet, your ankles..." He waited a few moments, studying her feet and lower legs. "In a minute I'm going to ask you to look up at the ceiling. Don't crane your neck, just move your eyeballs up." He demonstrated this maneuver and praised her when she duplicated it. "Now, keep looking up and slowly close your eyes—slowly... Good. Breathe deeply—let it out—

breathe deeply. Keep your eyes shut, but look ahead instead of at the ceiling. You're starting to float like a butterfly. It's warm. Feel the sun?''

The psychologist reached into his pocket and withdrew a coin. He took the young woman's left hand and turned it palm up. "Keep your eyes closed, Amy, while I put a quarter in your hand," Kimble told her. He did so. "Now concentrate on your left hand. You're going to feel your hand begin to slowly turn upside down so that the coin will fall out onto the floor. Don't you turn your hand, just let the hand turn itself." Nothing happened. Kimble appeared unperturbed. He kept telling her that her hand would turn and drop the coin.

Koepp watched with growing interest as the girl's hand at last began to rotate. Amy realized what was happening and giggled. Kimble kept encouraging her, until the coin slid off her palm and fell on the carpet.

He then started a counting sequence with the numbers in reverse order and instructed her to look at the ceiling once more, then to open her eyes. "Are you comfortable, Amy?" he asked.

"Yes, very comfortable," she replied.

"Do you feel as though your left hand has detached itself from the rest of you?"

She nodded her head.

Kimble continued to discuss her condition with her, stressing the concepts of relaxation and floating in a soporific voice. He kept repeating the same ideas over and over, then, satisfied that she was in a hypnotic state, he encouraged her to tell him what happened the night of the accident, the night Joanne Whalen was murdered.

Following his instructions, she adopted the present tense. "Debbie comes over to my house about six o'clock so she can hear a new CD I bought. It has medieval and renaissance songs played on the instruments they actually used in the fourteenth and fifteenth centuries. She's a music major, so she's really into things like that."

"But then the two of you leave?"

"Yes, we're going to a lecture at the university."

"What time do you leave?"

"The program starts at eight, so it must be about seven-fteen or seven-twenty when we go to the parking lot. We are oing to use Debbie's car, but her tires are bald. It's so slippery ve decide to use mine."

"Do you drive out to the street right away?"

"As soon as we get the snow off the car windows," the girl aid.

"Do you see anyone, a woman perhaps, going in or out of ne first condo, the one at the corner?"

"No, only Mr. Panetti. It was a bad night. Nobody else is round. We're not sure we should go because there are three r four inches of snow. Debbie thinks she should go home, but talk her into going to the lecture."

Panetti, Koepp thought. The man Schroeder saw was Panetti.

"Do you see a strange car, a Volvo, parked anywhere?"

"I don't know what a Volvo looks like," the girl said.

While Kimble paused, Koepp asked a question. "Did you ee a strange car that didn't have much snow on the windshield, ne that looked like it just got there?"

"No," the girl said with certainty. "All the cars are covered vith snow like ours."

Koepp began to feel the chill of doubt in his extremities. 'Amy," he said, "tell us about Mr. Panetti's car."

She paused for a moment. "The man who sells medical quipment? All right."

"Do you recognize his car?" Koepp asked.

"Yes, he drives a Mercedes."

"How do you know that?" Kimble asked.

Kimble's question was one Koepp wanted answered as well. Iow the hell could somebody who didn't know a van from a tation wagon identify a damned Mercedes?

"Debbie told me once that's what it was. She said it was a ery expensive car. Debbie is Europocentric."

Koepp was surprised to hear his own voice quaver as he asked, "Is Mr. Panetti's windshield covered with snow, too?"

Without hesitation, the girl replied, "Yes, all the cars are covered with a couple of inches of snow. His car is next to Debbie's and hers is next to mine."

Panetti was unloading his trunk at seven-thirty, but his car had been parked in the lot long enough that his windshield was covered with snow. And Schroeder had told them he saw a man leave Joanne Whalen's building when one of the Robbins women—which one didn't matter—went into it. His insides began to churn. How wrong he had been!

He suddenly stood up and made a slashing motion across his throat for Kimble's benefit. Then he looked at Margaret. She was on her feet, too, watching him with an intense but puzzled expression.

"Dr. Kimble," Koepp said, "I need to make a call."

"My office is next door. Use the phone in there." He didn't look at the two detectives; his attention was concentrated on Amy Shue.

Margaret followed Koepp into Kimble's office. He found Rose Robbins's phone number in his notebook and dialed it. When she didn't answer, he called Lisa. Again, no answer.

Margaret said simply, "You think Panetti's the killer."

In an anguished voice that sounded as if it belonged to someone else, Koepp said, "Yes, and maybe one of the Robbins women saw him come out. Maybe he saw her. I don't know. I don't even know which woman."

"Panetti knows."

SOMEONE HAD SET Wylie's clock to the correct time, Lisa noticed. Jenny Abrams, one of Wylie's patients to whom punctuality was a virtue above all others, had observed the clock as well. She threw a pack of cigarettes and a lighter into her purse, said good-bye and flounced out of the room, all, seemingly, in one continuous motion, precisely at the stroke of four.

Moments later Cathy Jakes buzzed Lisa on the intercom and

announced that her husband had dropped by and was waiting to talk to her.

"Okay, in here is fine," Lisa said. She assumed he had just arrived at the airport and was headed to his office.

Jack pushed tentatively at the door, but only thrust his head inside. "Is the doctor in?" he inquired.

She recognized that his question was an attempt at humor; he tacked panels from the Peanuts comic strip to the kitchen bulletin board whenever they featured the Lucy character and her "The doctor is in" sign. Lisa managed a small smile and waved him toward Wylie's sofa.

"Ah, the ubiquitous couch," he said, but he collapsed his lanky frame into it with a grateful sigh. "Can you spare a minute?"

"For you, yes."

He looked surprised, as though he had expected rejection. "I thought we should talk," he said.

"Yes, we should," she agreed. But not about divorce, she thought in a panic, not about that.

"You've been through a lot because of me," he said. He was going to add something else but she couldn't stop herself from interrupting.

"Yesterday was the most humiliating, the worst day of my life, Jack. Nothing else comes close. But the last few months—"

"It's because of her."

She wanted to strike at him with something, to punish him for what he had done to her. But her voice, bleak and controlled, was her only weapon. "No, Jack, it's because of you. Nobody but you cares about your mistress. Maybe you don't, either."

He studied his hands, folded awkwardly in his lap, for a long time before he spoke. "Of course I care. It was awful, finding her like that."

For the first time Lisa was able to imagine what it had been like for him to discover the mutilated body of Joanne Whalen.

Until this moment she had not been capable of any empathy for him, not since that moment when she heard his voice on the tape of the emergency call line.

He was speaking again. "I cared about her, but I never cared for her in the way I do about you. I love you, Lisa. It happened! God knows why. The important thing is, can you live with it?"

Lisa rose and went to the window, where she stared at the winter landscape, seeing nothing. Then she walked back toward him. "A week ago I didn't think I could. Now, after all that's happened, it doesn't seem that important anymore."

Jack reached out to take her hand as she passed behind the couch. "Is that the psychiatrist talking, Lisa?"

"No." Lisa's eyes welled up with tears. "Only me." She looked down at him. Her voice was barely a whisper. "I love you, too."

He stood up and for a moment she thought he was going to reach out and embrace her. She wanted him to, yet she was afraid of how she would react to his touch. God, she thought with odd detachment, how powerful emotions are, how easily they overwhelm reason.

Jack paused by the door. "Can't make dinner tonight. Sorry. Entertaining a client."

Thankful for his segue back to the safe subject of business, she asked, "Oh, which client?"

"Mel Rattner." He grinned.

Then she remembered. Rattner was CEO of one of their biggest customers—a "house account" who had always been handled by the deposed division president, Gary Cotney.

"I'm taking over all the house accounts," he said. "That's what the meeting in Chicago was about." He made no effort to keep the pride out of his voice. Clearly he was not only going to survive under the new management team, but thrive.

"Congratulations," she said, finding to her surprise that she meant it.

After he had gone and she had seen her quota of patients for the day, she stayed longer than usual to catch up on her neglected paperwork. Then she drove to Rose's apartment to pick up Kevin.

The last of the rush-hour traffic still clogged Collins Avenue, and vehicles were moving more slowly than usual because of a heavy fog. She pulled into the parking lot behind Rose's apartment building and parked so that she faced the back entrance. At first, when she realized no lights shone from Rose's windows, she became apprehensive. Then she remembered what her mother-in-law had told her about her schedule: she was to pick up Kevin at school, take him to his piano lesson, make his dinner—and what else? At length she remembered Rose saying, "The only time we'll be gone is out to fill a prescription for Kevin at the drugstore." Rose was taking Kevin's "flu" seriously; even though he was back in school, she feared a relapse.

It was almost seven before she saw the Buick edge into the garage behind her car. She climbed out and intercepted them as they started for the back entrance. Kevin was burdened with schoolbooks.

"Hi, Mama."

"Hi, honey." She gave him a perfunctory hug as he passed her purposefully on the way to her car. He was like his father in the singleness of his purpose: dump books in car first, hug later.

"Wanna come up for a cuppa?" Rose asked cheerily.

"No. I'm going home to a hot bath. I'm exhausted." Although that was true enough, she also wasn't ready to sit and gossip with a woman who had murdered someone.

Rose veered in front of the Volvo so she could wave at Kevin, who already occupied the front passenger seat. He pressed a mittened hand against the inside of the windshield to acknowledge his grandmother's good-bye.

Lisa climbed in her car and told her son to buckle on his seat belt. He began feeling around for the buckle end. Lisa tried to help him, but had no more success. She turned on the dome light, found the buckle jammed into the upholstery and strapped him in. Just as she was about to start the car she glanced at the back entrance of the building and noticed a man approach her mother-in-law. Something about him made her uneasy. He was tall, well over six feet, and had a high mound of black hair. Even at this distance of thirty yards or so she could see that he was much younger than Rose, so it was unlikely that he was a friend.

"Stay here, Kevin," she told her son, then she climbed out and walked quickly toward Rose and the stranger. When she saw the man grab Rose's elbow roughly, she increased her speed.

Rose saw her approaching and called out, "It's okay. I'm all right." The tension in her voice belied the words.

"What's going on?" Lisa demanded as she approached the stranger. She could see his face clearly. He was olive-skinned, rather handsome in a craggy, arrogant way, and he had dark circles under his eyes. He's not sleeping well, her therapist self concluded.

"Leave, Lisa, at once," Rose said in an unnatural voice.

Lisa heard some yelling inside the building. Through the glass doors and down a well-lit interior corridor she saw a group of teenagers heading toward the rear exit. The man also heard the sounds, which came from directly behind him. The voices spurred him to action. In an instant he transferred his hand from Rose's arm to her own.

She pulled back, freeing her forearm, but he had a firm grip on her coat sleeve. He started to move away from the building, dragging her behind him. "Both of you, get in the black car," he hissed. "Now! You drive, blondie. Either of you tries to run for it, blondie dies." She felt him press a heavily laden key ring into the palm of her right hand. She tried unsuccessfully to get her purse strap off her shoulder so she could offer him her money. It wouldn't have mattered. He wasn't there to rob them.

Rose, unaccountably, followed them even though the man could no longer restrain her physically. Then, in an instant, Lisa understood. For the briefest of moments she felt a flood of relief. Rose hadn't killed Joanne Whalen. This man had! Her relief disappeared as quickly as it had come when the man waved his free hand in front of her face. In it was an object he wanted her to see. A hunting knife.

Like the one that had killed Joanne Whalen.

AS THEY RAN to their car in the university parking lot, both Koepp and Margaret understood that they had to find Rose and Lisa Robbins and put them in protective custody. Once they did that, they could sort out which of the two had gone to Joanne Whalen's home. Margaret took the wheel of the car and roared out of the parking lot heading west.

"My guess is that Rose is the one who saw Panetti," Margaret said. "I believe Lisa."

"So do I," Koepp said. "Rose's place it is."

Because of the dense fog, it took more than twenty-five minutes to reach Rose Robbins's home. They said very little at first, probably because they were both preoccupied with the implications of putting Panetti back at the head of the suspect list. Koepp tried to understand why they had made such a mistake about Panetti. There were two reasons. First of all, he had made the assumption that because Panetti's DNA hadn't matched the Holloway killer's DNA, he was not the serial killer. Therefore, he couldn't have known about the tongue-slashing signature. So someone else, someone who did know about the mutilations, killed Joanne Whalen. Secondly, the coincidence involving the Robbins family was too beguiling. About the only thing that was certain was the realization that he was going to feel very foolish no matter how the Whalen homicide turned out.

"It never crossed my mind that three people were in Whalen's place that night," he said at length.

"Mine, either," Margaret said ruefully. "The man coming out—the man Schroeder saw—was the killer. Rose—assume it was Rose, not Lisa—finds the body and figures her son killed

Whalen. She takes the knife because she's afraid her son's fingerprints are on it, then plants it in Schroeder's van to frame him. The real murderer, Panetti, was probably dumbfounded to hear we found the knife in the kid's van. But he figures he's in the clear because we charged Schroeder.''

"Only, if he watched the news tonight, he knows we let Schroeder go on the homicide rap," Koepp said. As they drove toward the suburbs, Margaret lapsed into silence, probably looking for flaws in their reasoning. She hadn't found any by the time they approached the block where Rose Robbins's apartment was located.

Koepp checked in with the dispatcher, reported his location and said they were going to interrogate a suspect. He considered asking for a patrol car at Lisa and Jack's home, in addition to Rose Robbins's apartment, but decided against it; they would get there too late and wouldn't understand what was going on.

As they approached the driveway to the apartment complex, Margaret informed him in a tight voice that a black Mercedes had just exited. Koepp glanced back over his shoulder to look for it just as Margaret made a hard left turn, cutting off two approaching cars in the opposite lane. Koepp banged his head on the windshield. Car horns erupted behind them. The Ford bounced across the sidewalk and forged into the parking lot at thirty-five miles an hour. Margaret jammed her foot on the brake pedal.

Both of them saw the little boy standing outside the back door of the building at the same time. "Good guess, partner," Koepp said before he jumped out of the car.

The child turned to run toward the apartment building, but Koepp caught him and picked him up. The boy had been crying before. Now he erupted with a shriek of terror and kicked wildly. He clawed at Koepp's face, then landed a small fist on the approximate spot where Koepp had banged into the windshield.

Margaret pulled the squirming boy from his arms and set him down on his feet. Then she let him go. He didn't run away as Koepp had expected, but only began to cry louder than before. Margaret crouched down so that her face was level with the boy's. She reached inside her pocket and pulled out her detective's shield. "We're from the police and we need your help," she told him with exaggerated calm.

"A bad man took Mama and Gran," he cried. His little body was wracked with heartbreaking sobs.

"What's your name?"

"K-K-Kevin."

"Who took your mom, Kevin?"

"A bad man—"

The Mercedes was getting away. It might not be Panetti's car, but he had no choice but to go after it.

Margaret must have read his thoughts. She flipped the car keys to him. "I'll take care of Kevin," she called. Then, as Koepp raced back to the pool car, she called out, "Get backup. I'll call the lieutenant and tell him we have a hostage situation."

Koepp spun the car around and bullied his way back into the traffic. Another chorus of automobile horns accompanied his demonic driving.

He ran a red light at the Kimbrough intersection and a second one at the Valley Road intersection, hoping all the while that the Mercedes hadn't turned off on either of the other streets. Miraculously, he caught up with the black sedan and even got close enough to read the license tag. He radioed in a request for the name of the licensee. As they turned onto the West Branch Parkway, the dispatcher informed him that the car was owned by Nick Panetti. Should he ask for backup now? No, not until he figured out where they were going.

He fell back a couple of car lengths and tried to fit the disjointed pieces together. It looked as if someone was in the backseat of the Mercedes; the boy was probably right about Panetti taking Lisa as well as Rose. Rose was the only one who could identify him, so why had he abducted Lisa? The only explanation he could think of was that Lisa had somehow stum-

bled into the middle of the kidnapping. Now she was as much
of a threat as her mother-in-law. And she was going to suffer
the same fate as Rose.

Panetti was going to kill them both.

The car ahead, which had been headed southwest, turned
onto Merrill Avenue, an east-west thoroughfare running par-
allel in this area with the Metro Transit System tracks. The
railroad tracks and street were separated by a low ridge that
was covered by evergreen trees. The ridge flattened out into a
parking lot for the Hillside railroad station after several blocks.
The sedan popped out of the traffic into the half-empty station
lot and came to a stop about a hundred feet from the building.
Mercury vapor lamps cast an eerie orange glow everywhere,
but also provided sufficient illumination for Koepp to see the
three figures dismount from the automobile. Koepp nosed into
a space behind a pickup truck and shut off his engine.

He called for the assistance of the closest patrol car. The
dispatcher acknowledged his request, but he couldn't wait to
hear who was responding. He had to follow the trio on foot.

They had walked past the station a few yards, then turned
toward the railroad tracks. They seemed to sink into the ground
as they descended an embankment. Koepp started to run as
soon as they disappeared from sight. By the time he reached
the top of the embankment they had moved about two hundred
feet off to his left and were walking along the bottom of a
shallow ravine, through which ran a double set of railroad
tracks.

Both sides of the ravine were bare of any significant vege-
tation; there was nothing for him to hide behind. As soon as
he walked down the embankment, Panetti had only to glance
over his shoulder to see that he was being followed. Koepp
couldn't risk it.

In growing desperation he studied the terrain ahead of the
three figures trudging through the deep snow beside the railroad
tracks. Four more vapor lamps flooded the railroad cut for another two hundred yards or so. Then, about where the light

dropped off, a trestle began for the tracks which spanned the West Branch river. There was a small clump of trees near the trestle on the opposite side of the ravine from Koepp.

The trees would provide the cover Panetti wanted. It was a serviceable place to murder someone.

As if to validate Koepp's thoughts, the three figures who were moving inexorably away from him crossed the double tracks. The woman he was holding—it looked like Lisa—began to struggle. Panetti then encircled her at the waist and began to drag her toward the trees. The other woman attacked him from the back with her bare fist, but he only stopped for a moment to say something to her, before resuming his forward progress. Whatever he had said dissuaded Rose from renewing her harassment. *Don't fight him*, Koepp thought. *Don't fight him.*

Koepp chose the only option he had that offered any chance to get closer to his quarry. He crouched down below the brow of the ridge and began running toward the river as fast as he could. He would be out of Panetti's sight almost until he reached the trestle. But once he tried to move down the embankment to the tracks, Panetti would see him. There was nothing else for him to do. By the time he got to the trestle some other course of action might present itself. If no opportunity came to surprise him, Koepp would have to show himself and try to talk Panetti into giving up.

Thirty yards from the trestle the ridge flattened out, forcing him to stop and sprawl on the crusted snow to avoid being seen. The three figures were clustered again, sixty yards away but moving toward him now.

He pounded the snow in frustration. The moment he stood up Panetti would see him. He waited, his heart thumping with his recent exertion and the anticipated confrontation. What weapon did Panetti carry? He had killed with a knife, but did he have a gun tonight? Koepp slowly extracted his revolver from its hip holster. It wouldn't help him unless Panetti foolishly cut loose his captives. But the touch of chilled metal made him feel more secure.

His attention was arrested then by a glow of light behind him, from the opposite side of the river. He squirmed a quarter turn so he could see the trestle. Just across the river the huge headlight of a suburban train was probing its way through the fog and stand of fir trees. The sound of the onrushing locomotive changed abruptly as it began to forge across the trestle.

Suddenly giddy with excitement, Koepp began to push against the ground with his muscles tense. In a few seconds the locomotive thundered past and blotted from sight the three figures on the other side of the tracks. Koepp sprang up as the second to the last car passed and sprinted directly toward the trestle. As the final car sped by, he sprang across the tracks and hurled himself against the opposite embankment between two small evergreen trees. For a moment he must have been in sight of Panetti, but he had counted on the distraction of the train to divert the man's attention. He hadn't been seen, he discovered, when he glanced back at the three figures. They were still coming, but were less than thirty yards away.

Having secured cover for an ambush, Koepp turned his attention to his attack. The gun he held in his hand was useless, even dangerous, until he could separate Panetti from both victims. He thrust it into the pocket of his jacket. When Panetti was abreast of him, he'd attempt to rush him from the side and knock him off his feet, counting on surprise to enable him to bring his .38 into play before Panetti could use his own weapon.

He tried to shrivel in on himself behind a sheltering tree. Fifteen yards. Ten. They were going to pass within three or four feet of him.

Five yards.

Koepp froze, coiled behind his tree, as Lisa and Panetti came abreast of him. Then he drove with all his power at the taller figure. He hadn't counted on the slipperiness of the crusted snow. As he sprang at Panetti the soles of his shoes lost their purchase, robbing him of much of his power. He could tell by the limp, yielding feel of the other man's body that he had not had time to tense his muscles before the impact. But Koepp had not delivered as severe a blow as he needed. He had surprised the man but hadn't hurt him. And he knew instinctively that he hadn't separated Panetti from his weapon. Panetti grunted softly as his big body pitched sideways toward the railroad tracks. They crashed together into a tiny ditch. Lisa, also knocked off her feet, landed on her back a few feet up the slope.

Koepp frantically jammed his hand into his jacket pocket to grab his .38.

It was gone.

As Panetti rose to a standing position Koepp spied the revolver lying on top of the crusted snow of the ditch between the killer and himself. He tried to crawl toward it but the treacherous snow betrayed him again; he broke through and found himself mired in deep powder momentarily. His abortive effort to reach the revolver had attracted Panetti's attention to it as well. Both of them went for it.

Koepp had the sickening sensation that he was going to lose the race, but Panetti, standing upright, ignored the gun himself and stalked Koepp with a knife. A knife was quieter, Koepp thought with eerie detachment.

He looked around for some object he could use as a weapon, but there was nothing but snow. Snow, snow—

Even as he fastened on to the substance in his mind, a large chunk of it came from above them and struck Panetti on the side of his face. The big man howled with pain and turned to face his attacker. This time Lisa had scooped up two handfuls of granulated snow from beneath the piece she had broken free and thrown at Panetti. She flung it in his face. He was blinded momentarily, giving Koepp a precious second to lunge for his weapon. For an instant Koepp saw a glint of light reflected from the man's knife blade as he swung his arm in a downward arc. But the arm stopped when Koepp pushed the muzzle of his .38 into Panetti's groin. He curled his finger around the trigger and waited for the knife to move. It had a handsome pearl handle.

After a few seconds the hand relaxed its grip and the knife tumbled into the bottom of the ditch.

DETECTIVES ALFANTI AND DEMOSS from the second shift had responded to Koepp's request for assistance. They were running across the train station parking lot just as Koepp marched Panetti up the embankment. "I'm charging this man with the murder of Joanne Whalen," he gasped.

DeMoss nodded. "We'll attend to that, Sergeant."

"I'll be along momentarily," Koepp said. "As soon as I can gather up the Robbins family and my partner. Don't interrogate him until we get there."

"We wouldn't think of it, Sergeant," Alfanti said, glancing at his partner for corroboration.

"And read him his rights again," Koepp said.

Koepp drove the two women back to Rose's building. When they arrived they saw that the lights in her apartment were on. Evidently Margaret had located the manager and persuaded him to let her and Kevin wait there.

Margaret was crouched in the foyer with her pistol in her hand when Rose unlocked the door and swung it open. Her intense expression was replaced by a wide grin as soon as she saw Koepp. She holstered the gun quickly and put her hand over Koepp's wrist as he grasped the doorknob. She gave him a gentle but unmistakable squeeze.

"I arrested Panetti," he told her. "DeMoss and Alfanti are booking him now."

Margaret nodded without saying anything.

In the living room Kevin was submitting to a frantic hug from his mother. They were both oblivious to everyone else. When Rose moved toward the kitchen the two detectives followed her.

"I suppose you have a lot of questions," she said.

"Yes," Koepp answered. "And you'll have to come with us to headquarters. You broke the law, Mrs. Robbins."

Margaret quietly began to Mirandize Rose, but the woman interrupted her. "I know my rights. I'll tell you whatever you want."

"Do you know who that man who attacked you is, Mrs. Robbins?" Koepp asked.

"No, but I know where I saw him before."

"The night you went to Joanne Whalen's apartment and found her dead?"

"Yes, I met him on the stairs, but I didn't think anything about him." She paused as if she were trying to understand her own actions. "It just never occurred to me that that man was the killer."

"Because you were sure that your son had killed her," Koepp suggested. "Which is why you took the knife?"

She took a long time to nod her head. Perhaps she was trying to prepare herself for his next question.

"But you did something with the knife, didn't you?"

An expression of horror and revulsion seemed to constrict her features. She stared beseechingly at Margaret, as if the younger woman somehow held the means to absolve her. "I cut into her mouth—her tongue. I knew about that because I read the police reports in Lisa's briefcase. I saw them by accident when I was looking for Lisa's appointment book—to see if she was seeing a divorce attorney—" The words tumbled out now. "I wanted to make the murder look like it was the work of the same man—the one who killed those other women. I only went there to talk to her, to get her to leave my son alone—"

Koepp didn't need to inquire how she knew about Philip Schroeder's fetish about women's underclothing; the young man's medical file had been in the same briefcase. He had to grudgingly admire the ingenuity and resourcefulness with which she used those records.

Margaret the woman, not Margaret the detective, asked the

next question. "How did you know Joanne Whalen was the woman who was having an affair with your son?"

"She was the auditor for the Childrens' Hospital," Rose said. "My son is on the board. I saw how attracted she was to him whenever there was a social function. Women can see these things happening. I tried to reason with Jack—"

Koepp changed the subject. "Somebody put Joanne Whalen's groceries in the freezer," he said.

"I guess I did that," Rose said. "I was standing next to her body, trying to decide what to do. It was a reflex action—something like that."

"How did you get into her home?"

"I made duplicates of her keys."

"From the keys your son had?"

"Yes. I tried to talk to her, but she wouldn't return my calls. I thought if I let myself into her condo and waited for her, she couldn't ignore me." She avoided looking at Lisa, who had appeared silently in the doorway. For the first time the expression on Rose Robbins's face changed from resignation to curiosity. "He knew who I was because I was on TV, right?" she asked.

Koepp nodded. "He also knew you had to be the one who put the murder weapon in Schroeder's vehicle."

"He must have been infatuated with her, too," Rose said. Koepp noticed that she didn't use the word "loved," which by inference would have impugned her son even more. This delicacy was clearly for Lisa's benefit; he wondered if it would help save the Robbinses' marriage.

Then Lisa said in a low but distinct voice, "What's wrong with us?" Before either Koepp or Rose could answer, she continued. "You thought Jack was capable of killing her. I thought you did it to keep me from finding out the truth. We were both willing to let Philip Schroeder go to jail for it."

Rose, moving restlessly, took a long time to select the words for her reply. At last she said in a voice close to breaking, "We protected each other. That's what families do."

Margaret said softly to Lisa, "We contacted your husband through one of his business associates. He's waiting for you and your son at your home."

"Kevin and I can go home then?"

Both detectives nodded in unison.

Lisa stayed in the kitchen while Rose went to get Kevin bundled up again. When her mother-in-law was out of earshot she asked, "What will happen to her?"

"I'm sure she doesn't have a record," Koepp said. "Given her motivation, I'd guess she'll get a suspended sentence."

Her relief was evident in her tired face. "By the way, thank you for saving our lives," she said, smiling at Koepp.

"Same to you," Koepp replied. "Without your snow job, I'd still be lying in that ditch."

Lisa smiled again, embarrassed, but said nothing.

They gathered together in an awkward cluster near the door, long enough for Lisa to embrace Rose. "No matter what happens, Jack and I will be here for you—both of us," she said simply. "We'll take care of everything—bail, lawyers—"

"In the morning is soon enough," Rose said, tears welling in her eyes. "Take care of each other tonight."

Lisa embraced the older woman, then she and her son were gone.

Koepp and Margaret waited patiently while Rose went through her apartment shutting off the lights, turning down the thermostat, making sure the windows were locked. Margaret watched her with an amused expression on her face, but when she looked back at Koepp her faced clouded.

"You got Panetti, Ray," she said, "but it's not over. There's still a serial killer out there. I'm not quitting on Nancy Sorgel and the others."

He knew how much it bothered her, deep inside, to know that the murderer of three women was still free to kill again. But Koepp had no solace to offer her. "We can't win 'em all, partner," he said.

JACK MUST HAVE SEEN her headlights, or heard the garage door because he was in the garage waiting for them when Kevin popped out on the passenger side. He picked the boy up easily and hugged him so hard he squealed with delight. It was another of those rough rituals of male bonding that she would never understand, Lisa thought.

But she felt their relief, and shared it. The nightmare wasn't over yet; Lisa assumed that the police hadn't told Jack about his mother's actions. She had no idea how she would find the words to tell him, to help him live with the awful knowledge of her savagery. But they would survive. As Rose had said, they were a family. They looked after one another.

Jack put Kevin back on the pavement and came around the front of the car. They faced each other uncertainly for just a moment, then Lisa rushed into his encircling arms.

She felt the arms fold around her, gently, protectively. Finally, she began to cry.